T0354791

HOPEFUL
AT
THE HAY

This novel is entirely a work of fiction and my imagination. Any resemblance to actual events or people would be totally coincidental. This book can be read alone but it is the fifth in a series of novels. The reader should start with the first in the series called Paradox at Pebble Beach followed by Confusion at Cypress Point, then Suspicion at Spyglass Hill followed by Surprise at Spanish Bay.

OTHER BOOKS BY MICHAEL DOVE

CRIM 279

THE RUNNING LIFE (WITH DONALD BURAGLIO)

PARADOX AT PEBBLE BEACH

CONFUSION AT CYPRESS POINT

SUSPICION AT SPYGLASS HILL

SURPRISE AT SPANISH BAY

HOPEFUL
AT
THE HAY

MICHAEL A. DOVE

HOPEFUL AT THE HAY

iUniverse books may be ordered through booksellers or by contacting:

iUniverse
1663 Liberty Drive
Bloomington, IN 47403
www.iuniverse.com
844-349-9409

ISBN: 978-1-6632-6670-5 (sc)
ISBN: 978-1-6632-6671-2 (e)

Library of Congress Control Number: 2024918328

Print information available on the last page.

iUniverse rev. date: 09/18/2024

FROM THE HAY WEBSITE

A Reimagined Short Course Experience at Pebble Beach

The Hay has been a fixture at Pebble Beach since 1957, when famed Head Professional Peter Hay revolutionized the concept of a short course. Hay's vision was to create a fun place where juniors, families, and friends, regardless of their ability, could gather around the game of golf.

In 2021, Tiger Woods amplified Hay's vision in a way few could have imagined with his brilliant redesign of the property. The result is a course overflowing with fun, including an exact replica of the famed No. 7 at Pebble Beach Golf Links, as well as holes designed to be played with any club in the bag, and an additional 20,000 square-foot putting course that sprawls 100 yards, yielding endless routings.

It's Pebble Beach, the Tiger Woods way. Play The Hay!

THE HAY SCORE CARD

THE HOLES ARE ALL NAMED AND HAVE YARDAGES FOR
SIGNIFICANT EVENTS AT PEBBLE BEACH GOLF COURSE

1. After Peter Hay who started the short course in 1957
2. A replica, without the ocean, of the 7th hole at Pebble Beach
3. Tom Watson's U.S. Open win at Pebble Beach in 1982
4. After Bing Crosby, who started the Clambake event in 1947
5. In 1948, Grace Lenczyk won the second U.S. Women's Amateur played at Pebble Beach
6. Lanny Watkins PGA Championship win at Pebble Beach in 1977
7. Jack Nicklaus U.S. Amateur win at Pebble Beach in 1961
8. Tom Kite U.S. Open win at Pebble Beach in 1982
9. Tiger Woods, the course designer, won the 100th U.S. Open by 15 strokes in 2000 at Pebble Beach

THE HAY

HOLE	YARDS								
1	57				HAY				
2	106				SEVEN				
3	82				WATSON				
4	47				BING				
5	48				GRACE				
6	77				LANNY				
7	61				JACK				
8	92				KITE				
9	100				TIGER				
TOTAL	670								

"Golf is the closest game to the game we call life. You get bad breaks from good shots; you get good breaks from bad shots – but you have to play the ball where it lies." – Bobby Jones

"As you walk down the fairway of life you must smell the roses, for you only get to play one round." - Ben Hogan

"Golf is deceptively simple and endlessly complicated; it satisfies the soul and frustrates the intellect. It is at the same time rewarding and maddening - and it is without a doubt the greatest game mankind has ever invented." – Arnold Palmer

"Don't bother me, all I want to do is play golf." – Chipper Blair

THE CALM

Jenny Nelson, teaching golf professional at Pebble Beach and Spyglass Hill Golf Course, barely awake and conscious, felt a really cold nose on her naked back. Angus, her black Scottie dog, was under the covers rubbing his face against her. Angus then licked her neck and made a very quiet whimpering sound that was muffled by the covers over the dog's head. Jenny glanced at the clock next to her side of the bed and was surprised it was six fifteen already. The radio next to her husband, Walter "Chipper" Blair's side of the bed was on KWAV, playing 'Love is a Rose' by Linda Ronstadt. Usually the music on the radio woke them both up, but for some reason, the sound was lower than usual. Angus must have rubbed against the radio during the night. When Jenny glanced at the window, it seemed lighter than usual. Was it possible the sun was coming out? Spring was still a month away, and sun in the morning, rather than the usual fog and mist, was highly strange.

Chipper was still sound asleep. Jenny leaned over Angus, and gave Chipper a kiss on the lips. He grabbed her immediately, and squeezed Angus between them, as he attempted to hug her. She could tell immediately Chipper was aroused and she quickly said, "Not now, Chipper, it's late. We have to get going." Angus was very uncomfortable. Chipper stayed in bed for a few more minutes and admired Jenny getting out of bed and heading toward the bathroom. Jenny, at five foot ten inches was just a few inches shorter than Chipper. She had a fully-tanned body and short black hair. Chipper admired her for a few more seconds then hurried out of bed to the window.

He smiled when he saw enough light outside so that their morning golf shot would be visible all the way to the green. The last two weeks had been wonderful, nothing but golf and calm. He had been in enough trouble over the past year to fill a lifetime. And none of it was his fault. He just wanted to play golf and do his driving range duties at Pebble Beach Golf Course. He had to hurry to get to work on time. No shower this morning. No breakfast either. Angus was still under the covers but was moving and seemed agitated.

Chipper quickly dressed and headed downstairs. Their estate home bordered the fourteenth fairway of the famed golf course. He waited a few minutes near the back door until Jenny and Angus followed. She was singing "Love is a Rose and you better not pick it. Only grows when it's on the vine. Handful of thorns and you'll know you've missed it. Lose your love when you say the word mine." Chipper realized it was good Jenny was a great teaching golf professional and not a singer. He knew he would be hearing the song in his head all day.

Angus showed no fear in heading out the back door and descending the steps to the backyard. Only a short time ago, the two Dobermans and one pit bull, living next door kept the black dog from enjoying his outside time. Chipper didn't know what happened to the three dogs when the owners unexpectedly left and abandoned the house, but he was overjoyed that they had all gone. Pebble Beach Corporation General Counsel and Vice President of Community Relations, Richard Stein, and his girlfriend Debbie Rogers, were in the process of moving into the estate next to them. Each estate comprised several acres, so Chipper wasn't worried about being bothered by Richard and Debbie.

Just before Chipper walked out the back door, he grabbed two Slazenger golf balls from a large bowl, and fourteen dog treats for Angus, from a smaller bowl. Angus ran back and forth on the back lawn excitedly. Chipper and Jenny headed down holding hands and hugged for a while when they got to the lawn. Life was great and very calm. Chipper walked to the wooden cabinet and pulled out Ben Morris's old golf clubs: the long spoon for himself and the brassie for Jenny. As he handed the brassie to his wife, Chipper said casually, "I wonder if Ben would be upset if we had these clubs re-gripped with more modern grips. These old taped grips are really getting hard to hold on to. These are probably the original one-hundred-year-old grips."

Jenny quickly said, "You know the answer to that, Chipper. Ben would roll over in his grave if you did anything to these clubs."

Chipper said, "He was cremated, but I get the idea. We'll leave them as they are. Do you ever get the feeling Ben is looking at us and smiling when we do this every morning?"

"I do. Yes. He is certainly smiling, and I'm sure his spirit is around here, hovering over Aileen's memorial over there." Jenny and Chipper hugged again, then started warming up by swinging the long spoon and the brassie. Angus sat in the ready position, anticipating the morning shots to the fourteenth green. He was ready to go, almost like a sprinter in the starting blocks position.

Jenny hit first, and Angus took off, almost faster than the golf ball. Angus sensed the good vibes from Jenny and Chipper and was off like a shot. Jenny knew the ball would be close, hoping for the impossible hole-out. Chipper had promised her months before that they would try to have a baby if either of them made the morning shot. They both realized that when Ben Morris finally made the morning shot, after years of trying, he immediately swooned and died of a heart attack. That's the reason they lived in and owned the thirty-five-million-dollar estate they were given in Ben's will. Of course, Ben was in his nineties, and Jenny and Chipper were in their middle twenties. A heart attack was highly unlikely. Jenny wanted to have a baby and didn't want to wait until a highly unlikely hole in one. Today's was one of Jenny's best shots, and she knew it when she hit it. She sprinted up the stairs to look in the telescope mounted on the deck, and it was close, only a few feet away from the pin. She yelled back down to Chipper, "Almost, Mr. Chips! Only a few feet to the right. You can't possibly beat that one."

She continued to look through the telescope as Angus picked up the ball with his mouth and, without even slowing down, took a one hundred eighty degree turn, and came rocketing back the almost one hundred seventy yards to their backyard. Angus dropped the ball at Chipper's feet and was rewarded with seven dog treats. The little dog was ready to go again after he gobbled up the treats. He didn't even roll over for a belly rub, but got in his usual starting position, waiting for Chipper to take his shot.

Chipper took a few more practice swings then fired a nice-looking hook that curved around the big pine trees and headed toward the green.

3

Jenny was still at the telescope and yelled down, "Good shot, Chipper, but not nearly as good as mine!" She put a mark on her side of the board. There were too many marks to count now, but Chipper was still leading by a few: about two hundred marks each. Angus was back quickly and received seven more treats. This time he rolled over, knowing there were no more shots this morning, and expected a good belly rub. Jenny rubbed his belly while Chipper kissed Jenny goodbye and headed toward his golf cart. Jenny said, "See you at noon, Chipper. I love you."

"Me, too," was the last thing he said, as he replaced the golf clubs into the cabinet, winked at Aileen Morris's memorial stone, and headed out to the middle of the fairway with his cart. With his regular clubs, instead of the long spoon, he pulled out a six iron for the one-hundred-seventy-yard shot. It was a glorious day. The pin was just over the large bunker at the front left of the green. Chipper pictured a high draw and watched with awe, as it started exactly where he wanted it, turned just a few yards left, and came down softly, rolling about four feet past the pin. He calmly putted it in without even looking at the line. He knew how every putt broke on every green at Pebble Beach, because he had played it so many times.

On the fifteenth tee, he hit three metal for position off the tee, trying to avoid the bunkers on the left side of the fairway. He had nine iron left to an easy left-side pin and again hit a perfect shot to four feet. He made the putt, the first time he had birdied both fourteen and fifteen on his way into work in the morning. *Could life be any better? Really not.* He thought to himself. Rather than heading to the driving range after playing fifteen, he decided to play sixteen to see if he could continue his birdie streak. He pulled out his driver and tried to hit another draw to the left side of the fairway. He pushed it a bit, but was in good position for a second shot to a tough pin position on the right back of the green. Like his tee shot, he pushed his iron as well and was in a very tough position to the right of the pin on a severe downslope. He would have to use his great short-game skills to even get within ten feet of the pin. He hit a flop shot that landed in the fringe and hit so softly that it just trickled down slowly to a few inches from the pin. Not a birdie, but an easy par with a magnificent shot. Chipper said, "They don't call me Chipper for nothing." One of his favorite phrases.

It wasn't a birdie, so Chipper headed directly into his work at the

Pebble Beach driving range. It was a beautiful day, and he expected more golfers than usual at what he considered his driving range. He stopped at the pro shop to chat with head professional, Roger Hennessey. Roger had been a great supporter of Chipper during his trials and tribulations over the past year. Roger was always there to help, because Roger served in the military with Chipper's dad, Walter Blair, Sr. Chipper's dad had helped Roger, and Roger still felt he owed him several favors. He hired Chipper when no one else would, and he tried to have Chipper's back when he was in trouble, which was very often lately.

When Chipper drove up, Roger was outside the pro shop watching golfers getting ready to tee off on the first hole at Pebble. He smiled broadly and spoke first, "Good morning, Chipper. What a great morning, huh?"

"It certainly is, Roger. I birdied fourteen and fifteen, then made a par on sixteen that even Houdini wouldn't have made. I hit a flop shot from the right to a right back pin. Almost made it. Impossible shot. They don't call me Chipper for nothing."

"How is Jenny?"

"She's great. She'll be at my range at noon teaching Cindy more stuff."

"Still drawing a crowd at the lessons?" Roger asked.

"Yep, but they don't seem to be as rowdy as they used to be. I think they just enjoy watching Cindy get better. She's really doing great, and Jenny really enjoys it. Except for Duncan posting everything all the time. Do you know they get almost a million views every time he posts? It's crazy. Really crazy. Cindy is making a ton of money. She and Duncan have moved into Emily Hastings' old house."

"As long as Jenny is enjoying it, that's great. The Corporation raised her lesson rate again. I think she gets $1,100 bucks a lesson now."

"I don't think she even knows that. They don't tell her anything or how much of the lesson rate she gets. At least the Corporation let her cut back to four a day. They were having her give six to eight lessons a day for seven days a week. She is a little moneymaker for the Pebble Beach Corporation."

Roger commented, "Well, it seems the more they charge for her lessons, the bigger the demand."

Chipper called on his Stanford economics degree and MBA and said, "That's called demand inelastic. There aren't many alternatives to getting a lesson from Jenny. Not many things are demand inelastic these days. Only in the Del Monte Forest, maybe. I've got to get going, Roger. Beautiful day means more bodies at the range."

Roger said, "Before you go, why aren't you getting an award for saving the Corporation and maybe the entire PGA tour at Spanish Bay? In fact, you get nothing but grief and suspicion from the local newspapers."

Chipper didn't comment, but did wave as he got in his cart and headed to the driving range. Roger Hennessey shook his head and wondered why Chipper, the Stanford MBA, was happy just tending to the driving range at Pebble Beach, and why he didn't care about recognition for his insight and heroic actions that saved a lot of people's lives several weeks before. Roger said, "You see what you get with Chipper Blair, just wants to enjoy golf."

2011 PAGANI HUAYRA

Chipper spent the first few hours on the range replacing divots, moving the tee markers to new patches of grass, picking up broken tees and other debris, putting clean range balls into buckets, and making sure each hitting position was pristine. He was interrupted only four times by golfers who wanted buckets of balls to hit. When he saw a courtesy cart coming over from the golf course, he rushed back to the shack and had a bucket of balls ready for the golfer. Even though they only wanted a small bucket, Chipper gave them a large.

He deposited the broken tees, and always some dirt, into the automatic ball dispenser machine, so it would always be broken. The Corporation had given up on sending the repair man out to fix it every day and had given up on calling the machine manufacturer and telling them it was still under warranty but was ALWAYS broken and non-functioning. Chipper was hoping one day that someone would come and just truck it away. It was an eyesore in such a beautiful place. It didn't belong.

After his range cleaning was done, he amused himself by standing outside his range shack and commenting to himself about those hitting golf balls on the range. He was correct that several more golfers showed up, and there were more golfers than usual out hitting balls. Chipper started thinking of commentary, *"And here is what has to be a professional golfer stepping up to the tee. Look how he his dressed. Four-hundred-dollar slacks, expensive clubs, a Pebble Beach-logo windbreaker, just new out of the package. But....oh no! His swing is complete shit. Can't hit the ball with that swing. Let's see how he does. He's starting with his driver. A sure sign he doesn't know crap about golf. He swings, if you can call that a swing, and he actually hits the ball. It goes ten yards in front of him. He's looking around to see if anyone saw that. Uh oh, he's looking back at me. I'll turn my head so he thinks I didn't see it. Now he's jogging out ten feet to pick it up and bring it back to hit it again. I'm betting he doesn't hit this one any further...AND I'm WRONG!... He hits it about twenty-five feet this time. He's turning around again. I'm not gonna look for a bit. I'll just mess around with these buckets of balls. Now his friend is coming over probably to give him some tips. They are both laughing. The friend looks like he's saying keep your head down. That won't help, friend. Won't help at all. They are going to take seven hours to play the golf course today. Wouldn't want to be behind them. He swings again and connects big time! Had to be one hundred yards but almost directly right. It's very difficult to shank a driver, but golf fans, he has done that. He shanked a driver!"*

A bit later, the range was clear, and Chipper didn't see anyone else approaching, so he did what he always did in free time, grabbed a bucket of balls and a few clubs and walked out and warmed up. He liked to try different things on the range, hitting fades, hitting draws, low shots, high shots, aiming at different targets. He lived for his time on the range and his time on the golf course and, of course, Jenny Nelson. He was interrupted a few times by groups arriving at the range and wanting a bucket of balls to split, before they shuttled back to Pebble Beach to begin their $585 round of golf. Today, with good weather, they would get their money's worth. If it was foggy, as usual, maybe not. He hit balls until about noon when he saw Jenny drive up and, shortly after, Cindy and her boyfriend, Duncan.

The usual crowd of spectators was gathering at the end and back of the range, some yelling at both Cindy and Jenny. Cindy was now a willing internet star, with lots of sponsorship and NIL money coming in. Jenny was a reluctant internet star, just because of Duncan's constant posting of their lessons on every social media platform. Jenny was conservatively dressed today in slacks and a Pebble Beach-logo shirt and cap. Cindy was dressed as Cindy usually was, in very short shorts and a sleeveless Nike blouse that showed off her Nike golf bra, so she would get more NIL money. Duncan was, of course, filming everything on his cell phone for later posting.

Chipper smiled spontaneously when he walked up to Jenny, and, as they hugged and kissed, the crowd of mostly college boys booed loudly. Chipper smiled at that, too. He even waved back at the group of forty or fifty, who had become regulars watching the noon lesson. He thought to himself, *"Why on earth do they come every day to watch the two girls swing the golf club? Sure, Jenny was beautiful, and Cindy was girl-next-door cute with skimpy clothes, but didn't they have anything better to do? The group knew that both Jenny and Cindy were taken. Jenny, married, and Cindy with a constant boyfriend. I guess you get your kicks where and when you can."*

Chipper watched for a bit and was impressed with how well Cindy was hitting the ball and how much she had improved since Jenny started giving her lessons. Chipper was proud he still helped with short game lessons occasionally. She was finally swinging consistently in the inside to outside pattern that Jenny kept trying to drum into her. Virtually every shot was solid with just a little fade. As she improved her course management skills, Chipper thought, she might even have a chance to play number one on the California State University at Monterey Bay team by the time she was a senior. Maybe even a pro career.

As he was watching, he heard a loud muffler noise behind him, and a car screeched to a halt in a parking spot near the gathered crowd. All the guys there gathered around the strange car, as the driver opened the gull-wing doors and sauntered out. As Chipper walked over to the range shack, he heard the driver say loudly, "It's a 2011 Pagani Huayra. Only a few around. I paid a bit over three million dollars for it. Cash! I'm not supposed to be driving it much. It isn't street-legal because of airbag issues. My license is only a show and display license. I'm showing to you guys. You can walk around it, but don't touch it. Do you like the silver and gold colors? She's a beauty!"

Even Cindy and Jenny turned around and watched the young man walk over to Chipper. He looked to be in his early twenties, with a very confident walk, floppy dirty-blonde long hair, and expensive aviator shades on his head. He flipped them down over his eyes as he got closer to Chipper. He had on a matching black golf shirt and black shorts. No socks and what looked like Air Jordan sneakers. When he got close to Chipper, too close, Chipper stepped back. This guy was apparently a "close talker." Chipper stepped back again, as the man closed in and started talking, "Hey sport, it's a 2011 Pagani Huayra. Only a few around. I paid a bit over three million dollars for it. Cash! I'm not supposed to be driving it much. It isn't street legal because of airbag issues. My license is only a show and display license. You can go over and walk around it, but don't touch it. Do you like the silver and gold colors? She's a beauty!"

Chipper wanted to say, "I could give a shit," but he was having such a great day, he just didn't say anything. He just stared at the man's face until the Pagani driver spoke again.

"I just moved into the Forest and I figured I should probably take up golf. That seems to be a major activity here. It seems like a pretty easy thing to do. Just hit the ball with the stick. Never played before. Never had time. Too busy just working and making lots of money. I moved in a few weeks back. Paid twenty-three million cash for a big estate up the road."

Chipper commented calmly, "It's not so easy, really. Takes a lot of years to be able to play at all well."

The Pagani guy looked over at Jenny and Cindy and said, "How hard could it be? Look at those babes hitting the ball. The little blonde seems to know what she is doing. Just take it back, then club it. Boy, are they lookers. Look at the ass on both of them. I might like this game. Do you have a club I can try? Can you give me a quick lesson? I'll give you a ride in the Pagani. Did I say I paid three million cash for it?"

Before Chipper had a chance to say anything, and what he said would not have been nice, the Pagani guy started walking toward Jenny and Cindy. Chipper just stood there shaking his head. He was almost losing it. He wandered over a bit closer just to hear the conversation.

"Hi, ladies. My name is Nolan Lusky, my friends just call me No Load. You're both probably wondering about my car. It's a 2011 Pagani Huayra. Only a few around. I paid a bit over three million dollars for it. Cash! I'm not supposed to be driving it much. It isn't street legal because of airbag issues. My license is only a show and display license. You can go over and walk around it, but don't touch it. Do you like the silver and gold colors? She's a beauty! Do either of you want to take a ride in it?"

Duncan was filming, as usual, and Lusky looked at him and asked, "Hey, short sport, why are you filming these beauties?" Duncan didn't respond, and Lusky asked again, "Do you talk? Tell me what's up with the phone work?"

Duncan kept filming and said quickly, "I'm Cindy's boyfriend. I put some of her golf lessons on the internet. She's a star now!"

"I can see she's a star already, just by how she looks. Hey Cindy, do you want to go for a ride in my Pagani? How about you, tall girl? You would look nice in the Pagani. Are you a teaching person for golf?"

Jenny reluctantly said, "Yes. I am a teaching golf professional."

"I would love to have you teach me anything. How much for a lesson?"

"I think it's now $1,000 for an hour."

"Are you kidding me? Are you a hooker or a golf teacher? I've paid less than that for a half hour with some beautiful ladies. You should see my Angel."

Jenny just stared at him and said, "Go away, please. Just go away. You are interrupting us."

Chipper quickly went back to the shack and grabbed a five iron and a bucket of balls, and came running over, just to get No Load out of the way. "Hey, No Load. Can I call you No Load? I'll give you a free lesson. If you think the game is easy, try hitting a few, and I'll give you tips." Then he walked Lusky way over the far left side of the range and away from Jenny and Cindy.

Lusky followed him and was muttering, "I'd certainly like to take a lesson from the tall one or the short one. I've got enough money for several lessons. Maybe all night long."

Chipper had it at that point, and yelled, "Look, No Load! I'm married to the tall one. She's mine. Don't say anything more about either of them. And you'll soon learn something about the Forest here. What is said in the Forest is soon all over everyone's gossip. Best to keep to yourself. Just try to hit the golf ball here and be a good little boy. How old are you, anyway?"

"Twenty-three."

"You act like seventeen."

Lusky commented, "Do I call you range goat or range boy? I think I'd like to call you range boy, if that's ok with you? What do you make doing this? I made millions last year. Do you make minimum wage?"

Chipper almost swung the five iron at No Load, but restrained himself. "You're not making friends here, youngster. Just keep your mouth shut now. No more comments, or I'll club you over the head with this."

"To each his own. O.K. range goat guy," Lusky said.

Lusky was finally quiet. Chipper told him to grab the club, and Lusky held on tight with a baseball grip and swung the club like a bat, horizontal to the ground. Chipper said, "You can hold it like that if you want, but the proper grip is the overlapping grip." Chipper took the club and demonstrated, but No Load took the club back and continued to hold it like a baseball bat. Chipper put down a ball in a good lie on the grass, pointed at Cindy, and said, "Try to swing the club like she does."

Lusky's first swing ended up with Lusky on the ground. He started his backswing by picking the club up almost vertically, then swung down hard, taking a stride forward. The clubhead hit the ground about a foot behind the ball, bounced over the ball, and Lusky slipped in the grass and tumbled forward. Chipper didn't laugh, but merely said, "Easy game." Lusky did not seem to be embarrassed. He took four more swings, stayed upright on each one, and finally hit the ball on the last one...barely. The ball rolled forward about six feet.

Chipper again called out, "Easy game, for sure. You might want to invest in some golf shoes before you come out again." Then Chipper took the club and showed No Load how to grip it again and how to swing. Chipper's shot went about 200 yards with a slight draw, but Lusky didn't seem impressed. When Chipper looked at him and handed the club back, he was staring over at Cindy and Jenny again.

Lusky said, "I think I'll find out how to take a lesson from the beautiful girl, your wife, over there. Can't believe she's married to a range goat. Really can't believe that."

Chipper couldn't take it anymore, "Get the fuck out of here, No Load. Just fuck off. Take your little car with you. Just fuckin' get out of my driving range."

Lusky calmly walked over to where Jenny and Cindy were just finishing up the lesson and again asked, "Either or you want a ride in my Pagani Huayra? I can take both of you, if you want. One of you would have to sit in the middle near the gear shift, but that's ok. You might like the ride."

Cindy surprisingly said, "Duncan, how about a video of me standing near the car? It might be a good post." Then, without waiting for an answer she started walking over to the car, with Duncan following. Jenny was wandering behind, out of curiosity. Duncan filmed Cindy posing in front of the car, near the driver's door, and in back of the car. When she tried to put a bare leg up onto the hood, No Load started shouting, "No touching. No touching. Don't touch the car."

All the guys watching started shouting back, "Put your leg up, Cindy. Touch the car. Leg up, Cindy." And she did. Lusky took out his cell phone and started to video as well.

"You'll pay for that, young lady. You'll pay." Lusky was muttering as he took a rag out of the car and wiped his Pagani where she had put her foot.

JUDITH HITTEN

When Chipper finished his range duties later in the day, he decided to do one of his favorite things. He drove his cart out to the famous and beautiful seventh hole at Pebble Beach and planned to empty his golf bag of balls with shots to the green. At sundown it was glorious, with perfect shadows and lighting framing the seventh green. The pin was in the easiest spot on the green, about fifteen feet over the front bunker, and almost the middle of the green. It was only a few feet from where Chipper and Jenny got married several months before.

He grabbed all the balls out of his golf bag and found he had a dozen exactly. Chipper took a few practice swings with his pitching wedge. The plan was to hit each shot about ten yards past the pin and a bit left of it, and have the ball spin back and roll near the cup. On each shot, he was planning on "willing" the ball close to the cup. He was a firm believer that you could control the golf ball with your mind, and maybe by yelling at the ball, too. Maybe a hole in one today? There was just enough light so he could see the first shot land about ten feet right of where he wanted it and pull back to about ten feet to the right of the pin, exactly pin high.

It was so beautiful out that Chipper didn't want to go back to the estate. Their friend, attorney and estate manager, Judith Hitten, was due at his house for a quarterly update on his and the Ben and Aileen Morris Foundation's assets and expenses. He trusted Judith and was bored at the quarterly meetings. They were informal, but he still had trouble paying attention. The money just didn't matter that much to him. He knew Jenny would pay attention and react accordingly to the good news and the bad news, if any.

Chipper's second shot landed almost exactly where he was planning to hit it, and his adrenaline started pumping when it started rolling back toward the pin. It rolled back a bit too far and ended up about two feet short of the pin, from Chipper's view angle. "A good shot," he said. It turned out to be the best of his dozen shots. He couldn't hit any more closer to the hole after that one. He went down to the green, as darkness was encircling him, and putted all of them. Four birdies and eight pars. Not bad, but kind of what he was expecting. With no wind, he expected to birdie the hole one-third of the time.

He started driving back to his estate, knowing that Judith and Jenny would already be having a drink in the replica Dreel Tavern in his house. He was looking forward to seeing Jenny and having some of his favorite scotch. He parked the cart in his backyard, climbed the steps, and looked back to admire Pebble Beach Golf Course's green background, only visible because of the lights coming from his estate and others along the fairway. Inside the house, when he was going down the steps to the tavern, Angus was coming up to greet him. Angus rolled over on one step and accidently fell over the side of the step and rolled down a few steps. Chipper could tell Angus was embarrassed. Angus tried not to show it and just lay there like he intended that to happen.

"Good dog, Angus," he commented, then knelt down and rubbed Angus' belly long enough that Jenny had to beckon him into the room.

"We know you are there, Chipper. Come on down. You're late. We're already a drink ahead of you." Jenny and Judith were having martinis, and Chipper's scotch was already poured in a big glass and was sitting on the table next to Jenny. Judith had two big folders of paper, and her laptop was open in front of her. Chipper kissed Jenny on the lips and impulsively gave Judith a kiss on the cheek. Judith was surprised.

She said, "You seem to be in a good mood today. I'm going to make your mood even better."

Chipper took the seat next to Jenny, sipped from the scotch, and waited for Judith Hitten to start. He grabbed Jenny's hand, held it softly, and tried to pay attention. Angus settled in on the floor beneath his chair.

Hitten started, "I'll be very short. It seems the rich keep getting richer. Most of the holdings in your own account, Chipper, and most of the Foundation's, still have lots of Berkshire Hathaway, both Class A stock which is over six hundred thousand a share, up almost thirty percent from last year, and Berkshire Hathaway Class B stock, which is about four hundred dollars a share, also up almost thirty percent since last year. Your home expenses have only gone up slightly, and the Foundation's grants don't come close to the interest and extra value you accrued this past year. Both your own and the Foundation's assets are now well over four hundred million dollars. A few more years like this and you might be a billionaire."

Chipper did a fake yawn and drank a few more sips of scotch, "Thank you, Ben Morris and his brother. May they both rest in peace. How much is the Cypress Point membership costing me now?"

"The same monthly fee as always, about two thousand, and they haven't sent out the yearly summary fee yet. Last year it was an additional fifty-five thousand."

Chipper looked at Jenny and said, "We really have to start playing there more, now that we have more sunlight later in the evening." He took a few phantom swings, without a club in his hand. "So we are even richer than last year, Judith, even though the Foundation is giving away millions each year to golf-related stuff. It seems very easy to be rich. Kind of a life lesson. In golf, you have to practice for many years to get any good at the game. If you are wealthy, you don't really have to do anything, and you get richer. A sad comment on life as we know it."

Judith just sighed and commented, "Since when have you gotten so philosophical, Chipper? Just enjoy your life and don't feel guilty about it. You are making me and my partners rich, too, on the management fees for your estate. You can be happy about that. Any ideas, Jenny or Chipper, on what to try to fund this year for the Foundation? We're due for a meeting."

Jenny reacted enthusiastically, "You know, whenever I drive by The Hay par-three course, I never see any kids there, even in the summer. The Corporation allows kids twelve and under to play free, and teenagers are thirty dollars, unless they are part of the Youth on Course program, then they can play for five dollars. That's pretty generous, but I don't see many kids out there. The Northern California Golf Association, not the Corporation, administers the Youth on Course program, and it's thirty dollars per year. I don't see why our Foundation can't just provide free golf at The Hay for any kid nineteen and under. It would increase youth play and avoid the hassle of the thirty dollars to the Youth on Course program. The Corporation can just bill us for all the kids' rounds, or we give them money at the beginning of the year, and it goes toward the free green fees."

Hitten commented, "I can see you've thought about this, Jenny, but wouldn't the course then have nothing but kids all the time, keeping the seventy-five-dollar-paying adults off the course, or slowing them down? Will the Corporation go for this? I doubt it. No way would they allow it. It would cost them money, and I'm sure they would come up with other reasons that they don't want The Hay overrun with kids all day long."

Jenny said, "You are probably right, but I'll talk to Richard and have him bring it up at an executive meeting, or just talk to Donald Stevens about it. He sees him every day."

"OK, what else you got, Jenny?" Hitten said.

"What about a partnership with Golf Mart in Seaside, for free clubs for kids? They hardly have any inventory of junior sets. First Tee in Salinas lets kids have free clubs, but no such luck over here on the Peninsula. What about just free new sets of clubs for any high school golfer that makes their golf team? I think that's a good one. It wouldn't even dent the Foundation's money. Drop in the bucket. I for sure want to do that."

"You are just full of ideas."

Jenny said, "Let's go back to The Hay idea for a bit." And she took out her phone and tapped some buttons. "What if we just say our Foundation will pay for every round at The Hay?! All year long! For everyone! Adults and kids! We can make The Hay free for everyone! So let me guess that on average it's open ten hours a day. A foursome every eight minutes, so that's maybe seven groups an hour. So, maybe to estimate a bit high, that's three hundred players a day. Three hundred times seventy dollars green fees is twenty-one thousand a day. Take that..." and she tapped on her phone keyboard, "and multiply times three hundred and sixty-five days a year, and that gives us about seven and a half million dollars a year! That doesn't even make a large dent in the Foundation's interest income per year. I want to do that."

Chipper was laughing the whole time and said, "That's my girl. Very generous."

Hitten said, "You better add that idea to what Stein brings up at the managers' meeting. I don't think they could balk at that. It's probably higher than their actual yearly revenue at The Hay, and it would bring more people into the restaurant and bar for more revenue, as well."

Chipper took a few more club-less swings, and just said, "Let's play Cypress tomorrow afternoon, Jenny. I'll get Big Bill to watch the range for me, and you can move your lessons to another day."

"That's the Chipper I know," Hitten said, then she winked and took another sip of her martini.

Chipper started daydreaming about playing Cypress Point, and Jenny and Judith knew the meeting was over. Or, at least Chipper's part of it.

RICHARD STEIN

The next morning, Chipper had a rare hangover and slowly went down the back steps of his estate into the mist and haze. Angus was already on the back lawn, eager to go. Jenny was a few steps behind and chiding Chipper, "You shouldn't have finished the bottle of scotch, Mr. Chips. You are going to have a bad morning. Have you ever played a round drunk or hungover?"

Chipper stopped at the bottom of the steps, turned around and commented, "I'm surprised I never told you that story. Funny story. Well, maybe a sad story. One of the years I qualified for the State Amateur, here at Pebble, a good friend of mine took me to the Mission Ranch the night before the practice round. I don't remember anything after about six drinks there, but he got me to bed in the motel and woke me up in the morning, just in time to get us to the first tee at Pebble for our starting time. I felt awful. I was dizzy and could barely tee the ball up. Sick to my stomach. I swung and hit a decent drive. I'm not sure how I did that. Then I puked on the first tee. I had to get down on my knees, between the tee markers, and let it all out. It was disgusting. The two guys we were paired with couldn't believe it. The starter had to delay play and call guys to come out and hose down the teeing ground."

"That's awful. How did you play?"

"I don't really remember much, except when we got to the sixth tee, I barfed again and just lay on the bench and went to sleep. My friend picked me up again on the way back in the middle of fourteenth fairway. Funny, because we can see that bench, if it wasn't foggy this morning, from our backyard. From sleeping on the sixth tee, drunk, to owning this thirty-five-million-dollar estate, a few hundred yards away."

"Life is strange," Jenny said.

"I've never been drunk again before a practice round or a tournament round, since then. I learned my lesson."

Angus had stopped running around and was making like a pointer, standing ramrod straight, with his head facing into the mist, in the direction of the estate next door. He started barking. Chipper and Jenny stared through the mist as a man and another Scottie dog came walking toward them. When Angus saw the dog, a wheaten-colored Scottie, just a bit smaller than Angus, he started running toward the apparition in the mist. His tail was wagging, so Jenny knew he wasn't angry, just eager to meet the other dog.

As the man came out of the mist, Chipper could tell it was Richard Stein. Stein and his girlfriend, Debbie, must have finished moving into the estate next door. Strange, but maybe not so unbelievable, knowing Stein. He was dressed in knickers, long argyle socks that covered his lower leg, a matching argyle sweater, and a Ben Hogan golf-style hat. It looked like Bobby Jones, himself, was marching into Chipper's backyard. Before Chipper or Jenny had a chance to say hello, Stein started yelling, several times, "Hi, neighbors! Hi, Chipper! Hi, Jenny! Hi, Angus! I brought you a girlfriend!"

Jenny replied first, "Hi, Richard. You are up early. What a beautiful dog. Are you trying to copy us? Angus is one of a kind."

Stein watched as Angus and his Scottie dog, sniffed around and circled each other, with both of their tails wagging. "It looks like they are getting along already. Angus, this is Abigail, but we usually call her Abby. We've had her a week only. She's a beauty, isn't she?" Angus was busy sniffing Abby's rear end.

Jenny was embarrassed, "Angus, be a gentleman. Calm down, Angus. Is she spayed, Richard?"

"Nope. Debbie didn't want her spayed. She's been talking about having puppies around. She loves puppies."

Chipper watched as Angus and Abby continued to circle each other. "When did you move in, Richard? I'm surprised we didn't see any moving trucks or hear much noise."

"We didn't move much furniture in yet. Just the minimum. We couldn't move in until the chemicals in the bedroom the previous part-time owners used were clear and we got the go-ahead to move in. Debbie wants to get an interior decorator before we get new furniture. You know, the Arabs paid seventy-five million cash for the property, and I got it for a song. It's good to be an insider here in the Forest. We're just going to try to get comfortable living in such a big estate."

Jenny commented on Richard's outfit, "You look ready for golf, Richard. Very sporty."

"I knew you did the morning shot. If it's ok, I'd like to do it this morning, and maybe on some other mornings when I'm up early."

Chipper looked at Jenny, and Jenny said, "It's ok with me, Richard. I actually have some things to talk to you about that I want you to bring up at the managers' meeting: some proposals from our Foundation."

"I'd be happy to do that, but I won't remember anything so early this morning. How about emailing me your ideas? If they are too crazy, I won't do it, but I can't imagine them being too crazy."

Chipper was getting impatient, and Angus was losing some interest in Abby. Both wanted to get the golf shots in, and Angus was eager to run. Abby wanted to play and was running around on the lawn, but Angus didn't want to play. He had serious work to do in retrieving the morning golf balls.

Jenny warmed up and hit first, a decent shot, but nothing special. She knew it would be on the green, but nowhere near the hole. Angus took off, and Abby seemed fascinated by the sprinting black dog. Angus disappeared in the mist, then returned and put the Slazenger golf ball down at Jenny's feet. Abby came over and sniffed when Chipper gave Angus seven dog treats.

When Chipper hit his shot, Angus took off again, and Abby followed him about fifty yards before stopping and waiting for Angus to return. When Angus came back, golf ball in mouth, Abby followed Angus slowly back to Chipper. This time, Chipper gave Angus only five treats and gave Abby the other two. Angus seemed perplexed and not happy at all. He barked a few times at Abby, as Abby chewed the two treats.

Chipper had to go up the stairs and grab another Slazenger and seven more dog treats. Stein asked why he couldn't just hit one of the Slazengers Chipper and Jenny had hit? The answer from Chipper was "Ben Morris wouldn't like it, Richard. Only one shot for each person in the morning, and only one shot for each golf ball. Then they get donated. That was Ben's rules. Have to respect Ben."

Stein's shot wasn't very good. He did get it into the air, but it hit a tree about fifty yards ahead and bounded left into the fourteenth fairway. Angus, and this time Abby, seemed to race for the ball, Angus barely getting there first. Abby looked like she enjoyed the romp, but Angus looked furious. He was growling. He seemed to be thinking, "*This is my territory. This is serious business. Don't mess with me.*" When the dogs ran back and Chipper gave four treats to Angus and three to Abby, Angus lunged for Abby's face.

Chipper frantically grabbed Angus from behind, and no harm was done. Angus quickly ran up the back stairs and stood by the back door. Jenny said, "Sorry for that, Richard. Angus hasn't ever acted like that before. It's very strange for him to have another dog here. I'm sure they will learn to get along. I'll email my proposals. Say hello to Debbie for me. I'd love to go inside the house and see what it's like."

Stein said, "Any time, Jenny. It's pretty empty now." Then he turned and retreated into the mist with Abby. Chipper and Jenny heard him yell back, "I'll hit a better shot next time! That was fun!"

STEIN AT WORK

Richard Stein strutted into the Pebble Beach Lodge in the same clothes he wore for the morning shot. He went up the stairs to his office and looked at the name plate near his door.

RICHARD STEIN
GENERAL COUNSEL AND VP FOR
COMMUNITY RELATIONS

He was happy with his life. He had worked his way up from being an assistant to the evil Dorothy Golberry to taking her job and being promoted to VP. He had made millions in buying property and now in managing the NIL money and contracts for Cindy Springer. He had just moved into a prestigious estate off the fourteenth fairway at Pebble Beach Golf Course. All this had happened very quickly, and he was proud of himself.

He also had a good looking girlfriend in Debbie Rogers, and Debbie seemed to be happy and in love with Richard. He could wear whatever he wanted, and people expected his changing fashion statements: a cowboy one day, three-piece suit the next, Ben Hogan look today. Who knows what tomorrow? He was on top of the world. He looked out the picture window of his office and admired the view of the eighteenth green at Pebble and Carmel Bay behind it.

Richard then listened to his office phone messages, and his reaction was classic. None of his messages were related to Pebble Beach Corporation. There were three messages from Cindy Springer NIL sponsors, Nike, Under Armour, and Oiselle, all saying the same thing: *What the hell was she thinking in the latest posts on social media? We can't sponsor her anymore unless they are taken down immediately. We don't want her promoting our product anymore. This is absolutely awful.* Stein couldn't believe the messages. He hadn't looked at Cindy's Instagram, TikTok, YouTube, and Facebook posts for several days. He immediately looked at the latest posts and was incredulous. *What the fuck was Duncan thinking? This was awful.*

Stein immediately called Duncan Campbell, Cindy's boyfriend and the Instagram posting king in her world. Duncan was responsible for making Cindy and Jenny Nelson famous with his postings of their lessons and Cindy's quest to get better in golf. Cindy was making millions in NIL money, and now it was all in danger of slipping away. Duncan answered, and Stein started yelling, "What the fuck, Duncan? What the hell are you and Cindy doing? And I can't believe that Jenny posed like that, too. Are you fucking crazy?"

Duncan was calm when he said, "I saw it early last night, Richard. I've been trying to take it down since then. I've been up all night. I did NOT do this! Really, Richard, did you think I would actually do something like that? Cindy is so mad at me, she won't talk to me. She made me sleep in another room."

Stein yelled back, "Have you heard from Chipper or Jenny? Chipper will kill you, whether it's your fault or not. How could something like this happen? What kind of car is that anyway? Very fancy."

Duncan said, "I have not heard from Chipper or Jenny. There was some asshole at the driving range yesterday with the car. He was angry when Cindy put her leg up onto the car. He took some pictures. He might have done some kind of Artificial Intelligence or Photoshop thing, but so could any of the other forty crazy guys that always watch the noon lessons. AI is so easy these days that any of those idiots could have taken pictures and posted them. I can't figure out how to get rid of them."

Stein looked at the social media posts again and saw both a completely naked Cindy and a completely naked Jenny. Cindy had her leg up on the car, and her entire body was compromised and for everyone to see in all her glory. Jenny was standing, completely naked, in front of the car, but was sideways and in not as revealing a pose as Cindy. He finally said, "Duncan, sorry for asking this, but I don't think Cindy or Jenny have breasts as big as in the photos. And I don't think Cindy's legs are that long?" Stein paused and waited for Duncan to respond.

Duncan seemed embarrassed when he said, "You are right, Duncan. Her breasts are not that big, and her legs aren't that long. The bodies on both of them have been Photoshopped in. I'm sure Jenny's breasts aren't that big, either. This is awful, Richard."

"It's worse than you think, Duncan. Her major sponsors, maybe all her sponsors, will cut her off if these photos don't disappear now. You'll have to move out of your new estate. You'll default on your mortgage. You'll have to live in one of those limos you drive during the day. Get everything down, Duncan. By the way, what kind of car is that? I've never seen anything like that before. Does it have gull wings? Looks like it does. I might have to get one of those."

"The idiot said something about the car. It was a strange name. I do remember he said it was over three million dollars and he paid cash. What a guy! I don't care about the car. All I care about is getting the nude and semi-nude photos down. Maybe I can just take down every social media post and start over," Duncan said. "That's what I'll do. Since I can't seem to cut the offending photos out on their own, I'll just take all the posting down and start over. I hope Jenny doesn't see these. Give me an hour, Richard. Give me an hour."

Stein said, "What's to prevent this from happening again, Duncan?"

"Nothing can prevent it, Richard. It can happen again. AI is a curse."

Stein was happy to look at the photos of both Cindy and Jenny for another ten minutes. Then he shut off his phone and immediately contacted OnlyFans, asked to speak to the manager of the content department, and told him to take a look at the photos of Cindy and Jenny. Later in the day, he had another contract offer for Cindy from OnlyFans. Then he spent the next several hours calling Cindy's NIL sponsors and calming their nerves. He was trying to balance the best of both worlds. He took a look at Jenny's email to him about her ideas for Foundation donations involving The Hay golf course. He snickered as he printed off the email. He felt they would make for a good laugh at his next managers' meeting.

CHIPPER AT WORK

Chipper viewed his driving range time as play, and not work. He was in a bubble when he was at the driving range. It was golf all the time, whether watching, picking up balls, replacing divots, moving tees, or hitting balls himself when there was a chance. Today, he didn't play his way into work. He drove his Tesla so that he and Jenny could play Cypress in the early afternoon. It was a rare treat. He was hoping Jenny could cancel her afternoon lessons and they would head over after her noon lesson with Cindy Springer. Big Bill O'Shea had agreed to handle the afternoon driving range duties. Chipper was eager to talk to Big Bill about how Irene McVay was doing.

Big Bill arrived about thirty minutes before noon and found Chipper hitting balls on the left side of the range. Bill watched Chipper hit a few, then grabbed Chipper's driver and started pounding his usual big fade down the range. Chipper said, "You are going to break my driver. It's not used to that hard a swing." Bill was carrying it about two hundred and seventy-five yards, with his big high fade.

Bill's first comment was, "Chipper, I imagine you saw the photos of Jenny and Cindy on the internet this morning?"

"No. I never look. Jenny doesn't look, either."

"You should have looked. I never look either, but the pro at Spyglass showed them to me. They were both naked. Cindy, full frontal, with her leg up on some sort of sports car, and Jenny was from the side."

"You've got to be kidding me. Jenny would never do that in a million years. She would never do that. It had to be Photoshopped or something. I hope she didn't see it. If she did, she would have called me already. I'm sure she didn't see it. That fucking Duncan. Why would he do that? Maybe he needed more views. I'm gonna fuckin' kill him."

"I can't imagine Duncan would do it, either. It was pretty well done, though, didn't look Photoshopped. Had to be done by someone who knew what they were doing."

Chipper started looking at his phone, but Bill said, "It's down already. Photos aren't there anymore."

"I can see Cindy maybe doing that, or maybe at the prompting of Stein, just to get more viewers. Or it might have been one of those idiots standing over there, waiting for the noon lesson. Those assholes are here every day. Don't they have anything better to do? I'm still gonna kill Duncan when he gets here. How is Irene?"

Chipper grabbed his own driver back and started angrily hitting balls down the range. Bill started talking about Irene McVay. "She is much better. I had to push her around in a wheelchair for about ten days because her ribs hurt so much. Now she is getting out of bed and walking around by herself. Those Arabs really did a number on her. The police have been over three different times to talk to her. The FBI guys, twice. Her story is the same every time, which is good. She is a hero, just like you, but no one is recognizing that. Her memory is a little fuzzy, but coming back. She can talk ok now. She likes to stand in front of the mirror, naked, and talk about how good she looks. Hasn't been this skinny since she was in college. And, I have to say, she does look good. Her sixty-year-old body looks like a thirty-year-old's. She must still be hurting, though, because her sex drive hasn't come back yet. You know, she's usually a very horny woman."

"Too much information, Bill. It's nice of you to take care of her the last several weeks. I'm eager to see her. When do you think she'll finally allow me and Jenny to come over? I'm sure Angus wants to see her, too. That would cheer her up."

Chipper heard a large applause from the large group of spectators now gathered at the back of the range. He was surprised there seemed to be double the usual number. They were applauding because Cindy and Duncan were coming out of Duncan's work limo. Chipper couldn't hear all the catcalls, but there were several that were out of line, and he grimaced when he heard them. "Nice body, Cindy." "You are sooo hot, girl." "Give us some skin, Cindy."

Jenny drove up in her Jaguar shortly after and received similar catcalls. Chipper tried to keep his patience. It wasn't easy. Chipper walked toward Duncan, who was carrying Cindy's bag, and immediately started questioning him. "How did it happen, Duncan? How could you let that happen?"

"I didn't do it, Chipper. You know I would never do that. The photos were done by someone else and posted on the site. I had trouble taking them down. I spent most of the morning working on getting them to disappear. The person that posted had some technical knowledge to set it up so I couldn't erase them easily. Could be one of those idiots over there, or it could have been that idiot that had the fancy car yesterday. Who knows?"

"I never saw the photos? Do you have them? Bill told me about it."

'Yes, I have them, but you don't want to look, Chipper. You really don't."

"Let me see them, Duncan." Duncan reluctantly showed Chipper the photos on his phone. Chipper actually smiled when he said, "These obviously aren't Cindy and Jenny. The faces are, but not the bodies, but I guess no one would know that except you and me. Cindy's is much worse than Jenny's. Full frontal. Wow." Duncan just shook his head back and forth. They both looked at the crowd gathered at the back of the range.

Jenny came up to Chipper, hugged him, and hung her head. "So embarrassing, Mr. Chips. So bad. Who would do that to me? I really want to get out and play Cypress and try to forget all this. Can we take Cindy?" Chipper nodded yes. Jenny continued, "Angus was a wild dog this morning after you left. I had to drag him into the house and close the dog door so he couldn't immediately run out again. Then he just barked and jumped and scratched at the back door the entire time I ate breakfast and changed. I finally let him out and watched him go down the stairs, and he just bolted toward Stein's house. I don't know if he wants to kill Abby or he has other dishonorable intentions. He was crazed."

Chipper said, "I'm sure he has honorable intentions. Just wants to see his new friend again."

"But they didn't really get along at all. I'm not sure Angus likes Abby."

While Jenny was giving Cindy her lesson, besides the usual yelling from the assembled crowd, they heard some different kinds of "oohs" and "aahs" and turned to see the Pagani Huayra car parking near the crowd. They couldn't remember the guy's name, but he exited his car, waved to the crowd, took out his cell phone, and started to film Jenny and Cindy on the range. Chipper took off running, holding a golf club, but the stranger jumped into his car and backed up quickly. The car was moving back, even with the gull-wing doors still closing. The crowd was yelling, wildly, "Club him!" "Hit the car!" "Get him!" But it was too late, and Chipper walked back to the range muttering.

"It's got to be that guy who is posting the naked pictures. Duncan, make sure you look and see in a bit. How can we find that guy?"

CHIPPER AT PLAY

Duncan headed off to work as a limo driver. Jenny left her car at the range. Chipper, Jenny, and Cindy put their clubs into the Tesla and headed off to Cypress Point. Cindy was over the moon. "The only class I have this afternoon is Business Marketing. I can skip that. I learn more from Richard than I do in class. This is going to be great. Really great. Cypress Point. I know the team played there last year. Thank you, Jenny. Thank you, Chipper. I'm going to beat both of you, you know."

Chipper said his usual, "Calm down, Cindy. Just be quiet and enjoy the day. No need to gush all the time. It's kind of a spiritual place. The Sistine Chapel of golf. No loud noises." Chipper pulled the Tesla onto the grass parking area, very close to the first tee.

Cindy couldn't help it. "Wow. We're parking twenty feet from the first tee. And on the grass! On the grass! The clubhouse and whatever building that is, is much smaller than I thought it would be. Not fancy at all."

"It's just about the golf, Cindy. No special amenities needed," Chipper commented.

Jenny said quietly, "That's Bradenton, the club President, just getting ready to tee off. Irene dated him awhile. Didn't know he was married. He took advantage of her. What a scumbag. Usually carts aren't allowed, but isn't that the Admiral in the cart? Angus peed on his foot at our membership meeting visit last year at our house. Very unlikeable guy, but when drunk, he's very funny. Must be ninety years old."

All Chipper could think about was *we're about ten minutes too late. I hope we don't have to play behind these clowns. They should let us through, or we'll have to go around them and skip a few holes. We should have gotten here a few minutes earlier.*

When they exited the Tesla, Bradenton was teeing off, and the car made a loud quacking noise, right in the middle of his backswing. Chipper had the Tesla locking sound on random, and it could have jingled, applauded, made a goat scream, or the sound of an old-school "ahooga". The loud quack was unfortunate, and Bradenton topped one completely. The ball didn't even roll off the front of the first tee.

Bradenton looked right at the Tesla and said, "Fuck the Tesla. Fuck you, Blair. Did you do that on purpose? Damn electric cars. We shouldn't have let you become a member, with your damn electric car."

Chipper said, "Go hit a mulligan, Richard."

The Admiral, from his cart, yelled, "No fucking mulligans! We have a match. Big money riding on this. No fucking mulligans."

Bradenton, reluctantly, walked to the front of the tee, where his golf ball was lying, and tried to hit a fairway metal, again topping the ball.

Chipper said, "Can the three of us just tee off and get out of your way? We'll be quick."

Bradenton looked back and angrily yelled, "No way, Blair! No fucking way. And who is the little girl who is improperly dressed for this club?" Cindy was wearing a short skirt and a sleeveless top. "Get her some pants before she heads out." Bradenton and his caddie then followed the Admiral's cart and his driver down the fairway to the ladies' tees. The Admiral, very slowly, exited the cart, took about a dozen practice swings, and hit one about fifty yards down the middle.

They could hear the Admiral yell, "Right down the middle. Take that, Bradenton."

Chipper suggested to Jenny and Cindy that they walk over to number fifteen and start there with the par-three, then play through eighteen, before starting again on number one. They would probably still catch Bradenton and the Admiral while they were on the front nine. Cindy stayed dressed as she was.

On the walk down the paved 17-Mile Drive over toward the fifteenth hole, Cindy asked Jenny and Chipper if they were free on Saturday night. She was planning on having an impromptu housewarming and inviting all her golf team friends and others she knew in the Forest. She was going to send out an evite, but also walk over to her neighbors' estates on each side of her house and across the street and put invitations into their mail boxes. "It's going to be a great party. I love the house so much." Although Chipper was reluctant, Jenny immediately asked if she could help with anything and told Cindy both of them would be there.

When they turned off the 17-Mile Drive and onto the path that led to the fifteenth tee, Cindy went crazy when she saw the hole, "I can't help it, Chipper. I'm gonna scream. Look at this hole. This is the most beautiful hole I've ever seen. The ocean, the cypress trees, the sand. This is heaven." She started jumping up and down, dropped her golf bag, took out her cell phone, and started snapping photos. She handed her phone to Jenny and made Jenny take about twenty photos of Cindy with the green behind her.

Chipper ignored them both and started swinging his nine iron. The hole was one hundred and thirty-five yards. The pin was tucked over to the right side of the green…a relatively easy pin position. Jenny and Cindy soon joined him in swinging some clubs to warm up. The girls would play the same tees as Chipper. Chipper looked at Cindy and said, "Ok. What are you thinking when you set up to hit this shot?"

"I'm only thinking that I've died and gone to heaven. I don't care how I hit the shot. I just want to sit here forever." Chipper looked at her and had to admit that she was right, also that she had great legs, but it was time to get serious about her golf.

"No. Really. Think about golf. What are your thoughts?"

"The wind is not that strong, and it's coming in from the right. There is a lot of trouble on the right. Ocean, rocks, a bunker, ice plant. I'm not going to hit my shot out to the right and hope the wind brings it back to the hole. I'm going to club up, hit a seven iron, aim a bit left of the pin and try to hold a little cut up against the wind. I know from everything you've ever told me that I don't want a downhill putt, so I'm not going to hit it very hard. I'd rather be short of the hole than past it. Then I'm going to think very positively. Hit my own shot. Swing my own swing."

Chipper didn't say anything, but was proud of Cindy. She was definitely becoming a golfer. He watched as she put her ball on a short tee on the left side of the teeing area and hit exactly the shot she was trying to hit. It started toward the middle of the green, faded a bit to the right, then the wind caught it and kept it straight. It hit about five feet to the left of the pin and spun back about a foot. She was in birdie position. Jenny clapped, and Chipper said, "Don't encourage her, Jenny," but it was too late. Cindy was running around the teeing area yelling and jumping and sprinting back and forth. She was like Angus.

Jenny hit a conservative shot and was about twenty feet away. Chipper hit a dead straight shot to about ten feet short of the pin. Cindy was smugly saying, "I'm closest," several times when they walked around the inlet to the green. Jenny and Chipper both two-putted, with neither putt having any chance of going in. Cindy stepped up and knocked her putt into the center of the cup for a birdie. "Let's play this hole again. I don't want to leave this hole. Can we play it again?"

Jenny and Chipper picked up their golf bags and headed through the canopy of cypress trees on the dirt path to the sixteenth tee. Cindy was serious for a change and asked Jenny, "Did you see that shot I hit? Of course you did. Pretty good, huh? Do you think, Jenny, that maybe I could ever get good enough to try the LPGA tour? I'm afraid my NIL money will stop after next year when I graduate. Does NIL money stop when I graduate?"

Jenny said, "You'll have to ask Richard about the NIL money. I don't think it stops as long as Duncan keeps posting your photos on the internet. You'll remain a big star and make money. It might not be called NIL money, but it would certainly be sponsorship money. And realistically, Cindy, most LPGA pros started playing when they were very young. You have some talent and have come a very long way in a short time, but there is very little chance you can become an LPGA touring pro. If you love golf, then maybe another job in the golf industry: a teacher, like me. Look how much Paige Spiranac makes as an influencer. You should just concentrate on doing as well as you can on your golf team and getting better every day." Cindy dropped her bag and hugged Jenny.

"Thank you for always being so honest with me, Jenny. But I am going to be hard-working and optimistic. I am going to be a touring pro. You can bet on that," Cindy commented.

When they came out of the cypress grove and Cindy got her first look at number sixteen, she was uncharacteristically silent. Complete silence as she looked over the ocean chasm in front of her and at the green in the distance. Chipper finally bumped her to make her break her silence. "How am I supposed to play this hole? It's impossible. It's like hitting the ball over the ocean to China. This hole is unfair."

Chipper said, "You can make it with any sort of a solid driver. Jenny can make it, and you hit it as far as she does. It's two hundred and thirty yards to the middle of the green, where the pin is. Looks farther, but that's what it is. You need to just carry it about two hundred and twenty. You can do that from the men's tees. Just hit a solid shot. Don't be intimidated."

Cindy hit first and was talking to herself when she swung the club. She hit a weak slice and watched as the ball came nowhere close to the green and disappeared over the cliff into the water. "Oh, fudge! That one doesn't count. Let me hit another."

"You have to hit another. Hitting three now." Jenny said, "Not a very professional shot, Miss LPGA pro."

"Don't make fun of me, Jenny. I'll do it this time."

As Jenny was saying, "You have to be tough," Cindy was already hitting another ball. This time she hit a high fade and carried the front bunker. A short bounce forward and she was putting, with a long putt for bogey." Jenny hit one on the green, and so did Chipper. Although they felt like it, they didn't point out to Cindy that down on the rocks near the water is where Emily Hastings' son, Steven, fell and died after being shot by Condoleezza Rice's bodyguard. Hastings had been trying to shoot the CSUMB golf team members and Jenny while they stood on the sixteenth tee.

Instead, when they got to the green, Jenny showed Cindy the exact spot where Chipper proposed to her. Jenny asked Chipper to recreate the moment for Cindy and get down on his knees, but all Chipper said was, "We're putting now. Concentrate on the golf. Just golf." All three two-putted. Chipper and Jenny for pars. Cindy for double bogey.

When they started to walk to the seventeenth tee, Cindy said, "Why don't we just play fifteen and sixteen over and over again? I'm ready to walk back to the fifteenth tee. Next time we can play the whole course, when that guy on the first tee and the Admiral are not around. Let's play fifteen and sixteen again."

Chipper and Jenny agreed, and they all spent a very enjoyable afternoon playing the two great par-threes over and over again. Cindy lost several balls on number sixteen, but enjoyed every minute of it.

SPECIAL MANAGEMENT MEETING

Richard Stein wasn't notified about the special Pebble Beach Corporation management meeting until four in the afternoon. He thought it must be very important for a meeting to be called so late in the day. He headed into the Bench Restaurant immediately, as the small conference room off the restaurant was where the meeting would be held. He was happy about the location, as CEO Donald Stevens usually brought in expensive scotch from the bar for everyone. It made for a lively meeting, after everyone had a few drams. Stein surprised himself by remembering to bring a copy of Jenny's email about her ideas on the Ben Morris Foundation's potential donations and projects.

Stein found three very expensive-looking and old-looking bottles of scotch already spread out on the conference table. He was the third to arrive and found CEO Stevens and COO Catherine McDougall already nursing large glasses of the brew. Stein sat at his usual seat, third one on the far side of the table, and grabbed one of the bottles that was closest to him. Neither Stevens nor McDougall said hello. They were quiet. The bottle had what looked like an elk's head prominent on the side. He looked at The Dalmore 25 label and poured himself a substantial glassful. When Stein took out his phone to google the price of the scotch, he had barely typed in the D-A-L, when Stevens said, "Don't bother, Richard. It's about three thousand dollars a bottle. I hope you enjoy it. The bar charges four hundred dollars for a few sips."

Stein sipped slowly as the silence returned. He watched head golf pro Roger Hennessey and several other executive vice presidents of one thing or another enter the room and take their customary seats at the table. The silence continued. The head of security was the last one to arrive, and it was only then that Stein had some sort of an idea that the subject of the meeting would be something unusual.

Stevens waited until everyone had poured their scotch before he started, "I hope you are enjoying your scotch. It's a good one. We have two special subjects today. I want total secrecy about both of them. No one is to leak anything about this to anyone." Stein felt that Stevens was only looking at him as he said this. Stein looked both right and left and tried not to look suspicious. His relationship with Stevens wasn't the best. Nothing to worry about, but Stein wished it was better.

"The first item has to do with The Hay. We are going to be visited by the Duke and Duchess of Irvingtonshire. They are avid golfers and have a daughter who is eight and a son who is six. They have paid us a substantial sum to have exclusive playing rights at The Hay for five days. When I say substantial, I mean very substantial. They like privacy when they play golf, and the purpose of their visit is to teach their two children the game. They felt The Hay par-three course was a great place to teach their children the game. They are bringing teaching pro Chris Como with them..."

Roger interrupted Stevens, "Why aren't they using one of our teaching pros? Jenny Nelson would be perfect for them."

Stevens didn't look happy when he replied, "When they are paying as much as they are, they can have any teaching pro they damn well want, Roger. Let me finish." Stevens took a big swallow of scotch before continuing, "Como will be giving beginner lessons to the two children. The Duke and Duchess don't want anyone around. Security is going to put up a fifteen-foot commercial block vinyl fence around the entire golf course very soon. No one can see in. Our corporate statement to the press or anyone that asks will simply be that we are doing a few modifications to the golf course. Everyone needs to say the same thing. Just a few modifications to make The Hay even better. Does everyone have that?"

Stein felt that Stevens was looking at him again and he was the first one to grab a bottle of scotch for a second glassful. He was feeling pretty good and loose at this time and decided to bring up Jenny's idea, as long as The Hay golf course was the subject. "Got it, Donald. As long as we are discussing The Hay, I have been approached by a local nonprofit that is interested in promoting golf, and they wanted me to bring up an idea to see if there is any interest." Everyone at this point knew it was from Jenny and the Ben and Aileen Morris Foundation. He continued, "The Foundation is offering to pay enough money to the Pebble Beach Corporation each year to allow The Hay to provide free rounds all year to all those that play. It's a substantial amount of money." Stein didn't want to say the amount yet.

Everyone at the table looked at Stevens for a reply, and Stevens looked right back at each face at the table, waiting for someone to make a comment. When there were none, he said, "How much are they offering?"

Stein didn't want to offer up the seven and a half million amount so he said, "Five million dollars." Stevens looked at the Chief Financial Officer, and the CFO just shook his head to indicate "No."

Stein said, "How much would it take to make the correct offer and get the corporation more than is currently made in green fees at The Hay? Bringing in more people would also raise the business and revenues at the restaurant and bar."

"This is a waste of time," Stevens finally said. "We're getting more than five million from the Duke and Duchess just for the five days they are here. Making green fees at The Hay zero would bring in all the riff-raff. We don't want riff-raff here. No riff-raff. You tell Nelson and Blair the answer is no!" Stein knew when to stop and didn't continue.

Stevens stared at Stein, without saying anything for a long enough time that the entire table of managers were getting uncomfortable. Several started fidgeting, and many reached for a second glass of scotch. Stevens finally started again, "The second item is that we have been approached by a new tech state-of-the-art driving range company to be one of the first locations to have installed a totally technical, AI-based driving range. It would require minimal maintenance and provides a total golf learning experience for the user. Driving range fees would rise, and maintenance costs would go down. Because we would be a first early adapter they have offered us a great price, as well. I have some videos to show you what they are proposing which explain everything."

Stein watched, every second thinking that Chipper Blair would be out of work in his traditional driving range job if this were to happen. Chipper would be so much against this project and experience that he would go crazy watching this video or even hearing about the new idea.

The well-filmed and narrated video presentation showed a driving range that was totally artificial turf, from the immaculate teeing areas to the totality of the driving range turf in the distance. Each hitting area was equipped with a built-in state-of-the-art swing monitor that showed swing speed, ball speed, spin rate, distance, curve, elevation, face to path, swing to path, smash rate, and some other things Stein knew nothing about. The swing monitor made calculations that adjusted for wind speed and direction, air temperature, humidity, and barometric pressure. There were some "ooohs" and "aaahs" from the group during the video. Stein could tell by Hennessey's reaction that he was thinking the same thing about Chipper as Stein was.

The driving range turf area had pins placed every twenty yards with large flags that had the distance marked on them in very colorful and bold lettering. Very easy to see.

Each hitting area had a pay station where the golfer could pay for exactly the number of balls they wanted by tapping a credit card. They could hit the number of balls they wanted, then order more without heading back to the range shack or anywhere else. The balls were delivered immediately into a trough-like area. The golfer could also use the screen to elevate a tee to any desired height that they chose or to make it depress into the mat and disappear.

The artificial turf in the three-hundred-yard-long range was bordered by realistic-looking murals on each side and at the far end that looked like trees, clouds, and bushes. They also provided the additional benefit that any ball hitting the bordering mural screens would rebound back into the turf area. All areas and sides of the turf area sloped into several lower collection areas where every ball hit would roll into underground conveyer belts that would bring the balls back toward the teeing area.

The next part of the video was conceptual, as it showed graphics of the underground system. When the balls came back toward the teeing area, they went under a washing and cleaning process, much like a car wash. Then into a camera and sensitivity review process to determine if the ball was damaged in any way. If it was, it headed into the dead ball area, was immediately printed with a Pebble Beach Golf Course logo, and packaged with other such balls into groups of three. Because of the nature of the turf, there wasn't any chance for the balls to become muddy or very dirty, but some were always damaged by bad swings. Stein was actually pretty impressed by the process.

The company had statistics showing almost 100% of the balls remained in use, rather than packaged to be sold. The remaining in-use balls were then dispensed back underground to each hitting area, ready to be used again. It was foolproof.

When the video was over, everyone applauded except for Richard Stein and Roger Hennessey. When everyone left, they stayed after and finished the remaining scotch, the whole time guessing what Chipper would say or do if he ever heard about this proposal.

THE HAY

Jenny, Chipper, and Cindy finally played the seventeenth and eighteenth holes at Cypress Point, then drove to The Hay to meet Duncan and have some drinks. Cindy was kind of unimpressed with the last two holes at Cypress. "These aren't so great. After playing fifteen and sixteen, they are kind of a letdown, especially number eighteen." She had bogeyed both holes, a long way from being good enough to be an LPGA pro. During the car ride to The Hay, she wouldn't be quiet. Chipper finally had to turn the radio up really loud for Cindy to get the not-so-subtle hint.

When they walked to the outside deck area of The Hay, Duncan was sitting with Richard Stein, and they had the best outside table on the deck. Right near the eighth tee, behind the wind-protecting plexiglass. Debbie Rogers had already brought Chipper and Jenny's favorite drinks to the table: the Aztec Old Fashioned for Chipper and a Pom Watson for Jenny. Richard was obviously drunk already, and Duncan looked forlorn. Cindy started immediately enthusiastically talking about her shots on number fifteen and sixteen at Cypress. She stopped when Duncan held up his phone and showed her photos from today's range session at Pebble Beach earlier. Jenny looked over her shoulder as Cindy just said, "Oh, my gosh." several times, over and over again. Jenny had to look away.

Stein took the phone from Duncan and laughed heartily, before saying, "It's obviously not you guys. The breasts are too big, and who would ever hit golf balls completely naked on a driving range? Or anywhere, for that matter." Stein looked over at Jenny and Cindy and again said, "Obviously, not your breasts. Either one of you." Duncan took the phone back and turned it completely off.

Chipper said, "How do we stop this guy? It's obviously the asshole with the strange-looking sports car. Can we take it down immediately, Duncan?"

Stein said, "You're going to make a lot of money off of this, Cindy. It's not such a bad thing."

At the same time, Chipper and Jenny both said, "Shut up, Richard. Just keep your mouth shut." Stein was wearing the same outfit he had on the other morning, knickers with long socks, with a matching Ben Hogan-style cap. He looked ludicrous, but he did shut up and just sat there sipping his drink with a big grin on his face.

Duncan said, "I can't shut it down here. I have to wait until we go home in order to do it on the desktop."

"Can you go now, Duncan? Please, go now, then come back." Pleaded Jenny. Cindy nodded at Duncan to do as Jenny said.

Debbie Rogers came back with two more drinks for Chipper and Jenny and said, "They are not your breasts, Jenny or Cindy, I can tell. Nice breasts, kind of like mine, but definitely not yours." Stein then grabbed Debbie gently by the waist and made her sit down on his lap. The other patrons nearby were shocked that a server would do this and more shocked when Stein reached around and fondled her right breast. "Not here. Not now, Richard." And she stood up and said to Cindy, "And what can I bring for you, beautiful young lady?"

Cindy said, "Can you bring me what Jenny is drinking?"

"Two issues, Cindy. One is you are still underage, and the other is your non-alcohol golf team contract," Debbie commented, as she left the table. In a few minutes she came back and said, "This one is just cranberry/pomegranate juice. You'll like it." Cindy took a sip and smiled at Debbie. It was heavy on the alcohol, and she needed it after seeing the internet photos of herself and Jenny.

Jenny pleaded, "Richard, can we get some sort of legal restraining order against this guy? It has to be him. I don't know what his motive is. Just a crazy tech guy."

Stein should have stopped drinking already and was slumping in his chair, "There is no way we can prove it was him, Jenny. There are about one hundred other idiots out there watching you guys every day. It could be one of them. And, like I told you, Cindy might make even more money off of this."

"Richard, this is serious stuff. I don't care about the moneymaking for Cindy. Look at what this does to our reputations. We have to make it stop."

Stein took another sip of his drink, slid down in his chair, and said, "I don't know how bigger breasts are going to hurt your reputation, Jenny."

"You are a pig, Richard. A total pig."

Chipper looked at his phone and saw that the photos were no longer there on Cindy's social media sites, but knew that, obviously, once on the internet, always on the internet. "They are gone. Duncan took the sites down again, but I'm sure they are all over everyone's phones by now. I hope it doesn't make the Cindy or Jenny discussion on Golf Channel again, but I bet it does. Next time I see that jerk, I'm gonna club him with my driver."

Cindy finished her drink and signaled Debbie to bring her another. Debbie ignored her. Cindy blurted out, "Let's change the subject. Did you see that birdie I made on fifteen? The very first time I played it. What a great shot. What a great shot. Thrill of a lifetime."

It was just getting dark when Duncan returned. Debbie brought both of them the same drink that Cindy had. Debbie was cutting Richard off, but bringing him non-alcoholic stuff, and he didn't notice. Richard confided, "Some strange things happened at the managers' meeting today. I really wish I could tell you what happened, but I have been sworn to secrecy, and I am a good soldier." He made a signal with his hand that his lips were sealed. But he couldn't keep quiet. "I just wish I could tell you guys. It affects you the most, Chipper, and kind of you too, Jenny. I just wish I could tell you."

Chipper said, "I don't even want to know, Richard." He pointed at Jenny and Cindy, and said, "Go get a few wedges, a putter, and a golf ball, let's go play more golf. I feel an ace coming on."

Jenny said, "It's dark, Chipper, and I've had a few drinks."

Cindy yelled, "I'm in!" and started jogging toward Chipper's car to get her clubs. She got there before Chipper. Jenny stayed at the table with Richard, while Chipper retrieved her wedges and putter.

It was dark, but the holes were short, and there was just enough light to see the pin placement on the first hole, only fifty-seven yards away from the tee. There was a group of men sitting near the tee, drinking on the outside deck. One of them yelled, "Kind of dark, isn't it?"

Chipper shouted back, "Not dark enough, buddy!" The Hay used mats on each tee to save the turf. Chipper teed up just back of the provided mat, on the grass turf. He would never expect anyone to want to hit off of artificial turf on a driving range, and certainly not on an actual golf course. The group applauded when Chipper hit first to the Biarritz-style green. The pin was in the front, and Chipper hit it about three feet away. He said the usual, "They don't call me Chipper for nothing, buddy."

The group gave catcalls when both Cindy and Jenny stepped up to hit. Jenny hit it about ten feet away and Cindy twelve. One of the guys yelled again, "Do you mind if we follow you around?"

Before Chipper could respond, Cindy yelled back, "Come on, guys! We'd love to have the gallery."

Jenny lipped out. Cindy left her putt short. Chipper made his three-footer for birdie. The group watching had about ten guys, who brought their drinks, and they all applauded again when Chipper's putt dropped.

Number two at The Hay was named "Seven" because it was an attempted replica of the seventh hole at Pebble, without the ocean. It was surrounded by traps, exactly in the same position as the famous Pebble Beach hole. There was a beautiful tall pine tree behind it. Chipper asked if someone in the gallery could walk ahead to the green and shout back where the pin was. Two guys sprinted ahead to the green. The pin was in the front. Chipper had played the seventh hole hundreds of times. He took out a wedge, heard applause at the green and someone shouted, "Two feet away! Two feet away!" He made another birdie and was two under after two. Cindy and Jenny again made pars.

The drunken gallery knew at this point they were watching something special. These golfers, even the two women playing, were impressive. The third hole was called "Watson" and was eighty-two yards long. No bunkers. Chipper knocked it ten feet away, and both Jenny and Cindy were closer. The gallery groaned when Chipper lipped out and went crazy when Jenny made her birdie. Cindy left her putt short. Two of the gallery took off running back to The Hay bar to get more refreshments.

It was now very dark and hard to see even the short, less-than-fifty-yard holes four and five. The fourth hole was only forty-seven yards, called "Bing," and had a blind green over a slight rise. The crowd yelled the pin was in the back. Chipper hit sand wedge to one foot. The crowd became even more raucous, so loud you could hear it back at the restaurant. Stein decided to head out on the course, but when he stood up, he realized he couldn't go anywhere without assistance. He sat back down. Jenny made birdie as well.

Chipper tapped in and made birdie on the forty-eight-yard fifth hole as well. Cindy made birdie on five. After five holes, Chipper was four under, Jenny was two under, and Cindy, one under. The noise on The Hay made more patrons head out onto the golf course in the dark. On the sixth green, the gallery was up to about twenty-five. Cindy whispered to Jenny, "I've never played before this many people since the qualifying round at Spyglass, when Golberry got killed by the tree."

Jenny said, "Nice memory, Cindy. I'm hoping nothing bad happens today. Chipper is in the zone."

The sixth was called "Lanny" and was seventy-seven yards, with a bunker to the right of the green. All three were on the green, but none very close. All three two-putted for easy pars. The crowd groaned when Chipper missed his longish birdie putt.

The seventh hole headed back toward the restaurant and bar and was named "Jack." It was only sixty-one yards long, after Jack Nicklaus's U.S. Amateur win at Pebble Beach in 1961. It had a bunker behind the green, but not really in play. Chipper knew The Hay course record was six under, twenty one. He needed two birdies in the last three holes to tie that. During the day, it was an impressive score. At night, it was extraordinary. For some reason, no one knew or kept track of the women's course record. That had to be an oversight. Or, maybe not.

Chipper hit a good shot, but it drew back too much and was fifteen feet short of the pin. He had an uphill putt that he looked over from both sides of the hole. He took so long examining it that a few in the drunk crowd were getting restless. Finally, one of them shouted, "Hit the putt, already! Just hit it! It's dead straight." Chipper thought it was going to break about a cup length to the left, but when the guy yelled it was straight, he started second-guessing himself. He stood over the putt with uncertainty, but backed off and decided to hit it the way he saw it. When the putt broke into the center of the hole, he pumped his fist. So did Jenny, and so did Cindy.

When they took the very short walk to the eighth tee, they saw the manager of The Hay restaurant, Mathew Mackey, standing on the tee, with his hands on his hips. He didn't look happy. As Chipper approached, Mackey said, "What the hell do you think you're doing, Chipper? The course is closed at dusk. You can't be out here, and you're taking all these people, who should be ordering in the bar, out there with you. I can't let you continue."

Chipper explained calmly that he was five under par and needed one birdie to tie the course record and two to break it. The crowd was murmuring. Mackey wasn't sympathetic and stood his ground, "I can't let you continue. It's dark."

Chipper couldn't keep his cool and grabbed his sand wedge out of his bag and tried to ignore the man. The crowd started yelling, "Let him play! Let them play!" Debbie Rogers ran out from the deck and stood between Chipper and her manager, Mackey. She was good friends with him. She stood very close, on her toes, and quietly talked him into letting the group finish. She said it would be good for business if Chipper tied or beat the course record.

The eighth hole was the Tom Kite hole, ninety-two yards long, and a bit downhill. It was named after his 1992 U.S. Open win at Pebble. Kite had played the course and his own hole the previous December when he was in Monterey to play in the Monterey Peninsula Country Club invitational. Kite made par on his own hole.

Chipper was upset and did not hit a good sand wedge. It was a bit thin and left. He managed to avoid the two bunkers on the left, but he missed the green. The first green he had missed on the short course. Jenny knocked it close and had a tap-in birdie. She said, "I wish I could give you that shot, Chipper."

Chipper had a tricky left-to-right-breaking downhill shot that he had to chip. Of course, he hit a cut shot that bit, took the roll to the right and stopped a few inches from the cup. "They don't call me Chipper for nothing." The crowd laughed, but Jenny had heard it so many times she expected it and didn't react. Chipper needed birdie on the last hole to tie the course record.

Jenny had the honors on the ninth hole. It went back toward the restaurant/bar and was slightly uphill. There were no bunkers, and the pin was in the easiest position on the green. The green had a circular depression exactly in the middle of it. Shots that were on line short, or long, or left, or right, would funnel down to the pin position. The ninth was called "Tiger," after the course designer, and was exactly one hundred yards long. Jenny just missed the bowl and was ten feet to the right of the pin. Exactly pin high.

The green was now surrounded by gallery, most still drinking, and very raucous. Some wanted Chipper to make birdie and tie the course record. Some didn't. They wanted him to fail.

There were some bets being made. Chipper took his sand wedge again. He fully expected to make birdie. He just had to get it five or six feet on either side of the hole, and it would get close to the pin. As soon as he hit the shot, he knew it was a good one. He said, "That's a good one." It was right on line. He couldn't see exactly what happened in the dark, but when he saw it head for the pin and waited, he heard a huge roar from the crowd. He wished he could have seen it hit. The ball hit about five feet over the pin and backed up in the depression, toward the hole, and went in. Ace. Hole in One. Course Record. He saw many in the crowd jumping up and down. Several came toward Chipper and shook his hand. Others were already heading to the bar in anticipation of free drinks. Cindy was shouting at the top of her lungs and trying to hug Chipper. When she was done, Jenny came up and simply said, "Good shot, Mr. Chips." Then she hugged him and whispered in his ear. "It's baby time, Chipper." Chipper remembered promising Jenny that if either of them made an ace at the morning shot on number fourteen at Pebble they would try to have a baby. He thought to himself, *"This isn't fourteen. This is nine at The Hay."* But he just hugged Jenny and didn't say anything.

When he reached the green and bent down to pull out the ball he yelled, "Drinks on me!" He didn't care how much it cost. Then he repaired his ball mark. Then he repaired a few more ball marks.

It was a great evening at The Hay after that. Chipper's bill was astronomical, even when Debbie gave him the employee discount. She also refused to let him leave her a tip on the total amount. Chipper got a lot of pats on the back, handshakes, and congratulations. The Hay closed very late.

Duncan had to drive Stein and Chipper and Jenny home. Stein had to be carried into Duncan's limo. Chipper was able to hobble to it himself. Jenny propped him up. Debbie followed in her car. Jenny remembered at one point late in the evening that Debbie mentioned Angus had hung around the backyard of Stein and Debbie's estate almost the whole day. Debbie said she let their dog, Abby, out at one point, and the two dogs were frolicking most of the day, until Debbie left for work. Chipper didn't remember anything about The Hay after his round, or getting home, or trying to make a baby three times when they got home. Jenny was irresistible.

MONTEREY HERALD

The next morning's Monterey Herald newspaper had an article from the only remaining reporter on the staff, Jerry Devine. The Herald, for the past several years, seemed to just take non-local articles from the AP or USA Today news lines. Devine was the only one that did local articles and seemed to have an unlimited source of gossip and a preoccupation with news about Chipper Blair and items about the rich and famous who lived in the Del Monte Forest.

BYLINE DEVINE

Course Record at The Hay. Or Not?

It seems the infamous Chipper Blair makes the news whether he wants to or not. He keeps saying he just wants to play golf, but he keeps getting into hot water. But the man can certainly play golf. Last night - that's right, I said last night, not during the day, but in the dark, our friend Chipper aced the last hole to shoot a 20, 7 under at The Hay. A course record by one. It has been verified by several who were watching. At least seventy-five people witnessed his hole in one on the ninth hole. Many followed him the whole round and commented that it could have been even better. He missed a few putts.

It's also notable that his wife, Jenny Nelson, shot three under. No one seems to know the women's course record, but at least this one was witnessed by a large gallery, mostly all drunk. Good for Jenny. She is a teaching pro at Pebble Beach. Blair, as most of you know, is a driving range attendant, although he calls himself an assistant pro.

But it seems that Blair always gets in some kind of trouble. It's not clear that his or Ms. Nelson's course records will be verified. The course was closed. They should not have been on the golf course at night. The Manager of The Hay tried to escort them off, after the seventh hole, but was persuaded to let them stay by an angry gallery that was following the group playing. The third member was CSUMB golfer, internet star and influencer, Cindy Springer.

There are two issues with his and her course records. The first is that the round was illegal. It was at night, and even though both are Pebble Beach Corporation employees, they did not check in or pay. They also took Springer out onto the course without paying. The second is that none of them played the tee-off mats. Blair refuses to hit off artificial-turf mats, and teed off on the grass near the mats. The mats are to be used to save the turf in the teeing areas. Apparently he didn't believe in that. From previous discussions I have had with Blair, he is a golf purist. He won't hit off mats. Ever.

We will have to wait and see if The Hay management and the Pebble Beach Corporation recognize the new course records. Whether they do or not, Blair shot twenty, and you can't take that away from him.

MONTEREY COUNTY WEEKLY

A few days later, the next issue of the Monterey County Weekly didn't mention Chipper or Jenny's golf feats, but did have some mention of Cindy and Jenny on the driving range.

THE SQUIDFRY

...The Squid certainly had its gills in a tizzy a few days back, when a co-worker pointed out a few local girls on the driving range at Pebble Beach. It's not unusual for women to hit driving range balls, but doing it naked is worthy of a mention. And it was the middle of the day. Teaching pro Jenny Nelson, wife of Chipper Blair, was giving a lesson to CSUMB internet star, Cindy Springer. The golf balls were not the only things that were bouncing. The Squid has to admit that these two are very good-looking fishes. The Squid may have to go over there and watch the next noon lesson...

EMILY HASTINGS

Emily Hastings was quite content. She had been living at Mr. Takahashi's house on Scenic Drive in Carmel for some months now. She had freshened up his spartan furnishings with new furniture, colorful pillows, knickknacks, paintings, and new fresh flowers every morning that were delivered promptly by Swenson and Silacci Flowers. It was not unusual for a delivery van to visit many estates in Pebble Beach and in Carmel every morning with fresh flowers. Takahashi liked the flowers, despite the high cost, and the new, mostly seabird-themed knickknacks. His Carmel stone façade made his house a tourist favorite when they strolled or drove by in the early evenings. The setting sun shining off the Carmel stone was quite striking.

Emily and Tak were familiar fixtures every morning on walks or runs along the winding path above the beach that was next to Scenic Drive. Emily enjoyed seeing familiar, friendly faces and waved to everyone on their morning jaunts. When Takahashi took his business trips to Japan, Emily enjoyed being comfortable in the house by herself and walking up Ocean Avenue to her favorite shops and bars in downtown Carmel. Her late-morning Irish coffee was a particular pleasure.

Emily was still in mourning for her son Steven, even though she knew his character was questionable, and he caused many people a lot of pain and anguish. She never thought of her late husband, Wells. Mr. Takahashi was a nice calming presence in her life, and they had grown to love each other. She told people that he was a gentle lover. With her habitual morning walks and runs, she was feeling good about herself and her discipline. She looked better, and she felt better. Life was becoming good again, although she missed her Pebble Beach estate and reputation as an exquisite hostess and party planner. Her parties in Pebble Beach were once the cream of the crop for Del Monte Forest socialites.

Takahashi was on his desktop computer in their upstairs living room, while Emily Hastings sipped on a glass of early-evening, pre-dinner, expensive port. Takahashi was sipping sake, while catching up on emails. The view from the living room, out the picture window, was magnificent. There was a panoramic view of Carmel Beach and Carmel Bay behind it. The sun was heading down toward the water, and the reflections off the water were dreamlike. The view alone was a twenty-million-dollar view. Emily's choice of furniture was off-white, and the previously sparse room was full of comfortable plush chairs and one couch. Wooden seabird sculptures adorned several side tables in the room.

Takahashi said, "We have been invited to a party this Saturday by a Cindy Springer. Isn't she the whompalicious golf girl that Jenny has been teaching?"

Emily perked up. "I picked up the mail at the post office today and didn't see any invitations. Did I miss it?"

"No. It come by email. An evite."

"What is an evite?" Emily questioned.

"It an invitation by email. It come by email."

"How horrible. How gauche. Très gauche." Emily sighed. "Invitations are supposed to be printed. I always had mine hand-printed and delivered by special messenger. How unsophisticated. What is this world coming to? I can't believe this."

"Party at your old house, this Saturday. A housewarming."

"Really? Really? How can she invite people on a Tuesday and expect they will come on Saturday? And this is in my house? Oh, this is a horror. A complete horror."

"Nice of her to invite us, no?" said Tak.

"She should have contacted me for help in this housewarming. I cannot imagine what kind of party this will be. We certainly can't give it legitimacy by going."

"I think I want to go," Takahashi said quietly. "Look at all the people that be there. We know many."

"How do you know who is going?"

"Look at evite. List of people invited. List of people coming. Right here. Also list of people not going. Also those who say maybe. Look, Emily. Look."

Emily leaned over and said, "Well, I never. This is called revite?"

"No. Called evite." Takahashi started listing those who were already coming. "My golf teacher Jenny and Chipper. Bill and your friend Irene. Attorney Stein and waitress server Debbie. Limo man, Jim Tiffany, and guest. I think Duncan work for Jim. Also funny strange man, Ian Osterholm, and guests..."

Emily said, "You mean that crazy man Osterholm was invited and told he could bring others? That is crazy to have a party and not know how many are coming. Absolutely crazy. How will she know how many places to set on the table? How will she know what to have the staff cook? How will she know how many place settings and glasses to use?"

Takahashi continued, "There are a lot with guests. One, your friend, Serena Antonelli and guest. She on golf team with Cindy. These other girls must be on golf team, too. Maya Garcia and guest. Madi Harwood and guest, Isabel Plumber and guest. Makena Moller and guest, Tilda Swenson and guest..."

"I don't have to hear you say everyone's name. I can read very well myself. It says it starts at five o'clock. What kind of party starts at five o'clock? If we go, I wouldn't have any idea what to wear. None at all. I think I'll call Irene. I'm surprised she is going. She's barely able to walk, after her ordeal." Emily sipped the last of her port and walked over and poured herself another glass. She thought to herself, *This could be horrible. I wonder what she has done to my house? She is barely out of diapers, this girl.*

Emily drank half of her port, then called Irene McVay. "How are you doing, Irene?"

"Much, much better, Emily. Much, much better. I almost feel alive again. Some lingering pain in my ribs. My thinking seems to be coming back. I can see straight again. It's not blurry. The pain medication helps me, but I know I have to stop taking it. I have a doctor's appointment tomorrow. How are you doing?"

"We just got something called a revite from that little girl Cindy Springer, who for some reason, now lives in my estate. I hope she is enjoying my years of decorating and good taste. The revite said that you and Bill are going..."

Irene interrupted, "Oh, I forgot to tell you, we had sex. It's been a long time. Can you imagine having Big Bill on top of you, especially with my ribs? I just climbed on top. It was a relief after all these weeks. Can you just imagine that big man on top of you?"

"No, I can't Irene, and I don't want to picture it either. Good for you, Irene. Tak and I usually do it kind of spooning, cuddle-style. I like that."

"And I don't want to picture that either, Emily."

"Look at us, Irene. Two almost-sixty-year-old women, comparing sex habits."

"We're in the prime, Emily. In the prime of life. And I'm feeling better every day. I can't wait to show Chipper and those young golfers my body. I'm looking great at any age."

"I was going to ask you," said Emily, "What are you going to wear to this housewarming at five o'clock? Strange time. Will it be sit down?"

"The evite said it was casual…"

Emily couldn't believe it and exclaimed, "Casual! Casual! In my house? A dinner? Casual? This is going to be awful."

Irene said, "I'm going to wear something tight to show off my body. Maybe some tight jeans, or maybe some lululemon tights. Maybe a cropped sweatshirt with no bra. I have to fit in with the young girls."

"Well, I think maybe I'll wear some jeans, then, and an expensive sweater. Some expensive matching pumps. I wonder what she will be serving for dinner and what kind of dinner dishes? I hope she uses my fine china and the expensive tablecloth. We'll see."

Irene said, "Got to go now, Emily. I'm eager to see you. Bill is beckoning me. I just hope I'm not traumatized when I walk into the house. I certainly won't go down to the wine cellar. I am hoping to block all that out of my mind. I don't really know how I escaped and did what I did down there. I was ferocious."

At about the same time, in their own estate, Debbie Rogers was telling Richard Stein that, although he RSVP'd to the evite, she couldn't see herself going to the party. She had a vivid picture in her mind of going down to the basement wine cellar and finding the two dead men with all that blood on them on the floor. Irene wasn't the only one traumatized by the Hastings' wine cellar.

Cindy Springer had been looking at responses every ten minutes all day and was excited at all the people coming to her party. Virtually everyone she invited said they would be there. She also printed the evite and folded eight copies to put into the mailboxes of the neighbors across the street and the three estates both left and right of hers. Because of the size of the estates, she had to walk a mile in each direction in order to place the invitations. She hoped they could come. She wanted to be a good neighbor.

NOLAN LUSKY

Nolan Lusky, all alone in his huge fifteen-bedroom estate, felt lost and alone. He thought it had been a good idea to move to Pebble Beach, but he found himself bored and lost in his own home in the month he had been in the house. His real estate agent, Tom Wallen, had advised him the estate was a great deal and was probably worth at least ten million dollars more than he had paid. Like Chipper, money didn't mean that much to Lusky anymore; he had plenty of it.

He had grown up in Silicon Valley and started M.I.T. when he was sixteen and didn't really fit in socially. He majored in computer science and electrical engineering, but found classes boring as well. He dropped out at the beginning of his junior year and moved to San Francisco. He was nineteen and moved into a work/loft space in the South of Market area. He called Sean Kirins, CEO of Arrow Electronics, on the recommendation of a M.I.T. professor and impressed Kirins so much that he received a job offer in their relatively-new cloud computing operation about halfway through his interview.

Lusky only worked for Arrow less than a month before he determined that there were many ways to improve cloud computing other than the approaches Arrow was taking. He drew up a business plan in a day and a half, without sleep, and hired a few programmers he had met at Arrow. They all stayed in his loft and within a month had developed a conceptual approach for improvement. He filed a business license application with the City of San Francisco and State of California.

His two employees and Lusky brainstormed names for the company, and many they came up with, like Cumulus Networks, Nimbus Networks, Altostratus Networks, Cirrostratus Networks, and Cumulonimbus

Networks were, not surprisingly, already taken. He decided to just go with his nickname No-Load and chose the name No-Load Cloud Operations. His employees were not happy with that, but it was Lusky's final decision. He was in charge. He was always in charge.

Before he even received his business license, he contacted the five top venture capital firms in San Francisco: Sequoia Capital, Benchmark, Kleiner Perkins Caufield & Byers, Accel Partners, and Andreessen Horowitz. Kleiner and Andreessen were interested and, after reading the concept paper, offered Lusky multi-million-dollar offers. He thought Andreessen was the better offer and signed a contract immediately. All this was happening extremely quickly for the nineteen-year-old.

His programmers only had been working for a few days to try to show proof of concept when he was informed by his contact at Andreessen that Salesforce had made a fifty-million-dollar offer for his concept, even without proof that it would work. Andreessen took ten million off the top, before even investing any of their own VC funds. Lusky took thirty-eight million and paid his two programmers one million each for what amounted to a week's worth of work. So it went in the world of cloud computing, startups, and VCs in San Francisco. Lusky took a week off, went on a monumental alcohol, cocaine, and hooker bender. The high-priced hookers, one of them named Angel, stayed in his loft for almost the whole week. Then he started thinking about his next startup.

Searching the tech newspapers and the San Francisco Chronicle want ads, he quickly saw that Artificial Intelligence was the next huge thing. He had limited knowledge but managed to find a job easily at an AI company called Hex, a short bus ride or long walk from his work/loft space. He read the summary of the job description and decided it was exactly what he wanted. He could learn this stuff easily. He interviewed well. He bluffed well. He lied and padded his resume.

Lusky read the description and was happy. *Large language models are unlocking new possibilities for software of all kinds – including data analytics. At Hex, we were early to incorporate powerful AI features into our product, unlocking LLM-powered workflows for thousands of users. We're looking for an exceptional engineer to level up the execution of our AI team across the stack – from partnering with research to identify the most important experiments to architecting scalable back ends to shipping delightful features. This person*

55

must successfully work with a team of world-class subject matter experts and partner on a team toward success around a unified outcome that accelerates Hex's product strategy over the next several years.

He continued his paying relationship with Angel and constantly admired her "scalable back end."

But he had no intention of staying "several years." He planned to stay long enough to learn AI, then decide how to make it better, in order to quit and find his next startup. He overstayed his welcome at Hex, making some enemies among the managers. He stayed nine months, longer than he expected. His managers found him unmotivated, arrogant, and obnoxious. Not the best recipe for success at a company. He gradually increased his absenteeism and finally got fired, intentionally, at exactly the nine-month mark. They never made him sign a noncompete agreement.

A month later, he had started another company, applied for a business license, and hired a few programmers at a very high hourly rate. He was using his own money to pay them, on the bet that he would again have a business plan and idea that would draw VC interest. VCs were funding any startup that claimed to be involved in AI, no matter how much expertise they had. He had trouble finding company names again, as there were dozens with AI in their company names. He tried AI Experts, AI Associates, AI consultants, AI Specialty Company, and finally settled again on the highly predictable name of name of Lusky AI.

This time he confidently only went to Andreessen, and they agreed to fund him for thirty million dollars. Even before his business license under the name Lusky AI was approved and any proof for concept was finished, Andreessen had again arranged a deal with Salesforce for one hundred and eighty million dollars up front and an additional four million per year in fees for twenty-seven years. Lusky never knew how they arrived at the number of years, but he did not complain. Andreessen took fifteen million off the top, and, at age twenty, Lusky took one hundred and sixty million and again paid his programmers a million each. He was then set to receive four million a year in addition for the next twenty-seven years. This was too easy, he thought to himself as he paid twenty-two million in cash for his Pebble Beach estate and just over three million for his one-of-a-kind 2011 Pagani Huayra gull-wing, gold and silver sports car.

He entered his estate's computer room, where he had four desktops, and eight large computer screens. One system for gaming, one for day trading, and two for programming whatever he wanted in his AI skills. He had become obsessed with Cindy Springer and Jenny Nelson. He had a vendetta against Cindy, but he was covetous of both of them. He spent a few hours in the middle of the day looking at old Duncan social media posts of Cindy hitting golf balls with Jenny giving instructions. He tried various placements of naked bodies on each of them, always upset that he could not quite get the breasts correct. They were always too big or too small. He was determined to get it correct.

He spent another hour figuring out what his next project would be. He had several options in mind. He was still bored. Maybe he would sign up for golf lessons with Jenny Nelson. That would be a way of getting closer to both Jenny and Cindy.

He found himself falling asleep at his key board, and decided to go outside and look in his mail box for the first time in about a week. Most of it was junk mail, but there was a copied evite flyer, without a stamp, inviting him to a party. When he saw it was from Cindy Springer and Duncan Campbell, he could not believe his good fortune. Apparently they were neighbors. He emailed an RSVP, then spent the rest of the day looking at imagined naked pictures of Cindy and Jenny.

ANGUS

Chipper woke up with the worst hangover he had ever had. His head pounded. Jenny had turned off the alarm and let him sleep. She was not feeling very well herself. He looked at the clock on his phone and panicked when he saw the time. He had never missed work, ever, since he started working for the Pebble Beach Corporation. He tried to get out of bed, but stumbled to his knees, tried to get up, then just lay on the floor next to the bed. He groaned and couldn't get back into the bed. He rolled over on his stomach and curled up into a ball.

Jenny was downstairs, heard the rumble on the floor, and ran upstairs. Her head hurt as well, but she laughed heartily when she saw Chipper on the floor. "Was the ace worth it, Mr. Chips?" Let me help you into bed, then I'll get you some water and some aspirin. Lots of water. You need lots of water."

"I have to go to work," he mumbled, but didn't resist getting into bed.

"I called Roger and told him about yesterday evening. He congratulates you on the course record and the ace. I told him neither of us would be in today for our regular work. Big Bill is going to take the range for you. I'm going to go over to teach Cindy at noon, but do nothing else the whole day. I'll be right back." Then she went downstairs slowly and came back with a pitcher of water and three aspirin.

Chipper dutifully took the aspirin, drank a lot of water, and slumped down in the bed on his stomach. "Thank you, Jenny. I feel truly awful. We have to do the morning shot, you know. I'll rest a bit, then get up."

"We didn't do the morning shot when we went to Scotland. We don't have to do it every day."

"Yes, we do. Every day. Ben did it every day." Chipper watched as

Jenny took off her pajamas and climbed back into bed. She turned him over on his back.

"First things first," she purred, as she started stimulating him with her hands.

"I have a headache," Chipper said.

"I didn't think I'd ever hear that from you. That's supposed to be my line. We have to continue trying to have the baby you promised me. You were drunk, but I can tell you meant it. I'm ready." She climbed on top of Chipper and said, "You don't have to do anything. This is purely clinical. No passion. Just making a baby. Thank you so much, Chipper."

While Jenny was moving slowly on top of him, Chipper said, "Where is Angus? I don't remember seeing him last night or this morning yet. He's usually in the bed."

Jenny said, "Shut up, Chipper. Don't say anything. He's probably doing the same thing we're doing with his girlfriend, Abigail. I don't remember much, but I do remember he wasn't around last night when we got home. Maybe Abigail and I can be pregnant together. It would be nice to have someone to share morning sickness with."

CINDY'S PARTY

Emily Hastings planned on arriving fashionably late for Cindy's housewarming party. She felt it was so strange that this young frivolous girl would be having a housewarming in Emily's former family estate. She was extremely happy with Takahashi and the house on Scenic Drive, but when she thought about it, she felt she would still like to be living in the Pebble Beach estate. More panache. More social status. Bigger house. Servants. Being served.

When Takahashi drove up the driveway and parked near the Richard MacDonald sculpture, there were already several cars in the driveway. Car aficionado that he was, he immediately saw and recognized the Pagani Huayra. He walked around the car several times, inspecting every inch of it. He was eager to meet the person who was driving it. Emily was impatient, and kept grabbing his arm, pulling him toward the front door. Takahashi never got angry, but he wasn't happy with the tugging. "You go inside. I look at car. Impressive car." She waited, but impatiently.

Emily was very interested in seeing what her house looked like. When they entered the large foyer, Cindy and Duncan were there to greet them. Cindy was excited, as usual. "Oh, Mrs. Hastings. It was so good of you to come. We love this house. Thank you very much. We haven't changed much of anything." Emily looked around and saw dust accumulated on the top of the picture frames on all the artwork hung in the foyer. She thought to herself, *this little girl has no idea how much those paintings are worth.* Emily also noticed dust balls and an accumulation of dirt on top of the baseboards. She would have to advise the servants and cleaning staff when she saw them. She missed seeing an expensive vase that was on a custom-made table in the one corner of the room that wasn't a rounded corner. Neither the table nor the vase were visible.

She couldn't help herself when she said to Cindy, "You might want to make sure the cleaning staff dusts the tops of the paintings and the baseboards."

Cindy didn't feel embarrassed when she said, "Oh, we can't afford a cleaning person. Duncan and I did a real good cleaning yesterday to make sure everything looked great. Mostly for you and Irene. I knew you would look. See, Dunc, I told you we should have gotten a ladder somewhere. I'm sorry, Mrs. Hastings."

Emily Hastings was also upset that Cindy hadn't mention how nice she looked. Her top was a three-thousand-dollar blouse that was purposely casual. Her slacks were custom-made by Balenciaga, and so were her sandals. She noticed that Cindy was wearing short Levi's cutoffs, with holes in them, and a Nike singlet that showed off her toned arms. Emily Hastings was mortified.

Takahashi handed Duncan two bottles of very expensive sake. Duncan handed both Takahashi and Emily some sixteen-ounce big red cups that he took out of their plastic wrap. He also handed each of them a black magic marker and said, "Please write your name or initials on the cups. You can use them for wine or beer that we have in coolers on ice in the other room. Or you can pour your own sake in them. I'll go put the bottles into the ice chests with the wine. Emily looked at Takahashi as she reluctantly took the big red cup in her left hand. She held it in the air and looked at it from all angles.

Takahashi said, "Do you know who owns the Pagani Huayra outside?"

Duncan said, "The what?"

Tak replied, "The expensive sports car in the driveway."

Cindy said, "Oh. It's the obnoxious guy from the driving range. He must be a neighbor. His name is Nolan Lusky. I saw it when he wrote it down on his cup. He gave me a big hug and held on too long, which was kind of creepy."

"Where is he now?" asked Tak.

Cindy happily said, "There are a lot of people here already who are just walking around the house taking a tour on their own. Mrs. Hastings, feel free. I know that you know the house already, but feel free to look around. But not until I give you the name tag for the game we are playing for people to get to know each other."

Emily expected to be handed a name tag that said Emily Hastings to put on her chest, but Cindy walked around behind Emily, pressed a sticker to her back and said, "You have to meet new people and guess what the name tag says on your own back. I picked a good one for you." Then Cindy gave Emily a big hug from behind and held her for a long time. "I love you, Mrs. Hastings." The name tag said Annika Sorenstam. Cindy then went around Mr. Takahashi and put a sticker on his back that said, Collin Morikawa. Then she gave Tak a big hug as well from behind.

"Go get yourself some beer or wine before you walk around the house. We bought some good brew."

Emily was eager to see Irene as they wandered up the stairs to see the bedroom. The door was closed, and they thought the bedroom was off limits, but as they were just walking away, the door opened, and a young man in cargo pants with no socks, Air Jordan sneakers, and long dirty-blond hair almost down to his shoulders came slinking out of the room. His shirt had a Pagani Huayra logo on the chest. Takahashi immediately said, "You owner of Pagani?"

Lusky said, "Are you a sports car buff?" Emily Hastings immediately went into the master bedroom and left Tak talking to Nolan Lusky. Lusky continued, "It's a 2011 Pagani Huayra that I paid just over three million cash for. I'm not supposed to drive it on regular streets, but I drive it here in the Forest. It's very special. Not many around."

Takahashi just said, "I know. I know all about that car. Very special."

"My name is Nolan Lusky, and you?"

"You can call me Fred today. Some days I have different names, but today I Fred."

"Ok, Fred. And are you a neighbor? I just moved into a house a few estates away. I paid twenty-two million in cash, but my realtor said the estate was worth a lot more. It's a big one."

Tak said, "I live in Carmel. This estate used to be my friend Emily's house."

"And what do you do, Fred?"

"Oh, I do a little this and a little that."

"What does that mean?"

"Import Export."

"And what do you import or export?"

"Oh, a little of this and a little of that."

Emily came out and said, "Ok, Tak. Let's go back downstairs. Bedroom looks pretty much the same as before, except dustier, and the walk-in closets have barely anything in them. The mirrors are fogged a bit. The bathroom needs cleaning."

When Emily came out of the bedroom and stood at the top of the stairs, she saw most of Cindy's CSUMB golf team friends coming out of another bedroom, all together. When Serena Antonelli saw Emily, and vice versa, they walked quickly toward each other and hugged. As they hugged, they both started sobbing, much to the amazement of the other golfers. They hugged for a long time. Neither felt an explanation to those watching was necessary. Another teammate, Maya Garcia, knew that Serena was living with Emily's son, Steven, when he met his unlikely death in the chasm near the sixteenth green at Cypress Point Golf Course.

When they stopped hugging, Emily stood back and stroked Serena's hair to put it back in place. She took out a handkerchief and wiped her own eyes, then Serena's. They laughed at each other. Emily noticed that most of the girls had boys gathered behind them. Apparently their plus ones for the party. "You look wonderful, Serena. I have truly missed you."

Several of the girls went around behind Emily and looked at her name tag and nodded in recognition. Serena looked and then whispered to Emily that she was Annika Sorenstam. Emily said, "Who? Who is that?" Then the woman and the girl held hands as they went down the stairs, back to the foyer.

Chipper and Jenny arrived late, because Chipper wanted to play a few holes on his way home in his cart at Pebble Beach. Jenny wasn't happy, as she was ready to go. She was silent as they drove into the Hastings' driveway. She was also anxious to see what kind of party Cindy was going to put on and the reactions of Emily Hastings and Irene McVay to the festivities. When they parked, Jenny was the first one to spot the strange sports car in the driveway. "Chipper, that's the car of the guy on the range that we think is posting the naked photos on Cindy's site."

Chipper didn't say anything, but wished his Tesla had a key, instead of just recognizing his cell phone in order to operate. He would have keyed the side of the three-million-dollar car. When they walked by the car and entered the foyer, they immediately saw Irene and Big Bill. Jenny whispered to Chipper, "Irene looks great. She is so thin." At that point, Irene McVay was limping toward Chipper and Jenny. She limped past Jenny without saying hello and grabbed Chipper around the waist.

She stared in Chipper's eyes and just said, "So nice to see you, Chipper. Don't I look great? I hurt a bit, but I feel much better." Big Bill and Jenny stood by the side and smiled at each other. Irene, obviously, still had feelings for Chipper. "Bill and Jenny, would you excuse me just a minute while I chat with Chipper in the other room?" She said this without looking at Bill or Jenny and grabbed Chipper by the arm and led him into a sitting room off the foyer. The room was empty.

"Don't I look great, Chipper? I haven't been this thin since I was a teenager. You should see my body." At that point, she took Chipper's arm and put his hand on her waist, under her sweater. As she told Emily, Irene was braless. She then put Chipper's hand on her breast and kept it there, even as he tried to pull it away. He finally, somewhat reluctantly, just kept his hand on her breast, as Irene told him how difficult it was for her to come to Cindy's house, after what happened in the wine cellar. "Don't I feel great, though, Chipper? Skinnier and firmer than a high school girl."

Jenny finally came in, and Chipper was startled when Jenny came over and said, "I see, Irene, you are making my husband feel you up." Then Jenny reached under Irene's sweater and fondled the other breast. "Very bizarre, Irene. Yes, Irene, you look great and feel great for a sixty-year-old woman. You should be proud of yourself. Now, let's go into the other room to see what's going on. And keep your hands off my husband."

When they returned to the foyer, the entire CSUMB women's golf team came over to Jenny, and they started yelling, "Sea Otters! Sea Otters! Sea Otters!" Emily Hastings, nearby, was horrified. Jenny had been helping with lessons for all the players, as well as her special time with Cindy. The girls loved her. Cindy did not invite the coach, because she knew that all the girls had signed a no alcohol, no drugs contract, and she expected many would be drinking that night. Some were already on their second red cup full of wine.

Cindy asked a few of the girls and Jenny to help her and Duncan in the kitchen with dinner. Chipper was standing between Emily and Irene when Nolan Lusky finally came down the stairs into the foyer. He was upstairs for a very long time looking around the house by himself. Lusky walked down the stairs like he owned the estate. Chipper immediately, to the surprise of all those standing there, accosted Lusky and gave him a gentle push on the shoulder.

"I saw your car outside. I'd like to key the side of it. We are sure you are the one posting pictures of my wife and Cindy on the Internet. It has to be you."

"Not me. I don't even know what you are talking about. You're the driving range guy, right?

Big Bill O'Shea came over when Chipper pushed Lusky again. This time on the other shoulder. Lusky stayed calm and said, "What are you? Some sort of school kid? I don't know what you are talking about."

O'Shea grabbed Chipper's arm, as Chipper was about to push Lusky again, and said, "Chipper, leave the man alone. You don't want to get in trouble again. Let's go get a real drink."

DINNER IS SERVED

Lusky followed Chipper and Bill into the study. They found the room already filled with some college guys that came with the CSUMB girls. They were seated and drinking beer from their red cups. Lusky said to Chipper, "You have me all wrong, sport. I'm just trying to fit in here in the Forest. I've always had trouble making friends, because I'm basically a smart kid in a room full of adults. I've done ok for myself. Look at the car I drive and the estate I live in."

"I don't care," sneered Chipper. "I don't care what kind of car you drive or where you live. I'm not very friendly either. You rub people the wrong way, whatever your name is."

Bill went into the cabinet beneath the wet bar and pulled out several expensive bottles of various types of liquor. Some were open, and some weren't. He poured Chipper and himself weighty red cups of scotch. Lusky poured himself some rum from an open bottle. All of the college guys, except one, came over and either chugged the rest of their beer or poured it down the sink, then filled their red cups with the liquor of their choosing.

Cindy walked in and said loudly, "Dinner is served. Please come into the dining room." Then she left, and they all heard her saying the same thing in the foyer and more softly in the distance. Everyone headed into the dining room with their red cups carefully held in their hands.

When Emily and Irene walked into the dining room, Emily scanned the dining room and immediately said to Irene, "Jesus Christ, Irene, it's a buffet with paper plates." She walked closer and saw large bowls on hot plates on a side table, paper plates, napkins, and plastic utensils propped up in more red cups nearby. There were Kentucky Fried Chicken boxes that had been warmed up at the end of the table. Emily and Irene surveyed the food: a lot of fried chicken, chicken nuggets, chicken wings, biscuits, mashed potatoes, baked beans, sweet corn, coleslaw, and a huge container of bubbling macaroni and cheese. Emily finally said, "I can't eat this shit. Where is my fine china?"

Mr. Takahashi scoffed and said, "This great. All my favorites." Then he was the first one to start filling his paper plate with food, soon followed by everyone else. Irene talked Emily into at least having some of the corn, coleslaw, and a biscuit.

Everyone found a seat at the table or on side chairs along the wall. Emily was horrified when she heard one guy say, "This is great, Cindy. What a feast. You've outdone yourself." Emily looked over, and he had two paper plates full of chicken wings and a heaping pile of mac and cheese. Emily made a gagging sound, and put a few fingers in her mouth to emphasize.

Takahashi said, "You a snob, Emily. Different generation. Different times. Let them enjoy." His plate was brimming with chicken tenders and mashed potatoes dripping in gravy.

Emily said, "You're not touching me tonight, old man. No way."

The main table was full of the CSUMB group. The chairs around the side were the "older" people, including Jenny and Chipper. Nolan Lusky managed to find a seat at the table next to Cindy. Duncan was on the other side. Jenny noticed Lusky was leering at Cindy, and occasionally leering at the other girls. Jenny told Chipper, "Look at that guy. I don't trust him at all."

Everyone toasted Cindy and Duncan with whatever they had in their cups, and just at the end of the toast, almost on cue, Ian Osterholm entered the dining room and said loudly, "Let the party begin. Sorry I am late. The girls took a long time to get ready." He had his girl helpers, twins Charlene and Darlene, one on each arm, looking ravishing in their usual outfits: short black skirts and low-cut peasant blouses. Behind Osterholm was another younger girl, extremely beautiful, in more modest clothing: white tight jeans, and a gray tee shirt with a reverse Saint Laurent logo. Just like Irene, she was obviously braless. She was a bit shorter than her sisters, but had big eyes and was both cute and beautiful at the same time. Mid-length brown hair, no makeup, and gorgeous skin. She had a striking resemblance to Jessica Alba.

Irene whispered to Big Bill, "That shirt on the young girl behind the idiot is a six-hundred-dollar tee shirt. I've priced it before. I'm surprised Cindy invited the man. He is always a loose cannon."

Several of the college boys stood up when the group came in, and the girls with them had to tug at their arms to make them seated again. Osterholm said loudly, "Hello everyone. I am Ian Osterholm. These are my good friends, Charlene and Darlene. Some of you know them already. I want to introduce you all to their younger sister. She just turned eighteen and is now helping me in my estate up the road, as well. Her name is Merlene."

Cindy rose from the table and went up to Osterholm, "Thank you for coming, Ian. I am glad you were able to come and bring your friends. It's always fun to see you. And welcome Darlene and Charlene and Marlene."

Osterholm said, "Her name is Merlene, like mermaid, but Merlene. Common mistake to call her Marlene. But call her Merlene or just Mer." Merlene was quiet and looked embarrassed. Osterholm, as expected, then went in for a hug with Cindy. His hands went around her and grabbed her behind when he hugged her.

Jenny yelled, "Ian! Get your hands off the girl!"

Emily yelled, "You pervert, Ian! Get your hands off the little girl! She could be your granddaughter."

Cindy backed off and looked at everyone and said, "Isn't he just a kick? He is so much fun."

Lusky had gotten up from his seat and was walking up behind Merlene. "I'd be happy to help you get some food, Merlene. Can I call you Mer?"

Jenny rolled her eyes at Chipper and watched Mer smile and Lusky take her arm and lead her to the buffet table. All the young men were staring. Lusky grabbed a loose chair he saw and pulled it over next to his chair at the table. Cindy on one side and Merlene on the other.

When everyone was seated again, Lusky stood up and asked for silence by trying to click his plastic fork against his red cup. It was obvious he was feeling no pain at this time. He must have drained his entire sixteen-ounce cup of rum already. This time Chipper rolled his eyes at Jenny as Lusky started to speak.

"I wanted to introduce myself and thank Cindy for inviting me. I am a neighbor and own the estate a few houses down on the left. I paid twenty-two million cash for the house. I know I look young, and I am only about a few years older than you college students here. I started some tech companies and sold them for a lot of money. Cloud computing, then AI startups. I have a feel for what the next trend is." He waited for someone to say something, but there was complete silence.

He continued, "I know some of you here live in the Forest and for sure have money. Big money, like me. I'd like to announce that I am starting a new company, pre-venture capital funding, and if any of you want to get in early and participate, that I am sure you will make a ton of money. I'm sure I'll get VC funding because of my reputation. Even some of you college kids may want to contact your parents for this once-in-a-lifetime opportunity."

Lusky waited in silence again, until the silence lasted too long, and Osterholm finally said, "Well, get on with it, champ. What is it? I might be interested. Always looking for a good investment."

Lusky finally said, "Drones. It's drones. Not really a new thing, but my drone will be the fastest and most maneuverable ever. And it's going to work from a burner phone that shows you on the screen where it is and what it sees. You can also control the direction and speed from the screen. Ryan Lademann set the record in the Arizona desert with his XLR V3 drone. Fastest ground speed of only two hundred and twenty-four miles per hour. My drone, which will be named the Lusky Drone, will go over five hundred miles per hour. Yes, you heard it, five hundred miles per hour."

No one was particularly excited, especially the CSUMB women golfers. Lusky was surprised no one was excited, and he then launched into his car offer. He put his hand on Merlene's shoulder and said, "I am sure you all saw the beautiful sports car parked near the front door. It is a 2011 Pagani Huayra. Gold and silver color. I paid just over three million cash for it. Very rare. After I give a ride to Merlene, I would be happy to give anyone else a ride in it."

Merlene smiled. Takahashi said, "Me. I go for ride. Let's go now." Chipper and Bill headed back to the study to fill their cups with scotch. Emily Hastings frowned at Takahashi and slugged him on the shoulder.

When Chipper came back, all he said to the crowd was, "Let's talk some golf. What do you think about Nelly Korda winning four tournaments in a row? Amazing." That started a lively conversation at the table. Chipper asked, 'How many of you think you have the game to be an LPGA pro?" Several of the girls pointed at Serena Antonelli. She put her hands up in mock protest. Maya Garcia and Cindy Springer both stated that they would like to go pro as well.

Richard Stein appeared at the door and was wearing one of his signature outfits: knickers with long plaid socks, a Ben Hogan-style cap, and a baggy plaid sweater that matched his socks. He received a round of applause as he entered the dining room. He immediately said, "I am sorry to be late. I had to literally drag Debbie into the car. She's in the car and won't come in. Still traumatized by what she saw in the wine cellar last time she was here. I think she has to go down there to get over her fears, but she refuses to come in. Can a few of you help me get her in here? Irene, maybe you can talk her into coming in? You lived it. She only saw the aftermath."

"I'll try," said Irene, and she and Richard and Big Bill left the dining room and headed outside. Stein grabbed a red cup on the table that was filled to the brim with some sort of liquid. He figured it couldn't hurt to give Debbie some big gulps. Stein took a few sips and determined it was either very strong rum or strong whiskey. It didn't matter to him.

Irene found Debbie walking up the driveway, away from the house, and yelled at her very wisely, "Debbie! You have to help me get over my fear. Come with me to the wine cellar. We'll both confront this at the same time. I need you, Debbie. I really need you." Stein looked at Irene and nodded his head. He was impressed.

Debbie stopped in the driveway and turned around and stared at Irene, then came walking back toward her. They hugged and cried, then headed into the house. Irene said, "This is easy. We can do this, Debbie. We really can." There were several men outside around the Pagani at this point who had come out to see what happened in the driveway. Chipper. Osterholm. Takahashi. A few of the college boys.

THE WINE CELLAR

Stein and Big Bill guided the reluctant Debbie Rogers down the stairs toward the wine cellar. They were followed by Irene McVay, all the college girls, Cindy and Duncan, Chipper and Jenny, Emily and Takahashi. All were interested in hearing Irene's story. The college boys stayed upstairs to chat up Darlene and Charlene. Lusky stayed seated next to Merlene and wouldn't let her get up, even though she tried. Osterholm stayed in the dining room to watch over his girls. He was getting perturbed at Lusky.

In the wine cellar, Stein was the first to speak. "I made sure everything was cleaned up down here and immaculate. Look at the flooring." The floor now had an industrial padded cover that was a bright blue. It looked like a wrestling mat in a gym. Debbie unclosed her eyes and was happy there wasn't blood, but in her mind she still could picture the two dead men and pools of blood. She was the first to find them after Irene's heroics.

Irene said, "Thank you, Richard. I think I can do this. I'm not sure how many of you know that I was held in captivity down here by dark-complexioned men claiming to be part of LIV Golf leadership. I'm not sure how long I was held in this room, actually. I lived, no pun intended, on champagne." She pointed over to the champagne section of the wine cellar, and the girls could tell there was enough Dom Perignon for an army still on the shelves. Emily Hastings could tell what they were thinking and started wagging her finger at them. It kept them from immediately heading for the Dom. That would come a bit later.

Irene continued, "I was drunk, tired, sore, and felt I had no chance to escape. I was delirious. I was singing to myself and don't remember everything. I do remember getting an inspiration, and I knew they had to come into the room to kill me at some point. I grabbed two Dom bottles and sat down like this…" Irene sat next to the door on the right side. Everyone was paying rapt attention. She had a bottle of Dom in each hand. Irene asked Big Bill to pretend he was coming in the door. He feigned fear.

When Bill stepped in, Irene leapt up, and pretended to hit him on the head with the bottle of Dom in her right hand, "I landed a perfect blow to his head, and he went down immediately. Then the guy with a chainsaw, making an awful chainsaw noise, came running at me, and I retreated to the back wall. I was petrified. He tripped, and the chainsaw hit his own arm. I laughed when I saw him in pain. Then I hit him with the other bottle of Dom, and it broke. I then jabbed him in the neck, and more blood spurted out. It was glorious." The group in the cellar applauded wildly and shouted.

"Then, with the broken bottle of Dom, I made sure the other guy on the floor was stabbed in the neck, too. He gushed. It was more glorious. Then I made my escape, and I am thankfully still alive to talk about this."

The group applauded again. Every one of the college golfers then headed to the Dom rack and grabbed two each to take upstairs. Ian Osterholm was happy to open them all carefully in exchange for a warm hug from each girl. The champagne started flowing freely into the red cups.

Cindy then asked everyone to take all their used paper plates and utensils in to the recycle bags in the kitchen. Several helped put all the leftovers into plastic bags. When she returned to the dining room, she had Hostess cupcakes, both chocolate and orange, Ding Dongs, Twinkies, and Ho Hos. Cindy set up big mounds of them on the side table. Then she yelled, "Who's up for beer pong?" Everyone started yelling excitedly, and Cindy set out the red cups on one end of the dining table; many filled with Dom, some with beer, some with hard liquor. She had ping pong balls in the drawer of the hutch, already prepared for the after-dinner festivities.

Emily asked Jenny, "What is beer pong?"

Jenny explained that the players would bounce the ping pong balls on the dining table in an attempt to bounce them into the red cups. There were ten red cups at each end of the table, set up in a pyramid shape: one, two, three, and four in successive rows. Serena had suggested that the two teams, split between each end of the table, should be the girl golfers against the boys they brought. When someone on one team "cupped" a ping pong ball on the other side, someone from the other team had to drink what was in the cup.

Emily exclaimed, loud enough for everyone to hear, "Jesus, Mary, and Joseph, that table is custom-made for this space; Villa Valencia, extra-length, triple-pedestal. I paid over thirty-five thousand dollars for that table. She didn't use a tablecloth. It already has water marks. Now it's going to have more liquor marks and ping pong ball marks. And the cups aren't filled with beer. The Dom is over two hundred dollars a bottle. I can't watch this. Tak, I'm hungry, take me out of here. Irene, Bill, Tak, let's go to Roy's or the Bench or the Beach Club for a real meal. Jesus, Mary, and Joseph!" Then she headed quickly toward the front door.

Takahashi couldn't do anything but yell back, "Thank you, Cindy! Food was good. Lusky, I ride in Pagani next time. I find you." Irene and Bill reluctantly followed. Takahashi rushed back in, grabbed a few Hostess cupcakes from the pile, and carried them out as he left.

THE PAGANI

When Takahashi walked out, it was Lusky's cue to stand up and say, "I'm going to take Merlene for a ride." Merlene looked over at Ian Osterholm and could see he wasn't at all happy. She liked the attention from Lusky. She thought he was kind of cute, but overbearing, and wanted a ride in the car. She looked away from Osterholm and followed Lusky through the foyer and outside.

When Lusky walked by a few other cars parked in the driveway and saw his car, he walked completely around it, then immediately started screaming and ran back past Merlene into the house. When he entered the dining room, he immediately confronted Chipper, chest-to-chest. "You keyed my car! You keyed the sides of my car! I know it was you!" Then he fell to his knees and said, "Why would you do that? Why would you do that?" Then Lusky started sobbing.

Chipper didn't know what to do. Jenny was happy Lusky was on his knees, because if he was still chest-to-chest with Chipper, she knew Chipper would have strangled him. Chipper didn't have much patience. Chipper said calmly, "I didn't key your car, Lusky. I would have liked to, but it wasn't me." Then Chipper looked around the room and examined people's faces to see if anyone looked guilty. Everyone had a pretty good poker face. No hints of guilt from anyone.

Lusky continued to sob on the floor. No one tried to console him. The pong game halted to watch the scene, but several were impatient to continue. Lusky crawled to the wall, sat on a chair, and continued to sob. Cindy, of course, came over and sat in the chair next to him and said, "Mr. Lusky. It's only a car. You can have it fixed." That set Lusky off again.

"It's not just a car. It's a Pagani Huayra. I can't just have someone repair the scratch marks and repaint. I'll either have to get Pagani people from Italy to come over here or send the car to Italy. I can't be without that car. I love that car." He then stood up and pointed at Chipper again and exclaimed, "You're gonna get your ass sued, you asshole! I know you did it! I know you did!"

Merlene started everyone laughing by saying, "I guess I don't get a ride today?" She said it seriously.

Lusky walked out and on his way turned around once more and said, "You'll hear from my lawyer."

Everyone but the lady golfers and their boy guests decided to leave, including Chipper and Jenny. The Dom Pong game didn't last very long as everyone was rip-roaring drunk and stumbling in the dining room. Some fell asleep in the chairs. Cindy and Duncan told everyone that they could sleep in the upstairs bedrooms, as they weren't safe on the road back to CSUMB housing. "We'll clean up in the morning. Just pick a bedroom." It was only about nine PM when they headed upstairs and went to bed.

Cindy and Duncan headed to their bedroom. Serena and her boyfriend headed to another bedroom. Madi and her boyfriend to another.

When Jenny and Chipper arrived home and went to the bedroom, they found Angus and Abigail in the bed already. They were asleep under the covers. Jenny petted both dogs and, before bed, texted Debbie and Richard that Abigail was safe in their house. She noticed the sheets were muddy with paw prints, but she was so tired that she just climbed in one side of the bed. Chipper barely had room on his side. Angus had slobbered all over Chipper's pillow. Chipper reached over the dogs and grabbed Jenny's arm. They all fell asleep peacefully. It was the last peaceful sleep or day they would have for some time.

FANS ONLY

Sunday morning at five thirty, Richard Stein's phone started ringing. His dial tone was the song, 'Take it Easy' by the Eagles. It took him a few times through "Standin' on the corner in Winslow, Arizona," before he woke up to realize his phone was waking him up. He looked at his phone and saw it was Wendy Stover, his contact at OnlyFans. He picked up the phone and sat up in bed. Debbie sat up next to him.

He listened as Stover said, "This is absolutely great stuff, Richard. How did you arrange this? There are already half a million hits, and it's barely dawn. I've got to hand it to you. I don't know how you talked her into doing this. And the other girl is unbelievable. I've never seen anything like that in my life. We'd like to offer her a contract, too. This is gold, Richard. Absolute gold."

"I have to admit, Wendy, I have no idea what you are talking about."

Wendy said, "Just now, as I've been talking to you, we're up over seven hundred and fifty thousand hits. People are sharing it like mad. Who is the other girl, sharing the screen with Cindy? I've got to look at this with my husband. He won't believe it."

Stein said, "Wendy, it's only five thirty here. Let me get organized and call you back. What should I be looking at?"

"Oh, you're a funny one, Richard. I know you were behind this. Call me back in a few, and we'll talk about money again. We've already copied it to our site. We're up over a million. We'll be at several million by the end of the day."

When Wendy hung up, Stein brought up the Cindy OnlyFans site, on his phone and clicked to make the video, or whatever it was, show up on the big screen TV in their bedroom. Debbie and Richard stared intently as the screen showed Cindy and Duncan getting ready for bed, both obviously very tired. Cindy stripped off her clothes next to the bed and lay on top of the covers naked. Duncan left his underwear on and tucked himself in under the covers.

Debbie said, "You didn't put a camera in their bedroom, did you, Richard? If you did, I'll frigging kill you. I don't think even you would do that. I know Cindy and Duncan wouldn't have done that, even for a ton of money. Not enough money in the world. By the way, Cindy has a great body, doesn't she? She's so sweet."

The sound wasn't great, but it was clear enough to hear Cindy say, "Don't go to sleep, Duncan. I'm so keyed up still that I need you a lot. It was a great party, wasn't it? I need you, Duncan."

Duncan rolled over and said, "I'm tired Cindy, love. Just go to sleep."

Cindy then pulled the covers aside and started rubbing Duncan's underpants. "Come on, Dunc. I need you."

She pulled off his pants and climbed on top of Duncan. Her back was to the camera when they started having sex. Cindy started softly at first, then loudly started saying, "Do me, Dunc," over and over again, as she moved rhythmically. Do me, Dunc. Do me, Dunc. Do me, Dunc. Do me, Dunc."

"I'm getting excited," Debbie said.

They watched as Cindy said, "Do me, Dunc." Then started pleading, "Take me home, Dunc. Take me home, Dunc," and moving faster. Then she disappointedly said, "Aw, Dunc. Too soon, Dunc. Aw, Duncan." Then she rolled over on her back, completely naked in front of the camera, and "took herself home" the rest of the way. She quickly fell asleep.

Debbie said, "Take me home, Richard Stein. Take me home, then we'll watch whatever else has been uploaded." Stein was happy to agree. He paused the video and had some fun with Debbie. When they were done, Debbie said casually, "Richard. We shouldn't have done that. You should call Duncan right away and tell him, so he can try to take it down. You should call the police, too. You have Officer Henderson's number on your phone, right? You aren't going to try to make money off of this, are you? Even you wouldn't do that, would you?"

Stein didn't call anyone. He wanted to see the rest of the video before he did anything. When they started the video again, one quarter of the screen was now Cindy, sleeping naked, next to Duncan naked. Another quarter of the screen was Madi Harwood, under the covers, sleeping with her boyfriend next to her. Just sleeping.

The other half of the screen was Serena Antonelli and her boyfriend, naked and sideways on the bed. Then they were kneeling on the bed. Then standing up. Then Serena was out of the bed, and her boyfriend still on it. Then vice versa. Serena was doing things to her boyfriend that neither Debbie nor Richard had ever seen. "Wow. Wow. Wow," Debbie kept saying. "Where did she learn to do that? Yikes. No wonder Steven Hastings had her live with him. Just wow. Isn't she tired at this point?"

Stein was engrossed in the video and didn't really respond until it was over. "I've never seen anything like that before. The girl has some moves. I think I'm excited again. Let's go again."

"Not a chance, Stein. You have to make some phone calls."

Stein put the Serena part of the video on again, with the sound on mute. He immediately called Wendy Stover. As soon as he said, "Wendy," Debbie pummeled him on the shoulder. "Wendy. I just watched the video."

"That second girl is amazing. That's going to be a big moneymaker for us, Stein. Can you get her under contract immediately? That video may revolutionize couples having sex. In all my years, I've never seen anything like that. You have to get her under contract. What's her name?"

"I won't give you her name. Let me talk to her first. How does it help you to get her under some sort of contract? What we've just seen is all over the internet now, for sure. What are the hits up to?"

"Three and a half million, and most people on your coast aren't even up yet. Where did she learn all that stuff? I think she made it up. Quite an imagination. If we have her under contract, we can make sure her follow-up stuff is only available with us. She can make millions for us."

"What a world! What a world!" Stein said.

Debbie said, "This is sick, Richard. Really sick. These young women are being exploited. This is really sick. It's a sick world, Richard. Get the fuck off the phone with that sleazebag."

Wendy said, "What did she say, Richard? I can hear her in the background. I think she called me a name. This girl could be a gold mine, Richard. Get her. Get her, for sure. And Cindy is going to continue to make money. What a cutie she is. She needs a new boyfriend, though. Bye, Richard. Call me back soonest."

Stein immediately called Duncan's phone. It rang ten times before Stein heard Duncan pick up. "What do you want, Richard? It's very early. I don't feel very good. Huge headache. Huge."

Stein thought about saying, "Do me, Dunc," but thought better of it. He said, "Duncan. Bad news. Someone from the party last night put cameras in your bedroom, and at least two of the other bedrooms. They posted videos of you and Cindy and Serena and her boyfriend on Cindy's social media. It's all over the place now, Duncan. All over."

Duncan gasped and looked around the room. "I don't see any cameras, Richard. Wouldn't I see a camera? This is a bad joke, Richard. It's a joke, right?"

"Afraid not, Duncan. Don't let Cindy look at the internet, or Serena. Just find a way to take everything down again, Duncan. I'm going to call Officer Henderson and have him bring a security guy out to inspect your house. I'm pretty sure he can do that, even though it's Sunday. And don't do anything, Duncan. You are all still on camera. And Duncan, can you give me Serena Antonelli's phone number, please? I would appreciate it."

Stein heard Duncan rustle and get up. As an afterthought, Stein said into the phone, "And you are a lucky man, Duncan." Then he hung up. He reached for Debbie, but she pushed him back and was out of bed in a flash. Stein laughed, then started the Serena video one more time before he called Henderson.

OFFICER HENDERSON

Deputy Sheriff Henderson was very surprised to receive a call on his cell phone early Sunday morning from Richard Stein. He was tired of responding to issues in the Del Monte Forest, among the very wealthy and socially-connected. Why couldn't these people just keep to themselves? It seemed like every few months he was called into the Forest to respond to some sort of emergency. Some involved death. He dreaded picking up the phone.

"Officer Henderson. What do you want, Richard? It's Sunday morning. I'm not working, and I'm off tomorrow too. Hopefully it isn't Blair again?"

"Thanks for picking up," Stein said, "We've got a case of someone placing cameras in a few bedrooms of an estate, recording sex acts, and putting them on the internet. I need you to come out and inspect the house to see if you can find all of them and remove them. Also maybe you can find fingerprints on them and identify who might be responsible?"

"I can't do it today, Richard, and my tech and security guy at work doesn't work today either. I'm off Monday, but as a favor, I'll see if I can get out tomorrow with him and take a look. Give me the address. Can you meet me there, and we can take notes and get a list of who might have done it?"

"Thank you, officer. Absolutely." Stein gave him the address. "What kind of crime are we talking about, and what might the penalties be?"

"Actually, not as much as you think, Richard. You can google it, but it falls under Penal Code 632. Eavesdropping or unwarranted invasion of privacy. It's called a wobbler, which means depending on what the DA says, it could be charged as a felony or just a misdemeanor. I'm sure, if we find the person, we can talk the DA into making it a felony. A fine and some time in jail, probably not much, unless whoever did it has been convicted before for the same crime."

"The jail time might be good, but the fine won't matter. I have a hunch who it is. The money won't bother him."

"Probably difficult to prove, if a lot of people go through the house all the time. How many people were in the house the last few days?"

"She had a party the night before with a few dozen people. I don't know how many people went up to the second floor. I got there late."

"We'll find that out when we go out there tomorrow, Stein."

SUNDAY MORNING

Stein followed Debbie out of their estate and started walking toward Chipper's back lawn. Since they were up early, they knew that if Chipper and Jenny weren't in the backyard preparing, that they would be soon. The sun was just appearing on the horizon. Debbie was worried about Abigail, as she hadn't been home in a few days. Even if she was at Chipper's, Debbie missed the dog. She missed the cuddling. Stein wasn't much of a cuddler.

Stein had on different plaids today but was so happy and comfortable in his new outfits that he continued to wear the knickers and long socks, sweater, and Hogan cap. Debbie didn't like it but knew he would get tired of the look and change to something equally or more bizarre in about a week. His sartorial look seemed to change every few weeks. At least this look wasn't as bizarre as some of his others. She even helped him pick out and coordinate the plaids. Stein didn't care about whose tartan he was representing.

They walked slowly toward Chipper's, and their timing couldn't have been better. Debbie saw Abigail and Angus coming down the stairs just as the stairs came into view. She yelled to Abigail, but Abigail was distracted by Angus's running around wildly in the backyard, then heading to the fourteenth fairway to run around more. Angus was feeling it this morning. Lots of energy.

Jenny followed, and Chipper was just behind her. They both looked very tired. Jenny smiled when she saw Debbie and Richard, but Chipper didn't. That was to be expected. Jenny greeted them both by saying, "You guys are up early for the night after a party. How long did you stay?"

Debbie said, "We left just after you guys. The young people were the only ones left. Can you imagine playing beer pong, actually Dom Perignon pong, on Emily's expensive dining room table? The kids have no idea. Emily was going bonkers. Bonkers over Dom pong. Hard to believe."

Richard said, "We're up early, because I got a wake-up phone call from some possible contract contacts for both Cindy and now, Serena. You won't believe this. Take a look at my phone." Stein set his phone up to Cindy's social media and handed the phone to Jenny. Chipper didn't care, and he started swinging his long spoon club to warm up. While Jenny looked at the phone, Richard took the brassie out of her hand and started swinging himself. He watched Jenny with intent interest as Jenny looked at the phone.

Jenny started saying, "I can't believe this. I just can't believe this. Who put the camera in the bedroom? This is awful. Has Cindy seen this?"

Richard said, "I called Duncan as soon as I saw this and told him to not let Cindy see it and to take it down as quickly as he can. But, by now, it's absolutely all over the internet. Before we left the house, it was over three million views and rising quick. Poor Cindy. Poor Duncan. This AI/hidden cameras/social media stuff is all sick. Dammit. What a world."

"Do we know who put the camera in their room? How could they not see it?" Jenny exclaimed. Then Chipper's interest was piqued, and he took the phone from Jenny.

Richard said, "I have my opinion. It had to be that guy Lusky. Had to be. Absolutely had to be. I've called Officer Henderson to go out and inspect the house. These new camera devices are highly undetectable and sophisticated if you aren't expecting them. Why would they expect this? I agree, this is horrible."

Debbie interjected, "Really horrible. I feel horrible for both of them. This will never leave the internet. Never."

Chipper just kept saying, "Jesus Christ," over and over again. "Poor Duncan. How embarrassing."

Stein told Chipper to look at the next video, after the Cindy video ended. Chipper kept saying the same phrase over and over again, then started saying, "Oh, My God. What the hell is Serena doing? Just what the hell is she doing? I've never seen anything like that before in my life." Stein smiled, and Chipper played the video again from the start. Angus and Abigail were getting impatient and were pacing around underfoot. Chipper watched the video a third time.

Jenny finally had to grab the phone from Chipper and watched it herself. She started gasping and exclaimed, "Wow. Just wow! How can she even get in that position? I can't imagine that feels good at all." She looked at Chipper and, before he said anything, she exclaimed, "I know what you're thinking, Chipper. Just no way. Absolutely no way on that one. No one has ever tried that before, and I certainly won't. I wish I could get that out of my head."

Debbie walked over and hugged Jenny. Angus and Abigail were now lying on the ground next to each other.

Chipper started swinging his long spoon, and Jenny went upstairs to get a few more Slazengers for Richard and Debbie. When she came back, Chipper was already putting his ball down and hitting. As soon as he hit, Angus and Abigail took off toward the fourteenth green. Chipper ran up the stairs to the telescope, knowing he had smacked a good one. He wanted to see it before the dogs picked up the ball and brought it back. When he reached the top of the stairs and looked into the scope, he could see his ball was just three feet to the left of the hole. He was excited and yelled down, "Just three feet! One of the best." Then he waited long enough for the group to wonder why the dogs weren't on their way back already. They impatiently looked up at Chipper.

Chipper yelled down, "Angus is mounting Abigail on the green! They haven't picked up the ball yet. Damned dog. Maybe he got turned on by the Serena video?" In a few minutes, he saw Angus let Abigail pick up the ball, and they were on their way back slowly.

Debbie said, "Looks like we'll be grandparents pretty soon. For sure, it will be a cute litter. I hope Abigail has a lot of puppies."

The dogs came back. Abigail put the Slazenger down next to Debbie. Angus looked proud. Abigail looked tired and embarrassed. She just lay down on the grass and didn't chase any more golf balls. Angus was pumped and ran faster than usual at the next three shots that morning. When Richard and Debbie headed back to their estate, and Chipper and Jenny headed up the stairs, the two dogs remained on the grass, just lounging.

MANIC MONDAY

Chipper's Monday went from bad to worse, then to total disaster. First, Jenny showed him the online version of the Monterey County Weekly.

MONTEREY COUNTY WEEKLY

THE SQUIDFRY

The Squid's infallible sources told me some great gossip about a special party in the Del Monte Forest on Saturday night. I'm swimming around in circles about this one, blowing happy bubbles. Seems that Cindy Springer, newly wealthy internet sensation, had a housewarming at her new estate. The estate was formerly owned by famed socialite and party-giver, Emily Hastings. And, believe it or not, Hastings was invited to the party.

Springer is not even twenty and invited her golf team friends, some neighbors, and a few old society matrons. Times have really changed. Hastings was known for tuxedo and evening gown-clad guests and silver service with some of the most exciting and perfectly-cooked food ever invented. Springer's idea of housewarming food was Kentucky Fried Chicken (remember Squid loves the word Fry) and accompanying dishes, served on paper plates. Can you imagine Emily Hastings eating KFC? Apparently she didn't. The Squid is happy there was no fried calamari served.

Hastings was overheard shouting expletives that cannot be repeated when dessert was not flaming Cherries Jubilee, or Baked Alaska, but Hostess Cupcakes and Twinkies. Can you imagine? Squid is trying to picture Hastings eating a Twinkie. Makes one swim in circles and almost drown.

To make things more interesting, Springer's neighbor who was invited, a newbie to the Forest named Nolan Lusky, drove his three-million-dollar car over and parked in the driveway. Lusky is a tech wiz, some call him a boy genius, who made millions in the Silicon Valley before moving to the Forest, to do whatever tech wizzes do in the Forest. And this is the good part. Apparently our old friend, Chipper Blair, who gets in trouble daily, took a dislike to Lusky and keyed both sides of his car. Needless to say, Lusky was very upset at Blair. More on this story later. Squid can't stand much more of this excitement. I have to come to the surface.

Then Jenny showed Chipper the online edition of the Monterey Herald. Second page banner headline.

MONTEREY HERALD

BYLINE DEVINE

Pagani Huayra Vandalized

An interesting item came by when scrolling through the police log on Sunday. All of our Concours d'Elegance regular attendees and just you usual car lovers will be horrified. II seems a one-of-a-kind 2011 Gold and Silver Pagani Huayra with gull-wing doors, estimated to be worth well over three million dollars, was vandalized in Pebble Beach on Saturday night.

The owner, Nolan Lusky, filed charges with the Sheriff's Department of Monterey County on Sunday against, and you'll recognize the name, Chipper Blair. The penal code for vandalism indicates that if the amount of defacement is four hundred dollars or more, then it can be a felony punished by a fine of not more than fifty thousand dollars and imprisonment for a time set by the judge. Lusky commented that the defacement to his car may cost several hundred thousand dollars to fix.

He filed further charges of criminal mischief and trespassing, with extenuating circumstances involving a hate crime. Lusky has also filed a restraining order that keeps Blair from coming within two hundred yards of Lusky or the car or any other property owned by Lusky.

Lusky apparently did his homework and already has an expensive Silicon

Valley lawyer under contract. The petition and filing also lists conspiracy, disorderly conduct, bullying, civil rights violations, and domestic terrorism. Blair seems to be in a lot of trouble over this incident.

Jenny was upset, but Chipper, as usual, laughed it off. "I didn't do it. I just want to go out and play some golf now on the way to the range." After the morning shot, he headed out to the fourteenth fairway and played his way into work. His three-putt bogey on fifteen bothered him more than the news stories.

When he drove his cart by The Hay golf course, he thought it was strange that there were a dozen workmen and trucks and other equipment putting up what looked like a very dark green, opaque, vinyl-looking, dense, twelve-foot-high fence around the entire golf course, including around the putting green. He would have to ask Richard or someone else what was going on. He hadn't heard anything about a renovation. Why would the Corporation be placing a fence around The Hay?

When Chipper drove up to the range shack, there were already two vans parked on the grass. Different vans than those around The Hay. These vans had big letters on the side in a graphic pattern that said:

MADRDI

In smaller letters underneath, the acronym was explained:

MODERN

AUTOMATED

DRIVING

RANGE

DEVELOPMENT

AND

INSTALLATION

Chipper walked over to the first van, even before opening the range shack, and saw two guys in the front seat drinking coffee. The driver saw Chipper and opened the window. Chipper said, "Hey guys, what's going on?"

The driver, who seemed very friendly, said, "Hi, there. You must be the attendant. Good morning. We're here to do some work."

"I'm an assistant golf pro. I enjoy working at the range. No one told me anything. What are you guys going to do? Replace the sod? It's pretty beat up."

Both of the van guys started laughing immediately. The driver opened his door and stood next to Chipper. He was wearing golf slacks and a shirt and hat with the same MADRDI logo as on the van. "Actually, the issues you mention will all go away. Every maintenance issue will go away. There's no sod involved. Just artificial surface all over."

Chipper looked skeptical and asked, "Go ahead and explain the whole deal to me, then. No one told me anything about this. Are you guys involved in the fence around The Hay, too?"

"I'll give you the quick explanation. First, we are not involved in the fence project. Don't know what that is. We have a lot of measuring work to do today. The range will be all artificial surface, won't ever need replacement in the range, but the mats the golfers use will need replacement occasionally. We put up realistic mural screens as tall as the highest tree, based on pictures of the area. They cover each side of the range and one at the end. Balls always then end up in the driving range. We take pictures today, so our guys can replicate the setting..."

Chipper commented, "So you replace the real views with a picture of them?"

"Yes. Cuts down on maintenance. No looking for golf balls off in the rough or trees. Then we slope the artificial turf away from the sides and back, so every ball rolls into a channel in the middle of the range and returns to a cleaning machine underneath the turf. No more dirty golf balls. No more range cart or having to pick up the balls. No maintenance."

"It won't work. What if the channel gets backed up or blocked?"

"It won't. Special material and no main..."

Chipper finished the sentence, "I know. No maintenance."

"Then when people come to hit balls, after they pay, by the ball actually, the clean balls pop up to their mat. There are also monitors that show them, on every swing, distance, ball speed, angles, clubhead speed. It's pretty amazing, actually."

A thoroughly disgusted and surprised Chipper just walked away back to the range shack. He didn't say anything. The MADRDI guy didn't say anything either. For the next several hours, the four guys, all in golf clothes, used lasers to measure what they needed. Chipper went about his business. He put the automated driving range in the part of his mind that was useful for forgetting any issue he didn't like. He compartmentalized. Great way of getting rid of his fears of the future. It was like saying to himself, "This will never happen, and if it does, it won't work."

Not many people used the range that day. When Big Bill showed up around eleven, Chipper was happy to see him. The first question Chipper asked was, "What's going on at The Hay?"

Bill answered, "Everyone is pretty clammed up about that one. I heard several people say exactly the same thing, that it was for some renovations. Minor."

"So, after I shot my course record, the powers that be must have decided that the course needed renovation? Making it tougher?"

"I'm sure it had nothing to do with you, Chipper."

"There were some guys here this morning measuring for an automated driving range here. Have you heard about that?"

"Nope. But I'm not in the loop. Everything I know is just secondhand from listening to others. I assume you've seen the videos that were posted this morning?" Then, Bill grinned when he brought up the Serena part of the video. They watched together.

Chipper explained the driving concept. Then they went and hit balls side by side. At eleven thirty, Chipper noticed a larger than normal crowd of guys gathering at their usual place near the side and back of the range. He commented to Bill, "This is going to be bad for the girls this morning. I hope Cindy hasn't seen the videos. She's usually pretty calm about things posted, but she can't be calm about this one. I think it was that guy Lusky. Had to be Lusky."

The group waiting at the back of the range had grown to twice the normal size. Chipper guessed close to two hundred were waiting. Many had their phones out in anticipation of Cindy and Jenny's arrival. Chipper asked Big Bill to walk over near the crowd with him, feeling that Big

Bill's presence might keep the crowd from getting too rowdy. It didn't help. When Duncan drove up with Cindy, she jumped out of the car even before it stopped moving. When she ran to the range, she had her golf bag held in front of her, rather than over her left shoulder. The catcalls were unmerciful.

"Do me, Dunc!"

"Do me, Dunc!"

"I can take you home, Cindy!"

"Let me take you home, Cindy!"

"How can I meet your friend?"

When Duncan ambled by, the catcalls increased.

"Don't do me, Dunc!"

"Can't do me, Dunc!"

Big Bill finally said, "Ok, guys, you've had your fun. Now, end it. I want you to end it. Now! Fun's over." It helped a bit, but not much.

Chipper followed Cindy to the range, and when she put her golf bag down, he gave her a hug. "Thank you, Chipper. How am I ever going to live with this? My parents will see this. Dunc is embarrassed, and he shouldn't be. It's out there forever. This is horrible. I just need to hit golf balls. Need to hit them hard! Need to whomp them!"

"I wish I could tell you it would be over in a few weeks, but I don't know. You're a strong girl, Cindy." There was commotion behind them again, and Jenny came jogging up. She embraced Cindy for a long time.

Cindy said, "I just want to hit the driver today, Jenny. Whomp it good. Whompalicious. Can I do that?"

"Sure," said Jenny, "But warm up first. You don't want to hurt yourself."

"Maybe I do, Jenny. Maybe I do."

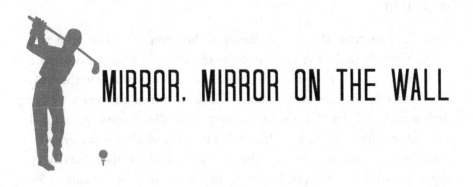

MIRROR, MIRROR ON THE WALL

Stein met Officer Henderson in front of Cindy's estate. Henderson had been there before, after Irene's escape from the wine cellar. He was quite familiar with the home. Henderson introduced Richard Stein to his security specialist, Wayne Simpson. Simpson was short, with glasses, and was not in uniform. He had a pocket protector with some pens in his jacket pocket. Simpson switched some sort of device that looked like a cell phone from his right hand to his left hand so he could shake hands with Stein. Henderson said, "Simpson is our security guy. Best in the county. If there are cameras in this house, he'll find them."

Stein said, "It's obvious there are cameras in the house. I'm very curious why Cindy and Duncan or Serena didn't find them."

Henderson couldn't help but say, "So the other girl is named Serena?"

"Yes, but don't tell anyone her name," Stein said, "Did you look at the videos?"

Henderson lied, "I did not." Stein knew he had watched them by his reaction to Serena's name.

Simpson said, "It's very easy to hide cameras these days. Very sophisticated. Especially if someone doesn't suspect it. Very, very easy."

They entered the house and headed up the stairs to the master bedroom. Simpson said, "I looked at the videos just to see what angle the photos were taken from. Strictly professional interest. I had to...and by the way, those are two foxy girls. That second girl, Serena, is amazing."

Henderson said, "Keep it professional, Wayne."

Simpson immediately started shining a light from his device, and waving it over a mirror on the wall, across from the bed. Within a few seconds, he had put on some gloves and was peeling off what looked like a contact lens from the mirror. Barely visible, even if you knew it was there. Simpson said, "I've only seen one of these before, and it was on a CIA-related case. Whoever did this must have a lot of contacts in the CIA, NSA, or foreign intelligence community. This is a mirror-glass color, totally undetectable, HD-quality, motion-sensing, multi-dimensional, directional microphone micro spy camera. It's smaller than the smallest commercially-available ones. It's smaller than the Tadpole. Much smaller. Very, very sophisticated. Easy to apply. Just sticks to the mirror. You can carry a lot of them in your pocket."

Henderson said, "Can you find prints on it, or on the mirror?"

"I can try, but the chance of finding prints on this thing are pretty slim. Let me look around the room for others."

Stein asked, "Can you get a search warrant for Nolan Lusky's house. He's the likely one that did it. Can you track the signals to his house? Or can you look at his computers to see what he has on them?"

Henderson answered, "It's not likely a judge would consider that we have probable cause to do that."

Simpson pressed a button on his device, and he waved it around different parts of the room. He explained that he was looking for HD signals that might be emanating from other parts of the room. "I would guess our camera-placing guy just had time to place one in each room, and probably on mirrors. Let's check the other bedrooms."

There were a lot of bedrooms on the same floor. Stein knew there were six. Simpson found identical mirror cams in the next two they looked at. When they walked into the third bedroom, Henderson said, "This looks like the bedroom Serena was in." Then he covered his mouth with his hand. "Sorry. Hard to forget."

Simpson easily found the camera, and it was the last bedroom he found anything in. The whole house examination had taken less than an hour. Henderson asked Stein if he could take a quick look at the wine cellar to see what it looked like. The last he remembered, it was a war zone: two dead bodies, chainsaw on the ground, broken bottles of Dom Perignon, and lots of blood.

Stein was proud when he led them downstairs. The room was pristine. Henderson was complimentary. The last thing Simpson said was, "It would take ten lifetimes to drink all this wine. I don't know how people make enough money to live like this."

Stein just commented, "It's a new world, Mr. Simpson. If you were a young blonde with a good figure, maybe you could live like this too."

MONDAY WOES CONTINUE

After inspecting Cindy's estate, Henderson drove directly to the Pebble Beach driving range, where he knew he would find Chipper Blair. The range was completely empty except for Chipper hitting balls. When the Sheriff's car pulled up near the range, Chipper was not surprised. He was actually pleased to see that it was Henderson who exited the car. Chipper didn't recognize the guy that got out of the passenger side.

Chipper stopped hitting balls and faced Henderson and the stranger when they approached. He said, "Hi, Officer Henderson. I was expecting you or someone else at some point. Don't you think it's strange that Devine from the Herald gets the information sooner than the accused?"

"Public record, Chipper. If you looked at the Sheriff's logs, you would be the first to know as well. You get in so much trouble that I'm surprised you don't start your day by looking at it. This is Deputy Simpson. I don't believe you know him?"

Simpson said, "Can I hit some balls while you deal with Officer Henderson?"

Chipper said, "Sure," and handed him a nine iron.

Henderson had a manila folder which he opened, as Chipper stepped back away from Simpson. Simpson took a swing, and Chipper said, "Try playing the ball about three inches back in your stance from where you had that one."

Simpson took another swing and hit one better. Chipper said, "Keep your left arm straighter. Don't bend it. Hit another one." The next shot was better still. Chipper continued, "Hit about five more like that, Simpson."

Henderson was getting impatient. He had papers out of the manila envelope and had a pen in his left hand. "I need you to sign this paper first, Chipper. It's verification that you received this restraining order. You can't get within two hundred yards of Nolan Lusky or any of his property."

"My absolute pleasure to sign that," Chipper said. "I don't ever want to see that idiot again. Ever. What are you doing to keep him from harassing Cindy and Jenny? I'm sure you saw the videos he posted of poor Cindy, Duncan, and Serena."

"No proof that he did it. Hard to prove," was all Henderson said.

Simpson, who was happy about the way he was hitting the golf ball, commented, "I'll try to see if I can find anything, but Henderson is right. Really difficult in this situation. Do you know both girls?"

"Yes, I do," Chipper commented, "Let's see you hit the five iron now. Grab mine out of the bag."

Henderson then waved the other papers in front of Chipper. Chipper paid attention to Simpson and heard Henderson say, "These are Lusky's attorneys' explanation of the charges against you and his petition that you be arrested immediately because you are a risk to his client. If you read Devine's column, then I know you read all the charges against you." Henderson waved the papers at Chipper again.

Chipper mockingly put his arms down behind his back and said, "Are you going to cuff me?" Then he said to Simpson, "Now, don't play the five iron like you are with the ball position the same as you did for the nine iron. Move the ball up a bit. About halfway toward your left foot." Simpson smiled when he hit a good one.

"What are you aiming at?" Chipper asked.

"I'm just hitting it. Not aiming at anything."

"Always have a target when you practice. Just like you would when you play. Aim at the second flag out there."

Simpson's next shot was about thirty yards to the right of the target. Chipper said, "Adjust your stance. You know that is pretty much where you were aiming. You might think you were aiming at the flag, but your body alignment is about thirty yards right of it."

Henderson, strictly business, said, "We have stuff to do. Enough of the golf. Concentrate on your alleged crimes, Chipper. You have to sign two more papers. One that you understand the charges against you. The other that you won't leave town. I am not going to cuff you. Not going to arrest you. You'll get a call from Deputy D.A. Sloane. You'll have to go in for questioning fairly soon. We know you aren't a flight risk. You should take these charges seriously. I know the fine doesn't matter, but you could have jail time."

"You know I didn't do anything. I didn't key the car. I would have liked to key the car, but it wasn't me. I just play golf, you know. When do you question all the other people that were there last night? All the college kids? All the other guests? It's a shame you have to spend time investigating this. Should I tell you now, or wait to tell Sloane, that I don't even carry a key. My Tesla doesn't use one. It uses a card. My house has a code. I don't use a key. I don't carry a key. What if I don't sign these?"

Henderson ignored Chipper's last comment and said, "You could have borrowed a key from someone or just picked up a jagged rock or something. The scratch might not have been from a key."

Simpson continued to hit golf balls and looked like he had no intention of leaving. "I've never hit the ball so well before. Thank you, Chipper."

In the car, driving away, Simpson looked at the list of charges against Chipper. He started reading them out loud and continued, even under the protests of Henderson. "Vandalism, criminal mischief, trespassing, disorderly conduct, bullying, civil rights violations, domestic terrorism, and with extenuating circumstances involving a hate crime." Then Simpson said, "He seemed like a nice guy to me. Sure knows his golf."

Henderson calmly said, "He is a nice guy. He just seems to get in a lot of trouble."

DRONE FLIGHT 1

Later in the day, still Monday, Chipper was hitting balls again, and there were a few others on the range. He heard the skidding noise of a car coming to an abrupt halt in the parking lot. Chipper and the others on the range looked back and saw a red Ferrari parked sideways, using a few parking spaces. The passenger side was facing the range, and Chipper smiled when he saw Tak struggling to get out of the car. He managed to roll to the side and ended up on the pavement. Looking embarrassed, he rose to his feet, and walked over to Chipper. Chipper assumed Emily was in the driver's seat, behind the tinted windows, and that the red Ferrari was Takahashi's.

"Hello, Chipper. You have to excuse me for who I am with. Please excuse. I want to see his drone. Driving range good open space to use new drone."

"Oh, Tak. You are with Lusky. He's a scum, Tak. Real scum. He filed charges against me for his car scratch."

"I know. I want ride or drive in Pagani, but Pagani now being fixed. He buy red Ferrari yesterday. Cash. He spend money like it water. I want to see new drone. Could be big moneymaker. He young and obnoxious, but he smart."

"Did you see the videos of Cindy and Serena?"

"No. What video?"

"It's good you didn't see them, Tak. Just make sure he goes way over on the other side of the range. Not anywhere near me."

"He also ask question. Don't know why? How fast your golf ball go? Strange question, huh?"

"For a regular PGA pro, probably one hundred seventy-five miles per hour. If I hit a good one with the driver, probably just over one hundred fifty, maybe one hundred sixty."

"Thank you, Chipper. We stay out of your way." Takahashi pointed to the far end of the range on the right. "Way over there. Over there."

Chipper watched Takahashi wander to the car, then stared as Lusky got out. Chipper continued to stare as Lusky grabbed a small drone in each hand. Takahashi held one as well. They looked much smaller than the usual drones Chipper had seen. Only about a foot across, and a foot wide. Chipper returned to hitting golf balls.

Takahashi watched as Lusky put the three drones on the ground and took out a cell phone from his jacket. Each drone looked identical and was completely shiny black, except for red lettering on the side that said *Lusky*. Tak watched as Lusky pressed a button on the first drone, and a few lights on it started flashing. Then he tapped in a few commands on the cell phone to sync with the drone. A few more lights started flashing.

Lusky said, "We can use stealth mode, with no lights, but I want to try to follow it now, so we'll leave the flashing lights on. Everything I need to control the drone is on this cell phone. The cell phone is not registered to anyone. It is stealth, as well. And take a look at the screen. A full-screen look at what the drone is seeing. It will be a blur, because it's so fast. And I can control it by just fingering a direction on the screen. I don't need to use any keys."

Takahashi said, "Who you sell it to?"

Lusky replied, "I have been talking to North Korea, Iran, China, some other independent drone dealers."

"Bad people. All bad people. Why not U.S.?"

"More money offered. Way more money. Also, they buy without the regulations that the U.S. insists on. More money, easier regulations, no hassle. Really big money. Selling to the U.S., even to the spooks, is too much bureaucracy and red tape."

"Why you need investors, then? Why you need me?"

"I don't, actually. But to get up to scale quickly, I need some investors. I'd rather not be dealing with venture capitalists again. Have to give up too much equity. You ever watch Shark Tank? These VCs are worse. Way worse."

"Why not use drones for good? Finding hikers. Delivering medical supplies. Deliver food. Watch out for fires in woods."

"No money there," Lusky said, quickly.

Lusky left the drone on the ground and pressed something on the phone that started the drone hovering a few feet off the ground. Takahashi was amazed at how quiet it was. Just a very hard-to-hear hum. Lusky then said, "Watch this. When asshole over there hits his golf ball, I'm going to knock it out of the air. You said one hundred sixty miles per hour. No problem. Watch this. The drone has state-of-the-art sensing devices. I just give it a target prompt, and it knows what to do. Watch this."

Takahashi watched as Chipper swung on the other side of the driving range. As soon as Chipper hit the ball, Lusky launched the drone. It took off so fast that Takahashi couldn't even see it. He thought he saw a little light flash, but that was all. Then he heard Lusky say, "Oh, shit. Dammit." Then Takahashi saw the drone tumbling to the earth on the other side of the driving range, apparently missing the golf ball and clanging into a tree, before dropping to the ground.

"What happen there?" Tak said.

Lusky only said, "Missed, and couldn't stop it or turn it fast enough to avoid the tree. The guidance and avoidance software still needs work, apparently. But did you see how fast it went? Amazing. My engineers said five hundred miles per hour and they are still searching for more speed."

Chipper, still hitting balls, was not aware that his golf ball was a target. He saw nothing and didn't even hear the drone hit the tree.

Lusky tapped on his phone again, pressed a button on the second drone, and it jumped to life and immediately started hovering. He said, "Attempt number two." This time the drone sped off and actually hit the golf ball, but then deflected out of control, and Takahashi could see it spinning wildly straight up into the air. Lusky again said, "Oh, shit. Dammit." He had to then try to gain control of the drone again, but it was last seen heading out spinning toward the far end of the range. Never to be seen again.

This time, Chipper saw the deflection in his golf ball and the drone heading up into the air, then spinning out of the back of the range. Chipper and the two other golfers on the range were now just looking at Lusky and Takahashi. When Lusky fired up the third drone, he had to yell to the golfers, "Hit a ball. Hit another ball." Chipper didn't, but one of the other guys did. This time the drone made a direct hit, and Lusky was able to control the drone enough that he made it return and hover over Takahashi's head before descending back to the ground. Takahashi clapped.

"Are you impressed?" Lusky asked.

"I not like that you sell to Iran, North Korea, China, just to make more money. What about Japan? You sell to Japan? Maybe if I invest, I get rights to sell new drone to Japan. I export, import."

"We can talk about that," Lusky said. "This drone still needs some work, but it is very fast. The fastest. Almost too fast. Now let's take the new Ferrari out on the highway again." Chipper watched them walking away. He then called Jenny, and they agreed to meet later and drive out to the seventh green at Pebble and hit shots before the sun went down. It had been a stressful day, and they both needed the golf and the view.

SEVENTH HOLE

On the way to the seventh green, Jenny started asking about baby names. "Chipper. We should start picking names for our baby."

"You aren't even pregnant yet. We have plenty of time. Let's just play golf. I had a horrible day. That guy Lusky was out showing Takahashi his new drone. It seemed to have some problems, but it's so fast you can't even see it. It had some flashing lights that looked like a blur."

"We should talk about baby names. That might help me get pregnant."

"That's not the way it works, Jenny."

"Ha, Ha. My parents want to name the baby after their parents. My dad's father was Shlomo and my mom's mom was Sadie. My mom texts me all the time. Just says Shlomo or Sadie. I've told her no, but you know how she is."

"Not a chance, although Sadie is kind of a cute name. Sadie Blair sounds kind of nice actually."

"Sadie Nelson Blair would be the name. Not just Sadie Blair. Sadie comes from the Hebrew meaning princess."

"What does Shoshona mean? I'm surprised I haven't asked you before."

"Rose. It means rose."

"What does Walter the third mean? I imagine my father wants me to name a boy Walter the third. That's why I haven't told them we're trying to have a baby."

Jenny googled it on her phone and said, "It's German in origin. Means power of the Army. Very strange. I guess that describes your father. I think we can agree that if we have a boy, the name won't be Walter the third."

"I kind of thought that we would name the baby after Ben or Aileen. Ben Blair is cute and Aileen Blair isn't bad."

"Ben Nelson Blair and Aileen Nelson Blair, you mean?"

"Won't your parents insist on the Nelsberg? Ben Nelsberg Blair has an interesting ring to it."

Jenny said, "Not a chance. And it won't be Chipper Nelson Blair the second either!"

Chipper said, "I was seriously thinking of Eldrick for a boy and Annika for a girl. Eldrick Tiger Chipper Blair, really sounds good. He would have a good start on being a star. Annika Blair is a great one, too."

"Now you're just making things up. I'm serious. Ben is cute, and it would honor Ben. May he rest in peace. Sadie is a good one."

They were now driving the golf cart up to the seventh tee. The wind was coming in from the ocean on the right in gusts. It was a biting wind. Not pleasant. Cold and blustery like Scotland. "Why don't we do this?" Chipper said, "I'm going to write the names we've talked about on each golf ball with my Sharpie, and we'll just see which ball is closest to the hole."

"We can't leave this up to fate, Chipper. A name is a serious thing. That's why I changed mine."

Jenny's name was something Chipper knew not to talk about. It was off limits for comments or arguments. He knew from experience not to say anything. He was quiet, climbed out of the cart, and grabbed his wedge from his bag. He took some practice swings, then took out as many golf balls as he had in his bag and started writing names on them. Jenny was swinging her pitching wedge and getting impatient. "It's cold, Chipper. Just throw me one that you've already written on."

They alternated shots and hit six balls each. Every shot was within twenty feet of the hole. The closest looked to be about three feet. Chipper drove the cart down near the green and walked to the closest shot. Jenny had hit it there. He laughed when he picked up the ball and looked at the name. Jenny said, "So tell me, already. What's my first child's name going to be?"

Chipper showed Jenny the golf ball. "It's Annika."

Jenny said, "You know, Chipper. That's not bad. Annika Nelson Blair. I like it." Then she gave Chipper a strange look and started unzipping her skirt. "Chipper, I feel right. I'm fertile today. I'm ripe. We were married here on the seventh green. Let's make Annika right here, too. It's very cold, though; hurry up. Take off your pants."

Jenny slid down her skirt, so it was around her golf shoes, then slid down her underwear. Chipper was pulling his pants down as quickly as he could. When Jenny bent over away from him, he couldn't help but laugh at the situation. Jenny wasn't happy. "It's cold, Chipper. Make it quick."

"Babies are supposed to be made in love."

"I love you, Chipper. Just make me a baby, already."

A big gust of wind came up, and both of them could feel sand from the bunker behind them blowing on their naked behinds. Then they lost themselves in a rhythm, and both were saying, "Annika. Annika. Annika."

When they were done, Chipper said, "If it's a boy, I think we should call him Sandy."

They putted out each ball, making four out of the twelve. Chipper repaired all the ball marks, and many more. Then they drove home. Jenny felt it would be good to raise her legs and rest them in front of her against the front of the cart. When they pulled into the backyard of their estate, she saw Angus and Abigail playing on the back lawn. She didn't pet Angus, but hugged Abigail and said, "Good luck to both of us, Abby."

D.A. REBECCA SLOANE

Chipper was happy he didn't have to go into the D.A.'s office to be interrogated by Rebecca Sloane. She went out of her way and was happy to arrange a meeting of everyone involved, except Lusky, at The Hay at happy hour time the following day. She told Chipper on the phone that she had some ideas about Lusky's petition against Chipper. It was out of the ordinary, but she was a friend of Jenny and Chipper and enjoyed coming into the Del Monte Forest for work.

Chipper had an uneventful day at the range. The fence around The Hay was almost done already. He made a vow to find out what was going on there. It turned out to be fairly easy.

Debbie Rogers placed a reserved sign on a large table inside the restaurant/bar area for the group. There was no benefit sitting outside, because the view was blocked of The Hay golf course and the ocean because of the large fence. It was an eyesore. Debbie had heard rumors about why the golf course was fenced, but when customers in the bar or restaurant asked, she kept to the company line, "The course is undergoing minor renovations."

Rebecca Sloane arrived first with a briefcase and looking very professional. She was wearing a dark pantsuit with a blazer. Debbie showed her to the table, and Rebecca quickly sat in the chair at the end and placed her briefcase under the table. Debbie knew her regular drink and hurried off to bring back an Arnie's Cadillac Margarita with Patrón Silver, fresh lime, orange-infused agave nectar, Grand Marnier, and Big Sur Salt. Debbie commented that Richard would pay, and the group would get the regular employee discount. The menu price for the margarita was twenty-two dollars. Most customers didn't mind the high price. The view and ambiance was worth it.

Richard sauntered in soon after Sloane and, as usual, handed out his General Counsel with Pebble Beach Corporation business cards to other Hay customers. He was still in his patterned knickers with matching socks, cardigan, and Hogan-type golf cap phase. Debbie put up with it and had to agree it was eye-catching, and he actually looked pretty cute. She never knew what Richard was going to order. He was unpredictable. Richard gave Debbie a hug and a peck on the cheek and just said, "Surprise me, beautiful." She left and brought him back an Ay Que Bueno that had Bacardi, mint, blackberries, lime, club soda, and a splash of Sprite. Menu cost was, by Pebble Beach standards, quite inexpensive at seventeen dollars.

Sloane immediately said, "Hi, Richard. Looking dapper, as usual. I like the look. What's the story with the Visqueen fence? Ruins the view."

"Minor renovations. It will be down in less than a week." He sipped his drink and didn't like the taste. He beckoned Debbie over while he poured the drink into a large flower pot with dirt near the table. She then brought the most expensive drink on the menu at twenty five dollars, the Pebble Beach Manhattan, with PB Knob Creek Single Barrel, Averna, Dolin Rouge, whiskey barrel bitters, and a Luxardo cherry. Not much of a risk this time as she knew Stein loved this drink. He would have several.

Chipper and Jenny came in holding hands. Sloane rose and gave Jenny a big hug, "You look wonderful, Jenny."

Chipper was surprised when Jenny said, "We're trying to have a baby, Rebecca. I'm very happy. I'm very hopeful. I don't want my man to be in jail, though. I need him to be around."

Sloane held Jenny's hands and looked her straight in the eye when she said, "I don't think he's going to be in any trouble. I have some ideas about the current charges against him from Lusky. I'm hopeful as well."

Debbie brought two drinks, and when Jenny sat down, she pushed her drink over to Chipper. He had two Aztec Old Fashioned cocktails in front of him. Jenny said, "Who knows, I might be pregnant now. I'm not going to drink anymore."

Chipper asked Richard, "Why the horrible fence, Richard, and don't tell me it's for a course renovation. It doesn't need a renovation, and the

Corporation wouldn't renovate in the spring, they would wait until the winter."

Stein wasn't really paying much attention, as Ian Osterholm was walking in with Merlene. In fact, most of the customers were staring at Merlene. She was wearing a very short pleated skirt, and was obviously braless under a plain white tee shirt with the Ralph Lauren logo on it. Stein mumbled, "Renovations, Chipper. Just renovations." Chipper was now staring at Merlene as well.

Osterholm sat at the table and said, "Isn't she a stunner? No question about that. Smart, too. Going to start college in late August at Brown. Ivy League. Her sisters graduated from Duke. Maybe pre-law. She might be able to help you in a few years, Rebecca."

Stein immediately said, "I'll hire her right now."

Osterholm put his arm around Merlene and said, "You know, people look at these girls and how beautiful they are and assume they are just lookers with no substance or brains. Charlene, Darlene, and Merlene are all incredible women, all very bright. These Pebble Beach types assume the worst when they see Darlene and Charlene in their maids' uniforms. They both majored in finance and actually help me with investments and money management. I pay them more than they would make at a consulting firm or as accountants. Merlene draws stares everywhere she goes. It can be a burden. Poor girl."

Sloane commented, "Well, we learn something every day. Thank you, Ian. I think that's the first time I've ever heard you say something serious. I'm impressed. We're waiting for several more who were at the party where the car was damaged, then we'll get started."

The rest of the invited group filed in: Cindy and Duncan, Emily and Takahashi, a few of Cindy's teammates. They waited patiently. When Serena Antonelli came in, the men at the table all rose at the same time. Some men in at the bar started whispering and one even applauded. Serena was embarrassed but didn't say anything. She just sat down next to Cindy at the table. Everyone was silent until Jenny asked, "How has school been the last few days, girls? I imagine it's been awful. Isn't there something we can do about Lusky, Rebecca? We all know it was him. Can't someone search his house?"

Serena said, "It has been awful. I feel awful. Our golf coach wants to suspend both me and Cindy. I was drunk and doing things I wouldn't normally do. Now I have to live with this video. Those idiots at the bar even recognized me. It just feels like everyone on campus is staring at me. Everywhere I go, I feel paranoid. Thank God my parents and brother haven't said anything. I feel like dyeing my hair and wearing a cap all the time. Dressing in baggy sweats."

Everyone swiveled when Big Bill was seen pushing Irene McVay in a wheelchair toward the table. Bill said, "I'm surprised there is no handicap parking here. Not even a place to park or let off someone who is disabled anywhere near the restaurant. I thought every place had to have disability access. Richard, why don't you do something about that? Try pushing a wheelchair across the street and up the ramp. Crazy."

Jenny said, "Are you ok, Irene? Still smarting from your injuries? You looked better last time. What hurts?"

Irene said, "Bill, please wheel me over to Serena." Cindy moved her chair, and Bill pushed Irene, in the wheelchair, as close to the table and Serena as he could. Chipper sensed what was coming, and he grabbed Jenny's hand and whispered to her, "This ought to be good."

Irene finally answered Jenny, "No, Jenny, not an injury from my kidnappers. I was feeling pretty damn good. This injury is Serena's fault. We watched her video, and I told Bill…"

Bill interrupted, "Irene. You are incorrigible. You don't have to say anything other than you hurt your back." Then he looked at everyone at the table and said, "She hurt her back."

But Irene continued, "I told Bill that I wanted to try some of the stuff Serena did in the video. You know the one where she stands on the bed and bends over forward from the waist and waves her hands under her legs. Then her boyfriend stands behind her, and she grabs him from under her legs…"

Everyone at the table was laughing now, including Serena. They had all seen the video. Then Irene got more animated, "Then while still holding her boyfriend, she leans forward and puts her head down on the bed…"

Bill finally said, "Enough, Irene. That's more than enough."

Irene sighed and said, "And that's when my back went out. I screamed from pain and slumped on the bed. How do you do that, Serena?"

Osterholm then rose from the table and walked around behind Serena.

He put a hand on each of her shoulders and said, "You, young lady, are a superstar. A real superstar."

Sloane said, "Now, that is the Ian Osterholm I know."

Jenny frowned and said, "Ian, take your hands off the poor girl's shoulders. Leave her alone. We should all leave her alone."

But Osterholm couldn't help getting in the last words, "Serena, you can make a lot of money doing that stuff. I can introduce you to some very important and rich people here in the Forest. In fact, some have called me already."

Serena made a comment that Chipper loved, "I just want to play golf. I want to be a pro golfer. Can you please let it go?"

Ian walked back to his chair and sat quietly.

Sloane finally started to get to the point, "Ok, everyone, let's get to the reason I wanted to talk to all of you. Every one of you was at Cindy's party. You all know that Lusky's car got keyed. Lusky has filed a criminal case accusing Chipper of doing it and adding a lot of charges. I don't want to go through all the charges now, but they range from misdemeanor mischief up to domestic terrorism. Strange as it seems, there is no precedent for punishment of domestic terrorism. It's a ridiculous charge in this case anyway, as are most of the charges. Lusky has a lawyer friend from Silicon Valley who is a bulldog. Lusky is probably paying him a lot of money for this."

Most of the group was listening intently, and Debbie was keeping the drinks coming. It was a usual Hay gathering. No one would be able to drive home. Not healthy. Cindy and Serena were not drinking, but the golf team boys that were there, without being carded, were already drunk.

Sloane continued, "I have two main things I want to talk about. One is that I know Chipper did not do this. I believe him. He doesn't even carry a key. His Tesla doesn't use one. It is controlled by his cell phone. So, whoever did this could be any of you. Which one of you did it or knows who did it?" Sloane then glanced around the table slowly and looked everyone in the eyes. Some matched her gaze. Some lowered their heads. She waited a long time, and the table was completely silent. No one confessed.

"Ok. The next item is that these criminal charges are so over the top, and no one can say they heard me give this advice, but I would recommend Chipper find his own high-powered attorney and file civil charges for defamation of character and malicious prosecution. You can't do this, unfortunately, until you go through with a case and are exonerated, found not guilty. I have some attorneys I can send you to."

Stein immediately said, "I can do this…"

Before he finished, Sloane interrupted and said, "You don't have criminal experience, Richard…"

"Yes. I can do this," Stein continued, "Right up my alley. Remember how I handled the obnoxious barrister in Scotland? I can do this."

Chipper, as Jenny knew he would, said, "I don't want to do that. I just want to get this over with. Like Serena, I just want to play golf. Let's just get this over with. The case won't take very long. I don't even have a key."

Stein stood up and said, "If the key doesn't fit, you must acquit!!" He then started laughing hysterically, but no one else did.

Sloane said, "I'm going to give you some names anyway, Chipper. We'll do the criminal case then, step by step. I'll try to talk to Lusky's attorney and get this dismissed. You have to come in and get booked again, though. You know the drill."

Chipper took a big gulp of his Aztec Old Fashioned.

Serena said, "Can't you do something about Lusky's unauthorized filming? Can I file something? Can Cindy and Duncan and I file something?"

"Yes. I'll help you. You need an attorney, too." Stein again volunteered.

Merlene said, "You know that guy kept putting his hand on my thigh when he had me sit next to him at the party. I kept moving his hand off, but he kept putting it back on my leg. I told him to knock it off a few times. He kept thinking I would be impressed with his money and his car. He's a nut job. A whacko. I just didn't know what to do in a strange home with strange people."

Osterholm surprisingly said, "Rebecca. What if someone confessed to keying the car? What would happen to them?"

Rebecca said, "Did you do it, Ian?"

"I'm not saying that. I was just wondering."

"With a car that expensive, some of the charges against Chipper might be felonies. Vandalism, destroying property. Could be a fine and jail time. If it was you, Ian, you probably shouldn't admit it. There is no way of knowing who actually did it. Do you have any prior convictions or anything?"

"He should. He definitely should," said Irene. Osterholm didn't answer.

While Sloane was talking, some at the table could hear Merlene whisper to Jenny, "Ian was mad at the guy for harassing me. Isn't that sweet?"

Stein made sure to get Serena's phone number before Serena headed back to school.

STEIN SPILLS

When the "legal" meeting ended, Chipper wanted to stay and try to get Stein to tell him what was happening with The Hay golf course and what was intended for his driving range. Jenny wasn't that happy staying, as she wasn't having anything to drink. Debbie brought her some appetizers, and Jenny snacked as Chipper kept trying to talk Richard into telling him what was going on. Richard kept saying, "Stop it, Chipper. I'm never going to tell you."

After several more drinks (a Hay Good Lookin' with Tito's Vodka, a Hay Beautiful with Tanqueray Gin, and a Hay Mary with New Amsterdam Vodka and chipotle tabasco mix) Richard was getting loose. When Debbie brought him, finally, an El Rey with Del Maguey Vida Mescal, Stein was ready to spill the beans. He probably wouldn't remember in the morning that he had told Chipper and Jenny.

He slurred badly, "The MADRDI, or something like that, company, has a new concept for a completely state-of-the-art driving range…"

Chipper interrupted, "I met their guys, and they filled me in. What are the chances this will happen? I hope none."

"Let me finish, Chipper, old sport. My friend, Chipper." Stein started sliding down in his chair and Chipper was afraid he would pass out before finishing. "You are my friend, Chipper, and my neighbor, in really expensive estates off the fourteenth fairway. Aren't we rich? Aren't we grand? Hey, neighbor. You have to promise you won't tell anyone about this. No one at all." Then Stein did a zipping his own mouth gesture.

"I promise, Richard. I promise."

"Then let me finish, neighbor. This MAD DOG company, or something like that, has measured your driving range and is going to make a financial presentation next week. Then Stevens will decide what to do. You know, no grass, no attendant. That's you, you know. Balls get cleaned automatically, come back to the hitting mats via an aqueduct, or something like that. Sounds pretty impressive. Pretty impressive. All green artificial turf. No mowing. No fertilizer. No work. Easy breezy. You, then, out of work, my man."

"They don't understand golf, Richard. Not at all. It's not golf. They want to cover the trees with a picture, a mural of trees. This is complete nonsense. Nonsense. Enough of that. This will never happen. What's the story with the HAY?"

"Oh, The Hay. I shouldn't tell you. Can't tell you. You'll tell. You'll tell. Na, na, na, na. You'll tell. Promise me you won't tell ANYONE!"

"I promise you, Richard. I won't tell."

Jenny leaned in as well and said, "I promise too, Richard."

Stein began, "You'll understand why Jenny's proposal to pay seven million a year to the Corporation wasn't even listened to. Timing was bad. Very bad. Unfortunately, it came at the same time as this, and they are paying more for just five days at The Hay." Stein slumped further down in his chair, He had finished his El Rey, and Debbie was going to give him another, but Chipper waved her off. Debbie sat down to listen. Chipper started sipping on the El Rey.

Stein continued, "Can you believe these people are paying about the same as Jenny's offer, but just for five days? It's a family that wants complete privacy when their two small kids get golf lessons. They don't want anyone watching or bothering them. They want complete privacy."

Chipper said, "Who the hell are they?"

Stein tried to remember, "They are royalty of some kind. It's something like the Duke and Duchess of Irvingtonshire and their small kids. Can you imagine?"

"How old are the kids?" Jenny asked.

"I don't remember exactly, but less than ten." At this point, Stein slumped completely in the chair, and Chipper had to go around the table and prop him up.

Jenny wondered, "Why didn't they tell me? I love teaching kids. I'm really good at it."

Stein said, "Let me remember. They are bringing some sort of hot shot teacher that used to teach Tiger. I think his name is Coma. Or maybe it's Cuomo. Oh, no, that's the governor of New York, isn't it?"

Jenny and Chipper said, at the same time, "Chris Como. He was Tiger's coach for a while. The Corporation should have told them they had me here, and they didn't need to bring in an outside teacher. I would have loved to do that. Even for free. The Duke and Duchess of Irvingtonshire. Wow, that's some title. When do they get here?"

The last word Stein said, before he faded completely away, was, "Tomorrow."

Chipper helped Debbie get Stein into the car. It was difficult because there was no place to park, other than on the main road, in front of The Hay. They still didn't have designated disability parking or even a drop off zone. Chipper had Stein by the arms and Debbie and Jenny had one foot each. Stein was entirely off the ground. "How am I going to get him into our place?" Debbie kept saying. Jenny offered to ride back with Debbie to help, then walk next door. Chipper would take a while to get home in his golf cart.

Debbie drove Stein home in her car, and when she parked, she shook him pretty violently. She had a water bottle that she poured over his head. That worked wonders. Jenny only had to help Debbie guide Stein toward the front door of the estate. Stein wasn't happy, but started muttering about legal matters. "Legal stuff. Got to do legal stuff. Have to get Lusky. I can get Lusky."

Jenny and Debbie hugged, then Jenny took the backyard route to her own estate. Meanwhile Debbie couldn't get Richard to bed. He insisted on heading to his office and doing as he kept saying, "important legal stuff." She finally left him in his office. When she awoke in the morning, Stein was asleep on the couch in his office with two neat stacks of paper on the floor next to him. She picked up the first stack and saw the title was:

CIVIL CASE COMPLAINT
BLAIR VS. LUSKY
MALICIOUS CRIMINAL PROSECUTION
$100,000,000

She read the first page after that and was impressed with the legal language and footnotes in italics but really didn't understand it. She put it down and picked up the second stack. The title was:

**CRIMINAL CASE COMPLAINT
ANTONELLI AND SPRINGER, ET AL VS. LUSKY
VARIOUS CHARGES DETAILED ON PAGE 3**

Debbie Rogers turned to page three and read six different charges that Stein had put in against Lusky. She glanced over a few of the other pages and again didn't understand all the legal terminology. She was proud of Richard. She kissed him on the forehead, then dressed in sweats and running shoes to get in a little treadmill time. They had a cardio room modeled after Chipper and Jenny's. She didn't have to be to work until four that day.

COMO

Chris Como was in the top echelon of golf teaching professionals. He had been Tiger's coach for a bit and was known for working with Jason Day, Bryson DeChambeau, and Trevor Immelman, among others. It wasn't known how much he charged the pros, but if an amateur went to him for lessons, it was $1,250 an hour. Dave Pelz, a short-game wizard and coach, received a rumored $20,000 per day for lessons. Hank Haney $15,000 per day. Butch Harmon $1,500 per hour. It was amazing that the Pebble Beach Corporation was charging $1,800 per hour now for someone to take a lesson with Jenny. She was ranked as the second-best woman teaching pro in the U.S. Mercifully, the Corporation cut down her lessons from eight a day to just four or five. Her notoriety, due to Duncan's Cindy Springer social media posts which often included Jenny, added to the demand. Most of the lessons were for wealthy men. It seemed her lesson rate went up weekly. She wasn't in control of it.

Jenny was old-style, teaching each person based on their current swing and making small adjustments each lesson to achieve the best results. Como had a unique holistic approach. He had a master's degree in biomechanics and also worked on each person uniquely, based on the swing they brought to him. Usually, the lessons he gave were to people that had played golf for some time. He was more of a swing consultant than a teacher of perfect elements of the golf swing. His association with Tiger Woods gained him national recognition, and he went from no-name to high-priced lessons.

Como wasn't that experienced in beginner lessons or working with kids. He had talked to a representative of the Duke and Duchess of Irvingtonshire to arrange this five-day gig, but had not talked to them in person. The money was too much to turn down, and Como knew it would be an interesting experience. They were paying for his beautiful room at the Lodge, as well as all food, as well as the lessons. He thought, *How difficult could it be to teach an eight-year-old and a six-year-old to play golf? And it's in such a beautiful place.* Como was from Dallas, Texas. A long way from Pebble Beach.

When he walked from the Lodge area to The Hay, a very short walk, it was cold and damp. He wasn't dressed for it. He walked up the parking lot around the Visqueen fence and was greeted by the head of Pebble Beach security, who introduced himself as Patrick Black. Black looked at Como's identification, then followed him through the gate of the newly-constructed fence. There were two other younger security guards who were introduced only as Jose and Jim. Black and the other guards had on golf clothes and Pebble Beach windbreakers. Each had a name tag pinned onto their windbreakers. They chatted and waited for the Duke and Duchess to arrive.

Black explained that The Duke's first name was Andrew, and the Duchess was Katherine but they were both to be referred to as "Your Grace." The children were the eight-year-old girl named Poppy, who was to be called "Lady Poppy" or just "Lady," and the six-year-old Archie, who was to be called "Lord Archie" or just "Lord." Como smiled, and Black commented, "The Corporation wants to impress these people. I was briefed for two hours on how to handle them. I won't bore you with anything other than what I told you."

Two large men in suits were the first to walk through the gate, quickly followed by the two children and then the Duke and Duchess. The two large men were obviously security guards and looked uncomfortable in their suits and ties. Lady Poppy was smiling and wearing a pleated skirt, golf shoes, a Nike shirt, and matching cap and carrying a golf bag that was too big for her. She was a cute little girl with a jaunty confident stride and a big smile on her face. Her brown hair was in a pigtail coming out of the back of the Nike cap. Lord Archie was in blue jeans and a sweater with an Izod logo, no cap, no smile, and looking sullen. He had on blue Crocs with several jibbitz on each one, including soccer balls, little rabbits, rainbows, and a Union Jack. Certainly not the best shoes for golf. He was dragging another golf bag that was too big behind him. One of the suited security guards leaned over to attempt to help Archie with the golf bag, but the Duke said, "Let him do it himself."

The security guard stood at attention and said, "Yes your Grace."

Black handled the introductions and even bowed. The Duchess said, "Please don't bow. Let's be informal here."

Black said, "Yes your Grace." And bowed again.

Como guessed the Duchess was about forty. A little on the plump side, but athletic looking, with a dark tan. She was taller than the Duke by a few inches and probably outweighed him by twenty or thirty pounds. She was dressed similarly to Lady Poppy, with a skirt, golf shoes, and a matching Nike polo and cap. She was pleasant-looking and had great posture. She stood up very straight and looked Como right in the eye, at the same level, when they shook hands. "Very pleased to meet you finally, Mr. Como. You come highly recommended. I hope my children have a wonderful week. You'll find Poppy very receptive. She loves the game already. Archie has a hard time concentrating. My guards will help you with that, I hope."

The Duke was thin and about five foot eight. Como thought he looked like a marathon runner. Not much fat. Athletic looking. Thin face. Bright eyes. Muscular arms that showed in his tight short-sleeved Under Armour shirt. No cap. Messy curly hair. Green eyes. The Duke stared at Como like he understood his soul and didn't say anything. Kind of creepy.

Como bent down to be on the same level as Lord Archie and Lady Poppy and said, "Let's start with short game, putting, and chipping this morning, then we'll take a look at your swings this afternoon on the course and have some fun. Just play for fun and a few tips. It should always be fun."

The Duchess said, "I think it best, Mr. Como, that we start each day at ten and end at about two thirty. Then the children can nap a bit, and then we can sightsee. Take them to the Aquarium. Go down to Big Sur. They want to play in the tide pools. Is that acceptable with you?"

Como said, "Yes your Grace. Perfectly fine." He was hoping that the Duke and Duchess weren't going to be around the entire time he was teaching the kids, but he was afraid to ask. He would play it by ear. It was very strange to give a lesson to two little kids with their parents watching, as well as five security guards. The security guards stood around the putting green, equidistant from each other, while he was on the green with the kids. The Duke and Duchess seemed to pay attention to what he was doing the entire morning. He felt like he was in a fishbowl. The Duke and Duchess stood apart, and Como never heard or saw them have any interaction at all.

Como told the kids to each grab their putters, and they followed him onto the green. He started with a little contest to see their skill level and whether they were competitive with each other. If they were, all the better. Their clubs were perfectly fitted to their heights, as he expected they would be. Poppy had a cut-down Odyssey two-ball putter and Archie had a cut-down Ping PLD Milled DS72 Satin that Como knew cost nearly five hundred dollars.

The kids were paying attention when he put their golf balls down about twenty feet from the hole he picked with a relatively flat putt. Archie putted first and, as soon as he hit the putt, started running after the ball. He hit it about ten feet by and was soon there, batting at the ball toward the hole in short little strokes. Como walked him back to Poppy and explained he just wanted him to putt the ball near the hole, then wait for his sister to putt. Whoever was closest won the contest.

Archie surprisingly listened. His next putt was about six feet by the hole. A better effort than the first one. A good sign. He started jumping up and down. The Duchess clapped. The Duke was silent. Poppy knelt down behind the ball and did a plumb bob, then put up three fingers, like Justin Rose, then she walked up and straddled her feet over the line of the putt in an attempt to do aim point and feel the break with her feet. She finally went back to behind the ball and looked again, took three practice strokes, then missed badly to the right. Still closer than her brother, though, about five feet away from the hole. She had an out-to-in putting stroke that was quirky. Como said to the Duke and Duchess, "It's obvious, your Graces, that she watches a lot of golf on TV." The Duchess chuckled. The Duke didn't seem to be listening. Archie insisted that he won, even though his putt was about a foot further from the hole than his sister. The Duchess came over and told Archie to sit on the green and not say anything until he was called on again. "Be truthful, Lord Archie."

Como took some time with Poppy to explain the proper putting stroke and placed tees down into the ground that would frame the stroke he wanted her to take. She conscientiously practiced while he then grabbed

Archie and had him repeat the same twenty foot putt a dozen times, in order for Archie to feel the proper distance on the putt. Then he moved Archie closer to the hole by about ten feet and had him practice while he went back to Poppy.

Como felt things were going well and could see the Duchess smiling, while the Duke had stepped back and was sitting on the small wooden railing fence around the putting green. Como was actually having fun. After putting, he basically used the same approach with simple straightforward chips with a pitching wedge from around the green. He could tell Lord Archie was getting a bit bored and unruly near mid-day while Lady Poppy was enthusiastically eager for more. The Duke was now lying on the grass napping. The Duchess was right with Poppy and asking Como questions about how it was to work with Tiger Woods.

The five security guards were still standing at attention around the green.

THE COURTHOUSE

D.A. Sloane made it easy for Chipper to go through the procedures he had been through a few times before. She guided him through arrest, booking, and arraignment before a judge, all before ten AM. He pleaded not guilty. He was released with no bail, on his own recognizance. He then headed back to the driving range, upset that he didn't get to play any holes of golf in the morning.

Stein wandered into the courthouse with both his criminal and civil complaints against Lusky. He filed the civil case in federal court and the criminal case in superior court. He was told that usually criminal cases had to be filed by a government entity, but they would accept his with the proviso that he would probably get a call from a judge telling him to do it over. Maybe not, but probably. The procedure, if accepted, would be that a grand jury would have to determine probable cause. An indictment of Lusky would be improbable.

Lusky would be informed of both cases against him, and Stein would have to pay for Lusky to be served.

As expected, Jerry Devine of the Herald, was all over these.

MONTEREY HERALD

BYLINE DEVINE

Pebble Beach Legal Squabbles

Our old, not of age but from familiarity, friend, Chipper Blair, may have found a new way of making money from his alleged criminal behavior. He has filed a countersuit against new Pebble Beach resident and wealthy young tech star, Nolan Lusky. Lusky had accused Blair of various crimes ranging from malicious mischief to domestic terrorism for allegedly keying his expensive Pagani Huayra automobile: a three-million-dollar car with gull-wing doors. The civil suit for malicious prosecution asks for damages of, believe it or not, one hundred million dollars.

Not a good day for Lusky, as he has another criminal complaint against him filed by Serena Antonelli and Cindy Springer, she of the internet golfing posts. This time for voyeurism, trespassing, and violation of privacy for allegedly placing cameras in Springer's estate bedrooms, then posting sexual activities that the two college girls were involved in for everyone to see. It seems the Serena girl already has a PhD for her activities. But seriously, if Lusky did this, he should be publicly shamed and sent to prison for a long time.

We'll follow both of these cases closely. There is never a dull moment in the Forest.

PLAYING THE HAY

Promptly at noon, one of the suited security guards for the Duke and Duchess slipped away through the gate in the fence, and went to The Hay restaurant and ordered several items for the Duke and Duchess and their children. The security guards wouldn't eat or drink. Just keep watch.

When he came back with food, the lessons stopped, and everyone found a bench in order to take a break and eat. He brought the Duke a Verano salad, the Duchess Pescado Tacos, and the two children split a Chipotle Burger and fries. The guard was chastised and lectured by the Duchess about why he didn't think of getting Como something to eat. He went back and got a Fiesta Bowl for Como.

After the lunch break, the Duke and Duchess retired inside to the bar while Como took the children, with the security guards in tow, to play some holes at The Hay. With the parents gone, Como asked the Pebble Beach younger security guards, Jose and Jim, to carry the golf bags for the kids. The Lord and Lady gave hugs to Como and the two guards. "Me mum always makes me lug me bag!" Lord Archie exclaimed, before the hugs.

Como was familiar with the course and the time they had left in today's lesson. He planned on having the royalty play holes one, two, five, and nine. The first was a fifty-seven-yarder, with a big green that sloped severely from back to front. He was anxious to see how the kids actually swung the golf clubs. Poppy was hitting first, and when she went to put her ball on a tee, Como said, "Let's play it down today, kids."

"What?" asked Poppy.

"No tee. Just off the ground," said Como.

Lord Archie said, "Don't call me kid, Sir. It's not polite. I am Lord Archie." When Como looked at him without a grin on his face, Archie said, "I am joking you, man." Como thought things were going very well at that point.

Archie surprised Chris Como, as his swing was actually better than his older sister's. Both used nine irons, Poppy hit it fat, and Como told her to put down another one and swing again. "Keep your eye on the ball, young Lady Poppy." She hit a better shot, but still short of the very short hole. Archie hit his on the front of the green and ran in circles around his sister yelling, "I'm better! I'm better than you!" He made clucking noises like a chicken as he ran up to the green. Jose chased him carrying the bag.

Como could tell Poppy was listening to him earlier in chipping practice, as she hit a good chip about five feet from the hole. Archie putted his forty-footer all the way off the green, and Poppy showed some personality by "clucking" back at her brother. Lord Archie started pouting, sat down just off the back of the green, and refused to get up again and putt. He continued pouting as his sister putted out, missing the five-footer, and everyone but Archie walked the short distance to the second hole. Archie remained behind, but in sight of everyone.

While they waited on the next tee, hoping Archie would follow, Como asked Poppy if she had ever been to California before. "I've been to New York, but never California. Me mum has been a few times lately, though. I think she likes it here."

Como came back and knelt down and said, "Mr. Lord Archie. This hole coming up is a replica of the famous seventh hole on the Pebble Beach Golf Course across the road. No ocean around the green, but the same distance and the same trap locations. Come on, lad, let's see how you play it. Come on, lad." Archie was intrigued and followed Como to the second tee.

Poppy hit a hybrid of some kind and rolled it into a large trap at the front of the green. Archie grabbed her club, instead of one of his own, and hit a majestically high shot, for him, that landed on the green and rolled to the back of the green. He was about thirty feet past the pin. Como and the security guards all clapped, and Lord Archie bowed low from the waist, then took off running all the way to the green, through the bunker, where he intentionally stepped on his sister's ball, and lay down on the green near his golf ball.

Como told Poppy to get her ball out of the trap. He would give them bunker lessons on day three. He told her to place the ball on the fringe and chip the ball close to the hole. She did as told and hit a good chip five feet from the hole again. This time she made it. Lord Archie two-putted for par.

On the forty-eight-yard fifth hole, the next they played, Como had them each swing their nine irons a few times. He wanted to make minor changes in ball position for Archie and wanted Poppy to take the club back more with her arms back from the ball, rather than a quick wrist hinge and taking the club back with her hands. He had them hit several balls from the fifth tee and corrected them each time they did it wrong. He didn't have them play the hole out.

The ninth was one hundred yards, uphill a bit, and he wanted to see each of them hit a driver. "Swing hard, both of you." Poppy hit a good one that flew over the green and hit the Visqueen screen that protected The Hay outside patio about twenty yards over the green. Archie swung hard, but never hit a good one until Como had him choke down a bit on the grip. He smoked one that hit the fence on the fly about one hundred and twenty yards from the tee. Como said, "Let's call it a day, little Lady and little Lord. It was a good one."

When the Duke and Duchess took the kids away and the security guards all left and locked the gate, Como was happy and felt like hitting golf balls. He walked across the road to the driving range and was hoping to borrow a few clubs there. His were back in the Lodge. He was surprised when he arrived at the range, expecting it to have dozens of golfers, to find only two hitting balls. One guy had a great swing, and one guy was a duffer. He walked up to the good swing and said, "Hi. Do you mind if I hit a few balls? I left my clubs in the Lodge and had a long day. Just feel like hitting a few. You have a good swing."

Chipper said, "Thank you." Chipper didn't recognize Como. There wasn't much of note to recognize him by. He was wearing a Ping golf cap. Athletic looking. Medium height. Probably worked out as he looked fit and muscular. Khaki pants and a golf shirt.

Before Chipper had a chance to respond, Como said, "Where is the driving range guy? No one appears to be in the shack."

Chipper proudly said, "I'm the driving range guy." And he pointed to his Pebble Beach golf cap. "Come on over, and I'll get you a bucket of balls."

"I just want to hit a few."

"I'm not supposed to do this, but about how many do you want?" Chipper filled up a basket and handed it to Como and didn't make him pay. "I hope you aren't a Pebble Beach Corporation spy." He said. "I know they would want the ten dollars."

They walked back to the range, and Chipper handed Como his nine iron and watched him swing. "You have a good swing yourself. Where are you from?"

"Texas. I'm here to give some lessons to some kids." At that point, Chipper knew it was Como.

"Oh, Chris Como. Sorry for not recognizing you. I heard about the royalty lessons. How did it go today? Very nice to meet you. I'm Chipper Blair, the driving range guy."

"It went pretty well, actually. I didn't know what to expect. A six-year-old and an eight-year-old. They paid attention most of the day, and they listened to me. I'm not that experienced working with kids." Como continued hitting balls while he spoke. He turned and gave Chipper back his nine iron and asked for a five.

Chipper said, "My wife Jenny is a teaching pro here. She's number fourteen on the Golf Digest list. Second ranked woman. She's very good. I don't know why the royals didn't ask for her or the Corporation volunteer her."

Como nonchalantly commented, "I'm number two. Maybe number one, Mark Blackburn, wasn't available. I've seen the internet posts of your wife giving lessons to Cindy Springer. I guess everyone has. I'd love to meet her. Maybe I can take her into the fenced area tomorrow to watch."

"I'm sure she would love that if she can reschedule her lesson time. I'll call her now. Why don't you come over here at noon and watch her give lessons to Cindy. Almost every day at noon right here. It's sometimes a zoo because of the internet stuff."

Como handed the five iron back to Chipper and asked for the driver. He said, "For sure, I'll make a point of coming over. I would love to meet both of them. Sorry for asking this, but will that other girl in the videos be here? The dark-haired one."

Chipper laughed and said, "No. She won't be here. She's a good player, though. Best on the CSUMB team."

"Oh. I've seen her play. Quite a player indeed."

Chipper and Chris Como hit drivers, alternating each time. Como would hit first and say, "High fade," then hit one, and Chipper would do the same. "Low hook." "Stinger." "Low fade." They matched shot for shot. "That was fun," Como said, "See you tomorrow."

But that didn't end up happening.

DRONE UPDATES

Nolan Lusky had read the Devine article in the Herald but had not yet been served with papers on either lawsuit. He was livid at Chipper, as well as Serena and Cindy. He knew there was no proof of his wrongdoing in the criminal case, and after talking to his high-powered lawyer, he was not afraid of the civil case either.

Lusky was very private and had only a few acquaintances and even fewer friends. More than his pending legal issues, he was tremendously worried about the possibility of not completing the task he had accepted a few months ago. He only had a few days left, and he was not convinced his plan would succeed. He would lose a lot of money if that happened. The men who had dealt with him were very private as well, and the woman they apparently worked for and protected was extremely strange. Strange in both her actions and her needs. She had bodyguards, but neither she nor the bodyguards would tell him what she did or where she made her money. Only that she needed an accident to happen to her husband. The money involved was enormous. He couldn't turn this down. Lusky didn't know how they found him to offer him the contract hit. Probably from the seedy contacts he had been making while trying to sell his drones.

He had to make it look like a total accident and had to cover his tracks. Maybe allow the evidence to point to someone else. He was happy he received a shipment from his tech wiz, Gopal, of a new supply of drones based on the specified changes he made after his first test at the driving range with Takahashi watching. His technical crew was very quick. As it turns out, very inexperienced as well. Lusky needed to use the new drones immediately without as much testing as he wanted. The speed of the drones made them almost impossible to control.

His tech guys told him they had adopted his suggestions, had improved the guidance system, and had juiced up the speed by about ten miles an hour. They were already twice as fast as any other drone in production, but his tech guys were always trying to get a few more miles per hour out of them. They told him the new drones were at the limit, unless he wanted a much larger drone. He didn't.

Reluctantly, Lusky, on this iteration, also had them take off the Lusky name. That turned out to be beneficial. The Russians, Chinese, and Iranians he was negotiating with didn't want the name on them. They didn't want any identifying names or markings on them for the production models when they were finally perfected. His ego almost got in the way, but the name was taken off the new models. They were totally stealth.

All of his customers wanted the capability of an explosive device carried below the drone, typically inside a small cage. The cage could be used to carry the explosives, as well as carry or pick up small items for transport. Lusky's technical guy told him they were very close to a production model of the drone, as well as a very small explosive device that could inflict huge damage on targets. He was expecting a shipment to arrive any day with a sample of the explosive devices.

Lusky was miffed that his United States Defense Department contacts didn't seem too interested in his price, or his device. They said it was too expensive. He knew they spent billions on planes and didn't understand why there was no interest in his state-of-the-art full-capability drone. He had received a few inquiries from some Midwestern militia and paramilitary groups that had promised, at some point, to send a representative out to view a demonstration.

Lusky was nervous when he packed up a few of the new drones in his Ferrari and drove over to the Pebble Beach driving range. He knew he wasn't really ready for this. He was winging it. He made a point of not parking in the regular lot, where he could be seen, and parked just off the 17-Mile Drive in some dirt. He walked through the trees to the right side of the range.

Chipper and Jenny were looking forward to meeting Como at noon. Jenny was more than excited about following him back to The Hay to watch the kids' lessons. She knew she would have a hard time holding back on giving advice.

The range was completely empty a bit after ten AM, and Chipper decided to put down some target markers behind the actual range hitting areas so he could practice some pitching at various distances. He put down his clubs at the left of the range and placed markers by pacing off thirty, forty, fifty, and sixty yards. He didn't want to use range balls because of their inconsistencies, so he went into his bag and pulled out some of his own. He laughed when he saw that the golf balls in his bag still had the potential kid's names still written on many of the golf balls.

Chipper started hitting at the thirty-yard mark to get a feel for what his swing should feel like to hit the ball thirty yards. He knew the thirty-to-sixty-yard pitches were key to scoring well, saving par, and making birdies. He wasn't happy with his first twelve shots at the thirty. The dispersion was too great. He went to retrieve the golf balls and walked back to start again.

While Chipper was walking back, Lusky was watching surreptitiously from the trees.

COMO AND THE ROYALS

Chris Como was ecstatic when the Duchess said that her children were really excited to start their day of lessons. She said they didn't sleep well and just kept talking about how much fun they had. Both kids, as well as the Duchess, gave Como hugs when they came through the fence. He decided to start them off with putting again and schedule the day much like the one yesterday.

The Duke and Duchess placed themselves standing near the green. The security guards were all in place, and Como started putting the Lord and Lady through their paces. He noticed that the Duchess, for some reason, kept looking over at the fence between The Hay and the driving range. The previous day, she was totally committed to watching her kids, but today she seemed distracted.

Lord Archie and Lady Poppy already had shown improvement in their strokes and judgment of line and pace on the first round of twenty-foot putts. The Lord and Lady were animated and showing their delight. Poppy was the first one to make a twenty-footer. She reacted by raising her putter up into the air and giving a fist pump, bowing to her mum and dad as they applauded.

Things could not have been going any better.

HORROR AT THE HAY

Chipper was just starting to hit his forty-yard shots in the large grassy area behind where the driving range blocks were set up. On his second shot, while his ball was still in the air, he could barely believe his eyes when a drone, almost too fast for him to see, swooped by and seemed to grab his golf ball. The golf ball disappeared from the air.

Lusky, in the trees, was overwhelmed that the guidance system and the small carrying device below the drone seemed able to grab, catch, and carry the target golf ball. All new systems and system fixes seemed to be a success. When the drone had the ball seemingly safely locked in the carrier, however, the 1.62 ounce golf ball apparently seemed to counterbalance the weight of the drone. The drone was so precisely calibrated that just the small weight of the golf ball affected the drone's flight. Lusky couldn't see what was happening with his eyes, but was looking at the screen on the burner phone. The screen enabled him to see what the drone camera was seeing. The burner phone was supposed to be able to control the drone, but Lusky was no longer in control. Watching the screen was making him dizzy.

Chipper had a full view of the drone spinning wildly, completely out of control, tumbling, tumbling, tumbling, at a great rate of speed, out of control, and heading toward the Visqueen fence surrounding The Hay golf course and putting green. It went over the fence very quickly and disappeared from sight.

At The Hay putting green, the tragedy happened so fast that no one could see it. The drone made a large crunchy noise as it made a direct hit on the Duchess's head. She was dead instantly from the collision. She crumpled to the ground immediately without a shout or a yell. Instant death. When they heard the noise, and the Duchess crumpled to the ground, the two security guards, based on previous training, immediately and spontaneously sprinted toward the Lord and Lady.

The Lord was covered by one, and Lady Poppy was tackled and covered by the other. They had practiced this scenario many times. Lady Poppy started screaming. When she was tackled, she was surprised, and her spikeless golf shoes seemed to stick in the grass on the putting green. Her right leg bent backward under her, and when she put her right arm down instinctively to brace her fall, her wrist bent back at an odd angle, as well. Her right femur and her right wrist were both broken. She writhed in pain under the heavy security guard. She was safe, but was in tremendous pain. No one ran over to protect the Duke. The Duke hit the ground and crawled toward his dead wife. Chris Como was stunned and didn't know what to do. He knelt down on one knee and just listened to Lady Poppy screaming. In another few seconds, the Duke was screaming too.

Jose, the Pebble Beach security guard, was closest to the dead Duchess. He crawled over and was afraid to touch the offending drone that was lying by her side. Her head was crushed in, but there didn't appear to be any blood. She was obviously dead. No question about it. He instinctively turned her over and was horrified. He mustered enough courage to touch the drone and saw the golf ball embedded in the carrying device below it. The golf ball said, "Chipper," written in dark ink. He yelled to Patrick Black, "Chipper! Chipper! Chipper!"

Meanwhile, in the trees to the right of the driving range, Chipper heard someone yelling, "Oh shit! Fucking shit! Fuck! Shit! Just Shit!" Lusky rubbed his burner phone against his shirt and pants, then dropped it into the dirt, then kicked it a few times until it was in the driving range, just out of the trees. He quickly picked up the two extra drones and took off running toward his Ferrari. He kept yelling, "Oh Fuck! Just flaming fuck!" as he ran. He headed his Ferrari out to the 17-Mile Drive and toward the Pebble Beach gate. He didn't want to go home. Lusky needed time to figure out what to do; he tried to hatch a plan. He just knew he couldn't drive to his estate. He had to get out of the area.

Chipper wasn't sure what had happened with the drone or at The Hay golf course, but he saw the cell phone come dribbling out of the trees toward his driving range. He jogged over to get it. Not a good idea. Not a good idea at all. He picked it up.

Patrick Black stayed at The Hay and called 911 as well as CEO Donald Stevens. At the 911 number, he called for a medical emergency, as well as police. At the same time, Jose and Jim took off running out of the gate and across the road to the driving range. They saw Chipper in the middle of the driving range holding a cell phone and sprinted toward him. Jose said, "Blair, what the hell is going on? You killed a woman over there. The drone hit her right in the head. She's dead. You killed a Duchess. You fucking idiot. You're lucky I don't carry a gun. I would shoot the hell out of you." Jose grabbed one of Chipper's arms, and Jim grabbed the other. They were pulling him apart.

Chipper could only yell, "I didn't do anything! There was a guy in the trees operating the drone. Probably Lusky. I don't know how to operate a drone."

"Where the hell is he then, Blair?" Jose said.

Jim repeated, "Yeah. Where is he then?"

"I heard a car take off and some yelling. I don't know where he is, but for sure it was him in the trees."

Jose loosened up on Chipper's arm and said, "Anyone else around here? Did anyone else see him or you?"

Jim said, "Put down the phone, Chipper. It's key evidence now. When the police get here, they'll put it in a bag and take prints. Just put it down on the ground gently. We have to take you in."

Jose called Black and told him they had Blair in custody and to send the police over to the range when they arrived. Chipper said, "Is it ok if I hit golf balls while we wait?"

Jose commented, "As long as you promise not to hit us with your golf clubs."

Chipper started hitting balls at the range with his driver. Jim was impressed. Jose didn't care. Jose said, "You are in a lot of trouble this time, Blair. We've caught you with the goods. This time you won't get out of it. I wonder what the penalty is for killing a Duchess. Even if it was an accident. Were you paid to do that for some reason?"

Chipper ignored him and continued hitting his driver. "Can I make a phone call?"

"Not until the police get here." They all heard sirens in the distance. The police arrived before the ambulance, but went immediately to The Hay.

It was Officers Kyle Anderson and Jackson Henderson again. They spent so long at The Hay, Chipper was getting some great practice with his driver. He felt that he was hitting the ball better than ever. He was practicing hitting fades and draws. Jose and Jim stopped trying to talk to Chipper and just stood by the side waiting for someone to show up and do something. What was taking so long?

ROSEWOOD ANGEL

Lusky drove out of the Del Monte Forest and headed north. By the time he had driven up to San Jose, about an hour from Monterey, he had figured out most of his plan for being safe from any possible investigation. He had a few items that were questionable, but most of his plan had been hatched.

He drove right to the Palo Alto/Menlo Park area, and turned off Highway 280 to the Rosewood Sand Hill hotel, a high class meeting place for the rich and famous of Silicon Valley. A lot of tech deals were made in the bar and around the pool of the Rosewood. Before Lusky had moved to the Del Monte Forest, he used to hang out at the Rosewood often. He used the Presidential Suite many times. In fact, he lived there quite a bit. The Presidential Suite was $3,700 per night, and he enjoyed staying there.

The Rosewood employees knew him by his nickname, No Load. When he arrived and checked in, he implemented the first part of his plan. He paid the desk clerk to make sure he was listed as staying in the Presidential Suite, not only the night he arrived, but the night before. He paid the desk clerk handsomely for the extra night's reservation, as well as paying the Rosewood for his suite the night before he actually arrived.

When he was comfortably in his suite, he texted his escort service to send over his usual "date," who was named Angel. He wasn't sure of her real name. He knew she was young, beautiful, more than beautiful, and was a student at Stanford that made a few extra dollars by being a high-priced escort, typically at the Rosewood. All he knew was that Angel would do anything he wanted if the price was right. Many times he tried to talk her into being his alone, but she was making too much money being with many others.

He didn't have any luggage and needed clothes. That was easy, and a short trip to Stanford Shopping Center, close by, was all he needed. Angel knocked on his door before 4PM, and he was eager to see her. Angel was about five foot six, a Barbie-doll blonde, with a beautiful figure, very smart, could talk about any subject, and was eager to please. She had been with No Load many times. He met her, through the escort service, when she was seventeen and a senior at Archbishop Mitty High School in San Jose. She pretended to like him as a person, although she found him arrogant and impulsive. He paid well and on time. She made a point of asking him about a full-time job after she graduated in three years. She was barely nineteen now.

Lusky made sure the escort company and Angel knew he needed her to say she was with him for twenty-four hours, starting the day before. He paid extra for that. Money was no object.

When Angel entered the room, she was wearing blue jeans and a Stanford sweatshirt. She soon took that off and was standing naked in the suite. Her body was extraordinary. Lusky complimented her.

"Nice to see you, No Load. When do I get an internship? What are you working on these days? I need a job for the summer. I don't need the money, just need the experience for my resume."

Lusky said, "You are truly beautiful. I don't need to give you a job. You are making plenty of money already doing what you do. Can we be exclusive? I love you. You have to remember, that if anyone questions you, you were with me in this suite, all day yesterday, and today also. Very important."

She said, "What kind of trouble are you in, No Load?"

"No trouble, just as long as you remember that. No trouble at all. Sit down on the bed with me. I need you. I'm very stressed."

Angel sat down beside Lusky, completely naked, and stayed there passively.

Lusky grabbed his laptop and found the videos of Serena Antonelli and her boyfriend. He made Angel look at the videos multiple times. She seemed to enjoy them and viewed with interest. Professional interest.

Angel said, "That girl is amazing. I've never seen anything like most of the stuff that she does. If you want me to do some of that, you are going to have to pay me a lot extra. I'm not even sure I can do some of that. She is in amazing shape. Where did she learn that? Her guy friend is a very lucky guy. Let me try the easy stuff first. You'll pay me extra? You won't last long enough to try any of the really weird stuff."

Angel stripped off Lusky's clothes and stood on the bed facing away from him, while he sat up, with the pillow supporting his back. Angel lay down on her stomach with her head well below Lusky's feet and slowly wiggled back toward him, at the same time saying sexy things and making sounds she knew Lusky liked. He was excited and "gone" even before he entered her from behind. Angel laughed and said, "See? Now how much time do we have to wait?"

Lusky ordered some room service. Champagne and caviar. Angel danced naked in front of him, standing on the bed. Lusky had no problem with his alibi, but still hadn't figured out how to place the blame on Chipper for using the drone and, even more complicated, for finding an excuse why the golf ball would be in the "catcher" device carried beneath the drone. Lusky didn't even know that he had lucked out by the golf ball saying "Chipper" on it.

"I think I'm ready again," Lusky said. They looked at the video a few times more, then he said, "Can you do Serena number three?"

Angel laughed and viewed that part of the video one more time. "I can try," she said. Serena number three was the one that Irene McVay was trying to do when she hurt her back and had to use a wheelchair after. Angel was much younger, though. Both of them stood on the bed. Lusky had to lean back against the padded headboard in order to keep his balance. Angel was able to bend over, facing away from Lusky, and touch her hands to the bed. Then she tried to stretch a bit more and put her hands and arms under her legs extending backward toward Lusky. He moved closer, and that's when Angel just started laughing uncontrollably. "This is stupid. This isn't worth doing." Then she tumbled forward on the bed.

Lusky told her to take a break and go use the spa in the bathroom or head outside and sit by the pool. "I think I have it. I think I have it," he told her. He went to his laptop, still naked, and composed a series of emails between himself and Chipper that he would later transport to Chipper's email account. Even if Chipper saw them and erased them, Lusky knew that any investigator worth their salt could find them. Lusky would save them on his laptop anyway.

Chipper: *Hi Nolan. I want you to know that I did not key your car. I don't know who did, but it was not me.*

Lusky: *Thanks for emailing me, but I think you did, and I am not dropping the lawsuit. If you look at the restraining order you received, you'll see you are not supposed to email me. Please desist.*

Chipper: *I have been thinking about your new drone company. I saw you and Mr. Takahashi testing them, and I am interested in maybe being an investor. Can I try one just to see if I can operate it and to see what it's capable of?*

Lusky: *I'm not interested in having you as an investor. I don't need you. You stay away from me, please.*

Chipper: *I am very interested. We don't have to see each other. Maybe you can leave a drone somewhere near your house with instructions on how to use it.*

At this point, Angel came up beside the bed, wearing a very small bikini and said, "I'm going out to the pool to get some sun. Come find me when you are done. I think I can do Serena number four without laughing. I think we'll both enjoy that one." Then she seductively walked toward the door of the suite. Lusky didn't even watch her. He continued with his fake email creation. He knew it was crude but felt it should work.

Lusky: *I'm going to reluctantly do this for you. I need to test the functionality anyway with someone who is a novice in this stuff. I'm sure that if you can figure it out using the instructions, then anyone can do it. Please be careful. They are very expensive. I'll leave one just outside my estate gate, behind the shrubs, to the left of the gate. Be careful how you use it.*

Chipper: *I'll be careful. I have an idea, though, that maybe you'll think is a good one. I want to try to use it to retrieve golf balls at the range. It would be useful if it could carry some golf balls or have a bucket or bag attached to the bottom that could grab golf balls from way out in the range and bring them back.*

Lusky: *We have one prototype that wasn't meant at all for golf balls, but might work for you. Be careful. I don't take any responsibility for what you might do with the prototype.*

Chipper: *Ok. I'll come get it and try it at the driving range, then.*

Lusky: *I won't be home for a few days. Leaving today and back Saturday.*

Nolan Lusky put in the proper dates of the emails. He knew it was very awkward and improbable, but it served his purpose. He had answered all the unanswered questions about dates and times and why Chipper Blair had the offending drone. Lusky was eager to go sit by the pool with Angel. He expected to be admired and looked at with jealousy by everyone else out there, but he realized he didn't have a swim suit. He had purchased some shorts, but no swimsuit.

Lusky remembered to call his attorney on his private cell number and ask general questions about his own liability if someone used one of his prototype drones and either injured themselves or someone else. His attorney guaranteed Lusky that his liability was limited. He shouldn't get in legal trouble for someone using his new drone, particularly if the person using it had asked to use it. Lusky felt he was safe.

He headed to the pool, wearing only his shorts, to see his Rosewood Angel, and bring her back to the Presidential Suite. Before he did, he took about ten minutes to place his undetectable little cameras on a few mirrors in the bedroom. They worked so well at Cindy Springer's, he thought it would be a good idea to film Angel trying Serena's tricks. They would be fun to watch later.

ARRESTED

Chipper was cuffed and arrested at the driving range by Officers Anderson and Henderson. Based on their conversations at The Hay and what Pebble Beach security guards Jose and Jim told them, they were sure there was enough evidence to justify the immediate arrest. Henderson put the burner cell phone in a plastic bag. They took some photos of the driving range and Chipper, and then took recorded affidavits from Jose and Jim. Chipper's dealings with the two officers in the past had never taken him to this point before. The officers were not even friendly. Very much silent and professional. No friendly banter. This was serious stuff.

Chipper said a few times more, "I didn't do anything. It was Lusky. Go find that bastard."

Anderson said, "We'll find him, but first we have to take you in."

"Do I get a phone call?"

"Not until we take you in to Headquarters," said Anderson.

Henderson said, "Just don't say anything more, Chipper." Anderson looked upset at Henderson after the words came out. The ride to the station was silent. Chipper was thinking to himself, *What now? What happens now? Who do I call first?* As usual, Chipper wasn't too concerned. He knew he had nothing to hide. They just had to find Lusky. *I wish I had actually seen him or seen his car drive away. I recognized his voice. Don't know if that means anything. I have to call Jenny first or Bill and have her get my golf clubs off the ground. That's the first priority. That has to be done.*

Chipper finally said, "Can one of you call Big Bill O'Shea and have him go get my golf clubs?" The answer was no. Chipper was now very upset. He wouldn't feel right until he knew his golf clubs were safe.

At the station, Chipper was taken directly to what he figured was the interrogation room. He was read his Miranda rights by Anderson and was handed a form to sign stating that he knew the charges against him. Anderson said it would be involuntary manslaughter or criminally negligent homicide. Another officer came in and said his name was Officer Kennedy. Kennedy was a small man in a business suit with a narrow checked tie. The tie matched the color of his plain blue shirt. He was not an imposing man, and he smiled at Chipper.

"I'm Officer Kennedy. I'm here to ask you a few questions after we let you make one phone call on this landline phone. It will be recorded." Anderson and Henderson stayed in the room.

Chipper asked, "Do I need an attorney here?"

Kennedy said, "I don't know. Do you?"

"I didn't do anything. As usual, I seem to have been in the wrong place at the wrong time."

"I'm aware of your previous problems in the Forest, Mr. Blair. You seem to get in a lot of trouble, but nothing seems to stick."

"I'm going to call my wife. Can I have some privacy?"

Kennedy laughed, "You have given up your right to privacy, although you might get a lot of privacy in a jail cell for a long time now, unless you manage to skate out of this one." Kennedy laughed again, and so did Anderson.

Chipper called Jenny, "Hi, Jenny. I love you…"

Jenny broke in immediately, "I heard what happened over there already. There have been group emails from Stevens saying no one should talk to the police…"

Chipper broke in again, "Too late, Jenny. I'm at the station now with the police, and they are listening to this call. I've been arrested. I'm innocent again…"

"I know you, Chipper. You didn't have to tell me you are innocent. I love you, too. The email from Stevens said that Roger has been immediately fired for not firing you…"

"Oh, shit. Poor Roger. Maybe Richard can do something about that."

Kennedy broke in, "Get on with it. Enough of this nonsense. Just finish the phone call. Give her some instructions or whatever you want to do, but just do it quick. Now!"

Jenny said, "Who was that?"

"My new friend, Officer Kennedy. Nice guy."

Kennedy said, "Get on with it, Blair. Hurry now."

"Jenny. First thing is please go over to the range and make sure my clubs are there and all of them are in the bag. They should just be lying on the range. I hope no one has taken them. There should also be a few of my own golf balls lying about forty yards away and near the bag. Make sure you get those, too. It would be awful to not have my clubs at home. Worst thing ever. Then please call Richard to see if he would come down here and be with me. I need advice."

"Richard isn't a criminal lawyer, Chipper..."

"I know, but he has savvy. I think I need him here anyway. I can ask him if he can get Roger reinstated."

"Twenty seconds, Blair. Fifteen seconds. Wrap it up. Mrs. Blair. Please call this number back when you find out if this guy Richard is coming here. We have to know how long to wait. Thank you, Mrs. Blair."

Chipper finally said, "Ok, Jenny. I love you. I'm sure I'll be home and see you later. Just get those clubs and call Richard. I love you."

Kennedy said, "You might not see him tonight, Mrs. Blair." Then he hung up the phone.

The group sat in silence for eight minutes peering at the clock on the wall. Kennedy kept calling out the minutes, then the landline rang. Jenny said Richard Stein would be there in about twenty minutes.

Kennedy hung up, then said, "Shit," and quickly left the room, followed by Anderson and Henderson. Henderson came back in and gave Chipper a bottle of water, but didn't smile.

THE CORPORATION

CEO Stevens had called a crisis meeting of his management team. He was steaming. He had already fired Pebble Beach head pro Roger Hennessey, without even talking to him. Stein didn't go to the meeting because he was headed in to help or at least try to help Chipper. Stevens held up the meeting for a few minutes waiting for Stein. Richard, wisely, didn't tell Stevens where he was headed. He just didn't show up at the meeting.

"Where the fuck is Stein? We need him here. How the fuck did this happen? That fucking Blair. I told Roger to fire him. Why was he still at the driving range? Why did he have a fucking drone? This is impossible. The worst. The absolute worst. Can't possibly have happened."

The management team sat in silence. There was nothing to say. Some weren't entirely aware of what had happened that had made Stevens so angry.

Stevens started again, "Where the hell is Stein? Maybe I'll fire him too. Hennessey was supposed to fire Blair. I might fire anyone who is a friend of Blair. What about his wife? Can I fire her?"

The Director of Golf said, "She's a big moneymaker for us, Donald. Big moneymaker. Not a good idea to fire her. And I'm not sure you can fire her just because she's Blair's wife."

"Don't tell me what I can and cannot do. This is a huge mess. I'm not sure there is a solution here, except trying to keep it out of the press and downplay it."

"I think it's too late for that," the COO said.

"Shit again, then. For those of you that don't know, we had the Duke and Duchess of Irvingtonshire here for private golf lessons for their two little kids at The Hay. We fenced it off. A high fence. They paid very big money for the five days at The Hay. Very big money. For some reason, Blair was on the driving range using some sort of drone, and it went out of control, flew over the fucking fence, hit the Duchess in the head, and killed her. What are the chances? What are the fucking chances? What the fuck was Blair doing on the range with a drone? This is impossible to deal with. We probably have an international incident. We're going to get our asses sued for so much money. So much money."

Still, no one answered or said anything. Stevens finally said, "So, none of you have anything to say? You are my executive team. You must have something to say. Where the hell is Stein? We need Stein. Where is our General Counsel? Someone say something."

COO Catherine McDougall finally said, "I think we have to issue a press release giving our condolences to the Duke and his family for the tragic accident that was completely unexpected and completely out of our control. We should offer to compensate them for any expenses due to her tragic death. Flying the body back to England. Burial and funeral costs. Reimburse them for the money they paid to rent The Hay golf course for five days, etc. etc."

All Stevens said was, "I'm not going to do that. I'm not going to do any press release, and I advise everyone here not to respond to the press or the police or anyone. Refer any questions to me. Everything related to this goes to me. Tell me everything. Where is Stein? I need to talk to Stein."

RICHARD STEIN

Stein walked into the interrogation room with Officer Kennedy. Now it was just Kennedy, Stein, and Chipper. Chipper noticed that Kennedy didn't seem happy. But he didn't seem very happy before, either. Kennedy opened by saying, "Mr. Blair, are you sure you want this guy as your lawyer? He isn't even a criminal attorney. He has no experience in this area at all."

Stein said, "You don't have to answer that, Chipper. Always look at me before you answer any of Officer Kennedy's questions." Then Stein came over and hugged Chipper. It was something Stein had never done before, and it took Chipper aback. Chipper sat in a chair at the table, and Stein sat down next to him. Kennedy was on the other side of the table. Stein looked at the wall to the left and was sure there were others looking in through the one-way mirror and listening. He had seen a lot of interrogations on TV shows. That was the sum of his experience.

Kennedy said, "I just asked him if he was sure he wanted you. That's all. I'll assume the answer is yes, for now anyway."

Chipper looked at Stein, then didn't say anything. Neither did Stein.

Kennedy started again, "You should know this conversation is being videotaped. As we said before, anything you say can be used against you in court."

Chipper looked at Stein again, and again said nothing. Stein was smiling broadly. He was having the time of his life. He had his phone out on the table in front of him in case he had to look up something that he didn't know about the law.

Kennedy was glum. "The first thing I have to check on is if you had any reason to kill the Duchess on purpose. Did you?"

Stein interjected, "Of course not. He didn't kill the Duchess. He never met the woman and didn't know her. And you are assuming that Chipper had something to do with the Duchess's death? That is a very bad assumption. He had nothing to do with her death at all. He is completely innocent."

Kennedy stood up and glared at both Stein and Chipper, "I'll be the judge of that. We have officers out investigating right now. Did Blair know that the Duchess had picked Chris Como to teach her kids golf, rather than choosing Blair's wife, Jenny Nelson, even though Nelson teaches locally at Pebble Beach? Were you upset about that, Blair? Were you upset with the Duchess? Were you upset with Chris Como?"

Stein stood up as well, looked at Chipper, and said, "He didn't know the Duchess. He didn't know how the selection of golf teachers was made. He didn't care that Jenny wasn't chosen. He probably didn't even know if she was a possibility. It's a stupid question, Kennedy."

Kennedy was infuriated at this point, "Mr. Stein. You are not supposed to give all the answers for Blair. Let him talk."

"He doesn't have to talk. I know him very well."

"I need him to speak. I am addressing the questions to Blair. Not you!"

Stein said, "Ok, Chipper, go ahead."

Chipper just said, "What Mr. Stein says is correct." Then he looked at Richard and said, "Richard, can you make sure that Roger keeps his job? There must be something in the Human Resources Office that talks about reasons for firing someone. He's worked there for years, and I'm sure has no other issues on his record."

Kennedy looked at the one-way mirror and frowned, then came around to the back of Stein and Chipper and said, "If you two don't start concentrating on my questions, then I'm going to keep you here overnight in jail, Blair. And you too, Stein. You have to let me lead the questioning and keep on subject."

Stein started fiddling with his phone, and after a bit of delay said, "You can't do that, Kennedy. If you have charged him with something, you have to allow bail and let him go."

"No I don't, Stein. No I don't. Just watch me. Blair, after we're done here I'm going to have you locked up as a flight risk. You'll spend at least tonight in jail."

146

Chipper said, "I didn't do anything. Richard, if this happens, please tell Jenny and have Debbie go over and console her tonight, for sure."

Stein asked, "What are you charging my client with?"

"It depends. Murder in the first. Maybe involuntary manslaughter or criminally negligent homicide. Depending on our investigation." Stein started googling again frantically.

Chipper asked, "Are you looking for and bringing in Lusky? He's the one who should be here instead of me. He did it."

Stein looked up from his phone and said, "Am I right that in California the penalty, if found guilty of the last two charges you mentioned, is either a two, four, or six-year sentence? And that being a total accident, even if it was found that someone was the drone operator, is a good defense?"

Kennedy replied, "You tell me, counselor. Blair, you should find someone else. Stein, are you saying your guy here might be guilty?"

"No. I am not saying that. I am saying that with his high-priced lawyer, if Lusky is found guilty, he might get off with just a fine, or he might get off completely because it was a total accident."

"You're the lawyer, Stein. I'm just a poor police officer trying to bring someone to justice. Now, Blair. You claim you weren't using the drone, but this guy Lusky was?"

"Yes."

"Did you see him?"

"No."

"How did you know it was him?"

"I heard his voice, and I know he is working on a new faster type of drone."

"How do you know that?"

"He told me."

"So, you are a friend of Lusky?"

"I met him a few times. Definitely not a friend."

"So, why did Pebble Beach security find you with the drone operating device?"

"Lusky must have thrown it away out into the driving range, and I went out to see what it was. I like to keep my range clean."

"Why did you pick it up?"

"I was curious what it was, and I didn't want it to sit out on the range."

"How did you know it wasn't an explosive device or something like that?"

"I never thought of that. I guess I was lucky. I won't pick it up next time Lusky does that."

"Why was the drone, when it crushed the Duchess's head and killed her, carrying a golf ball that said Chipper?"

"Bad luck. Chance. Lusky's drone grabbed the golf ball out of the air before it went out of control and went over the fence. It could have just as easily said Annika or Ben."

"Do all your golf balls have names on them? Do they all say Chipper?"

"No. Just that one."

"Why just that one?"

"Strange story, actually, we were picking baby names..."

"I don't need this now, Blair. We'll have plenty of time tomorrow after we track down Lusky to answer questions. You'll be locked up tonight, Blair."

"You can't do that," said Stein, "I must protest."

"Go ahead and protest, Stein. Protest all you want." Then Kennedy walked out of the room with Chipper.

LUSKY MISCHIEF

Back in the Rosewood Presidential Suite, Nolan Lusky was surprised he hadn't received a phone call yet from the Monterey County Sheriff, Pebble Beach security, or hadn't seen anything on the news about The Hay incident. He and Angel had come back inside, and she had tried Serena positions seven, eight, nine, and even ten, some successfully and some not. It had taken all afternoon and into the evening.

"I have to leave now, No Load. I really have to go. I have another client in the hotel I have to go to."

Lusky wasn't happy. "Don't go now, Angel. Really, don't go. Why don't you be exclusive with me?"

"It's strictly business, No Load, strictly business."

"But we have fun. I can tell you like me. It's not strictly business. How can you go now and be with someone else?"

"Business."

"Promise me not to do any of the Serena stuff with anyone else. Promise me."

"I can't do that, and you know you have to pay me extra for all this stuff. A lot extra. It's more than the usual, you know. Very special stuff."

"How old is your next friend? At least tell me that. I'm probably the only one near your age that can afford you."

"You'd be surprised, No Load. Very surprised. But my next friend is about sixty. And an old sixty. None of the Serena stuff for him. He would die. And very quickly."

Lusky laughed and reached for Angel as she exited the bed. He was resigned to her leaving. "Come back after. And remember that we have been together in this room for at least forty-eight hours. Very important, Angel. Very important."

"I know. I'm pretty smart, you know. Stanford student. Just trying to pay my tuition and get a summer internship and a job after graduation. Something legit." Lusky watched her leave the room, then immediately grabbed his laptop.

He looked at the videos he had captured in his suite of Angel and himself doing various Serena stuff. He was amazed at the quality of the videos and the sound. Even though he was sexually satiated, he found the videos very hot. He was sure others would too. Lusky used AI to add various faces from previous videos and the internet to his and Angel's faces in the recent session. Notably, he used Cindy Springer and Jenny Nelson to replace Angel's face. He tried various others to replace his own. After a few hours work, he was gleefully ready to post some new videos on Cindy's social media accounts. Angel became Cindy Springer, and after a lot of experimentation, he ended up using Rory McIlroy's face in place of his own. He buffed up his own body a bit, as well. He knew this would result in a lot of views, and all he wanted to do was embarrass Cindy Springer. The first time he met her at the Pebble driving range, she had put her foot up on his Pagani. That was a no-no.

At that point, his cell phone rang, and it was the call he fully expected. It said private number, and he picked up. The voice said, "This is Officer Anderson, with the Monterey County Sheriff's Department."

Lusky smiled and said, "What can I do for you, sir?"

Anderson was playing it cagey and didn't tell Lusky specifically what he was calling about. He wanted to see if Lusky volunteered any information or asked any questions that showed he knew more than he should have about the situation. "We were looking for you today at your estate to answer some questions. Couldn't find you. Where are you?"

Lusky countered, "I've been away for a few days. I hope you are going to tell me you found some evidence on Blair and proof that he keyed my Pagani. Boy, I miss that car."

"Where have you been? It isn't about the car incident." Anderson waited for Lusky to reply.

"I've been up at the Rosewood hotel in Menlo Park to do some business the last few days. I'm sorry to hear you haven't found anything about my car yet."

"When did you arrive there?"

"I checked in the day before yesterday. Nice place. Weather is warmer than in Pebble Beach. I do a lot of business here. I stay here a lot. Nice place. Very expensive."

"About what time did you check in?"

"Mid-afternoon."

Anderson was taking notes, and said, "Tell me about your drone business. How is that going?"

"I'm surprised you know about that. Trying to keep that a secret. If you have any money to invest, I am looking for serious investors."

"Who might have access to your drones, besides you?"

This was going exactly like Lusky planned. "I reluctantly let Blair use one. He was supposed to pick one up in front of my estate. I didn't want him to, but I'm kind of afraid of him and didn't want to piss him off. Who knows what he is capable of doing?"

"Interesting," was all Anderson said, then there was a long silence. Finally, Anderson said, "Will you be there tomorrow? I think I'll drive up and ask you some questions. Is that ok?"

"Certainly."

"It'll be about noon, then."

"You'll probably find me at the pool." Lusky said. "If I'm not there, go to the Presidential Suite."

Anderson hung up.

Lusky then posted his videos on Cindy's social media accounts.

JENNY

While Chipper was in a jail cell, he tried to keep busy by standing up and pretending to play Pebble Beach in his head. He was happy that Kennedy didn't put him in a holding cell with other "convicts." Chipper played each hole in his head, without the walking between shots. He swung his fairway metal on the first tee and hit a great shot, then an eight iron to six feet and made a birdie; the putt was dead center in the hole.

On the second hole, he hit a three-hundred-yard drive, then a hybrid on the green and made a twenty-footer for eagle. He was three under after two and definitely thinking of beating Wyndham Clark's course record from February. After Chipper birdied number three and number four, he made a hole in one on the par-three fifth hole. He was having fun. When he made the hole in one in his mind, he let out a "whoop" that was so loud he heard grumbling voices from other cells nearby telling him to "shut up" or "keep quiet."

While Chipper was having fun in his cell, Jenny was distraught at home. Stein had called and told her Chipper was spending at least one night in lockup, but that Debbie would come over to keep her company. Jenny didn't know that Richard had also called Big Bill and Emily Hastings. Debbie had called in sick from her serving at The Hay and arrived first. Jenny and Debbie went down to the bar, and Debbie made martinis for both of them, as Jenny just sobbed on a bar seat. "Extra gin, please," she said to Debbie. "Thank you for coming over. I can't believe this is happening to us again. Poor Chipper." Angus was lying on the floor next to the bar, a few feet away from Jenny.

While Debbie was making the martinis, she asked Jenny, "So, I assume you aren't pregnant yet, and that's why you are having a martini?"

"That's another depressing thing. I was hoping to get pregnant right away, but I started having my period a few days ago. Martini drinking is ok for now."

"Well, some good news on that front. I took Abigail to the vet yesterday, and she is pregnant." Debbie leaned over the bar and said, "Angus, you are going to be a daddy." Angus didn't even look up. He was on the edge of sleep. No movement or reaction from Angus at all. "Show some excitement, Angus. You knocked up Abigail, you little rascal." Still nothing from Angus.

Jenny said, "Well, I'll drink to that." Then she got off the barstool and knelt down and hugged Angus.

Debbie continued, "I'm really excited about the new pups. I could tell Abigail was adding a bit of weight and was lethargic. And her nipples were getting redder. That's a sure sign. We're going to be grandparents, and share granddogs, Jenny. Isn't that great?"

"What did Richard say about Chipper? Is he ok? Why did they keep him there overnight? As usual, he didn't do anything."

"Richard said the officer was a putz and a schmuck. Richard's excited, though. He stayed home to study being a criminal defense attorney. He's home doing research. He said Chipper had nothing to worry about."

"Maybe Chipper should find a real criminal defense attorney?"

"You know Richard, Jenny. He's a bulldog. He'll make sure nothing happens to Chipper. He can do anything."

Jenny heard some footsteps coming down the stairs into the bar. She was happy to see Big Bill helping Irene McVay down the stairs very slowly. She was still recovering from her bad back. They were followed by Emily Hastings and Mr. Takahashi. Jenny was grateful for the company and the support. When Irene reached the bottom step, she immediately said, "Jenny, Debbie, you have to see this. Really have to see this. Can you hook up my phone to your big screen TV?"

Jenny was expecting a different conversation, but said, "Sure. What do you want to show me?"

While Jenny was setting up the video, from phone to TV, Irene kept saying, "You really have to see this. It's a kick. You'll enjoy it."

Irene hit play, and the Lusky video of Cindy and Rory McIlroy came up. Jenny was in shock. Irene was laughing. Irene said, "This is ludicrous.

It doesn't look like Cindy's body, and for sure it's not Rory McIlroy. And Cindy is doing a bunch of Serena stuff. Watch this next part…"

Jenny said, "We have to call Duncan, so he can get this down. Poor Cindy. Poor Rory…"

Irene interjected, "Rory seems to be enjoying it a lot. Really a lot. Cindy is very talented. Even though it obviously isn't Cindy."

Jenny stopped the video and called Duncan.

Duncan's first words on the phone were, "I know, Jenny, I know. We've seen it. Cindy is laughing now. I wonder whose body that is. How do we stop this guy Lusky? What a monster. We've got to get the police to do something. I'm working on taking it down. He's done some stuff this time that makes it even more difficult to get down. The method I used before isn't working. By the time I get this taken care of, it will be all over the internet with millions of views. I'm sure Rory, and especially his wife, will be very upset. I'm sure Cindy will get a call from his lawyers. This is a nightmare. A real nightmare."

Jenny finally said, "Did you know Chipper is in jail? I'm going to try and visit him, and I'll talk to whoever is in charge down there in person."

Duncan said, "Why is he in jail?"

"It's too ludicrous to even talk about. I'm sure he'll get home tomorrow. When I'm calmer and things have been sorted out, I'll tell you."

Irene was still looking at the video on her phone and laughing. Big Bill was trying gently to take her phone away, but she kept turning to the side so he couldn't reach her phone.

Debbie changed the subject by saying, "Look at Angus over there. He's going to be a father, and Jenny and I are going to be related by our dogs' kids. Abigail is pregnant by Angus. What a stud he is."

Emily asked, "How long does it take for a dog to have a litter?"

Debbie said, "The vet said probably 7 more weeks, only. Dogs usually deliver nine weeks after conception, and Abigail is probably a few weeks along. Depending on how many pups she has, I might keep them all. Of course, I'll let Jenny and Chipper have a few, depending on how many there are."

"This calls for champagne," said Big Bill, who went behind the bar and grabbed a few bottles of Dom. Jenny didn't feel much like celebrating. She was wondering what was happening with Chipper.

CEO STEVENS

Donald Stevens was finally able to meet with Richard Stein. They were in Stevens' office, very early. There was no chance of doing anything to keep the situation quiet. Stevens was busy showing Stein online articles from virtually every news outlet in the world. Most disparaged the Pebble Beach Corporation: New York Times, USA Today, London Guardian, Reuters Press, Al Jazeera, Associated Press, Wall Street Journal, Dow Jones, Golf Digest... The list went on and on. They were all, unfortunately, based on Jerry Devine's Monterey Herald post that appeared online overnight.

MONTEREY HERALD

BYLINE DEVINE

Horror at the Hay

A horrific incident happened at The Hay golf course at Pebble Beach Resorts yesterday. The Duchess of Irvingtonshire, here at The Hay for a private golf vacation and lessons for her two small children, was killed in an apparent runaway drone accident. The fast-moving drone, apparently coming from the driving range nearby, was clearly out of control when it cleared a temporary fence around the Tiger Wood's-designed par-three golf course. It crashed into the skull of the Duchess and caused instant death. Her husband, the Duke, and her two children were watching when it happened. They are all under sedation and have left the area, with the body of the Duchess, in a private plane.

The Pebble Beach Corporation refused to comment on the incident, and we have not been able to contact the Duke or his press secretary. The Monterey County Sheriff's Department has jailed and booked a familiar character, calling him the suspect who was operating the drone when the accident happened. Details are few, but it appears Walter "Chipper" Blair is the suspect. Why he was operating a very-high-speed drone on the driving range is a question the police hope to answer. Blair is being held for interrogation, and no bail has been set. A call from this reporter to Blair's wife resulted in a hang-up.

Top-rated golf teaching professional, Chris Como, was giving the golf lessons to the children. I was able to reach him for an exclusive interview. He has also left the area and is back in his hometown in Texas. Como said, "It all happened so quickly. One minute she was standing by the side of the putting green, smiling at her kids' progress, and the next she was lying on the ground dead. It was stunning. The poor Duke and the children were in shock. Their security detail quickly covered the children, and I think the little girl, the Lady Poppy, was injured when her big security guard tackled her to protect her from more potential mayhem. We all didn't know whether there would be more drones coming over the fence. It was horrible and frightening. I'm sure the poor children are traumatized. The noise of the drone hitting her head was like a well-struck driver shot. Even louder. The drone had a golf ball in it that said, 'Chipper.' All very, very strange. I met Chipper. Seemed like a nice guy, and has a good golf swing. Very into his golf. Too bad for him."

This reporter will give updates daily on any follow-up to this horrific story.

Stein was supposed to go see Chipper and be with him when he answered more questions, but he couldn't possibly get away from Stevens. Chipper was going to be on his own. Stein hoped that Chipper didn't say anything to further incriminate himself. Stein knew this wasn't the time to talk Stevens into rehiring Roger Hennessey; maybe he could just go to Human Resources and cancel the firing. They probably hadn't done the paperwork yet, anyway. He decided to do that.

While Stein was preparing to get up and leave Stevens' office, Stevens received a phone call. Stevens looked extremely upset, and all he did was nod his head at the phone. He didn't say a word. Stein stared at Stevens intently, waiting for some sort of comment or reaction. Stevens hung up the phone and just walked to his window overlooking the eighteenth green at Pebble Beach Golf Course. Carmel Bay was behind it, and the waves looked as turbulent as what was going on in Stevens' head. He finally yelled, "Oh, Fuck! Oh, Jesus, Fuck! We are being sued by the Duke for six hundred million dollars for wrongful death, negligence, and pain and suffering. We can't possibly win this one. We are fucked. We can't stand this sort of financial loss. The Duke may end up owning the Pebble Beach Corporation. You have to find a way to get us out of this one. We need to get out of this one, Stein."

"Don't worry, Donald. No problem. I'm on it. No need to worry; we can fight this one."

Stein walked out, extremely worried. There was no way to win this one. The Corporation was going to lose big. No chance at all.

CHIPPER IN JAIL

Chipper didn't sleep much on his jail bed. It wasn't really a bed. It was just a hard bench. When he saw light coming in through the hallway, he started walking around his cell. He was taken back to the interrogation room and hadn't had food or drink for a very long time. He was hungry, thirsty, and a bit confused. He yearned for a conversation with Jenny.

He found himself confronted with Officer Kennedy again. Kennedy looked refreshed and was drinking a cup of coffee. Chipper had nothing. Kennedy looked pleased with himself. "How did you sleep, Blair?"

Chipper didn't answer.

"You might be wondering where your attorney is. He won't be here to help you today. Why don't you just tell me the truth? You operated the drone. I know now that the only fingerprints on the phone were yours. No one else. You are the only one that could have operated the murder weapon. Were you paid by anyone to kill the Duchess? Why did you do it?"

Chipper didn't say anything.

"Are you tired, Blair? Of course you are. I'm not going to let you eat or sleep or have anything to drink until you confess."

"I didn't do it. Lusky did."

"We'll find out later today about Lusky. Your friend, Officer Anderson, is going up to talk to him. Lusky's been in some expensive hotel in Menlo Park for three days. Has an alibi. You might as well confess. The judge may go easier on you."

"I didn't do anything. I was just out there hitting golf balls. That's what I do. I hit golf balls. Can I talk to my wife?"

"No phone calls, Blair. You know, you made almost every newspaper and online news report in the world today, already. Your name will live in infamy." Kennedy turned off the recording equipment in the room. "I hope you fry, Blair. I'm going to get you. Now, tell me why you did it. Things could get really tough for you, Blair. Who paid you off to kill the Duchess? Those poor kids saw their mother just lying there. How awful. Did you think of that?"

"I didn't do it. How many times do I have to tell you that?"

"If I had a dollar for every guilty suspect who told me that, I'd be a very rich man."

Chipper said nothing and wished he were back in the cell, rather than with Kennedy.

"You're rich, right, Blair? You inherited a fortune from a guy they thought you did away with?"

"I don't have to answer any questions from you, do I?"

"No, you don't, but that just makes me think you are guilty."

"How long before I get out of here?"

"Maybe a lifetime. I'm taking you back to your cell." Kennedy walked Chipper back to a different cell and waited while Chipper entered the cell. There was another man in the cell already, a scruffy looking man that looked homeless, like he had been living on the street for years.

Chipper paced back and forth and stayed on the other side of the cell from the man. Didn't say anything. The man said, "Sorry if I smell, been down on my luck lately. My name is Charlie. My friends call me Dizzy. What are you in for?"

"I didn't do anything. I'm being held for no reason."

"They don't hold people for no reason. I'm in here for trying to take a few bucks from a man on the street. I needed money to eat. He stopped to give me a few bucks, nice guy, probably, and I grabbed his wallet and tried to run. I can't run very fast anymore, and he caught me and held me down while he called 911. I just needed money to eat."

"Tough luck, Charlie."

Charlie asked again, "What did they bring you in for? You look like you're just off the golf course, or something."

Chipper was pretty sure, at this point, that Charlie was a shill, probably a police officer posing as a homeless guy, trying to get Chipper to tell him about his supposed crime. Chipper decided he wasn't going to say anything more. Chipper started playing Spyglass Hill this time, in his head. On every shot, he would take the kind of swing that the hole he was playing required, including putting. In his head he did the narrative. When Chipper started doing this, Charlie backed away.

Chipper even walked between shots, and lined up putts by kneeling down. Charlie was miffed. It took about three and a half hours, and Chipper shot 61, a course record.

Still no food, water, coffee, or phone calls for poor Chipper. He was starting to play Cypress Point, made a birdie on the first hole, with a gimme putt after a great iron, when Kennedy came back. Kennedy took Chipper back to the interrogation room.

ANDERSON AND LUSKY

Officer Anderson pulled into the Rosewood Sand Hill hotel and walked right to the pool area. It was about thirty degrees warmer in Menlo Park than it was when Anderson left Monterey. There were several people lounging around the pool on chairs and chaise lounges, and he had never met Lusky. Anderson was overdressed. He wasn't in uniform, but was in long pants and a leather jacket, covering a black long-sleeved shirt. He walked over to a middle-aged man and said, "Are you Nolan Lusky?"

The man sat up and said, "He's the guy over there next to the doll in the bikini."

Anderson walked over, across the pool deck, and Lusky stood up, as he was expecting Anderson. "You must be Officer Anderson. Glad to meet you. Nolan Lusky." He pointed to the lounge next to him where Angel was lying on her stomach with her bikini top unhooked, so her back would get tan with no line. Anderson stared. Lusky said, "This is my girlfriend, Angel. We've been here, just hanging out, for the last several days." Anderson continued to stare at Angel's back.

"Can we talk? Can we go somewhere private?"

"I have no secrets from Angel. We can talk here, if that is ok?"

Anderson was uncomfortable for several reasons, but sat down next to Lusky and started asking questions. "When did you get here?"

"A few days ago. You can check with the front desk for verification. Also, Angel and I have been together almost the whole time. Isn't that right, Angel?" He tapped Angel on the butt to rouse her in case she was actually asleep. Lusky knew she was probably listening, though.

Angel feigned waking, struggled a bit to pull up her bikini top, and sat up. She said, "Nolan and I have been here for several days. Yes. Together all the time."

This raised suspicion in Anderson. The answer sounded practiced and staged. Still he wanted to believe her. He couldn't help staring at her body. "Do you know the exact time, ma'am, that Mr. Lusky checked in the other day?"

She laughed, "He called me ma'am, Nolan. Just like in the movies. Can you imagine that? Ma'am. I'm not even twenty, officer. What's going on with my Nolan?"

Anderson became more suspicious, as she was obviously expecting a police officer. Lusky had briefed her in what to say. She was going to be no help with Lusky near her. At some point, he was going to have to question her alone and try to intimidate her. "Mr. Lusky, I'd like you to come to the front desk with me, please. Ma'am, you can stay here and work on your tan. I'd like to talk alone to your boyfriend."

Lusky got up reluctantly and brought his laptop that was sitting on the small round table next to him. Lusky said, "I read about the incident at Pebble Beach. Too bad for the Duchess and her family. It's all over the news and the internet. I feel bad that I let that Blair guy use my drone. I hope I'm not in any trouble."

Anderson said, "Let me be straight with you, Lusky. Blair says it was you. He doesn't know anything about using a drone. Why did you let him use the drone on the driving range? Why would he want to do that?"

Lusky said, "I have the emails where he asked me to use the drone." He stopped and lifted the laptop and showed Anderson the email string he had created. Anderson again thought it was a little suspicious that Lusky was able to immediately find the emails.

"Can you please forward that to me? Here is my card. Just use the email on the card. Send it now, please." Lusky happily agreed.

When they arrived at the front desk, Lusky lucked out again, as his friend was the desk clerk. The desk clerk knew exactly what to say. He had been paid handsomely. Anderson said, "Can you show me the record and print them off for me? Thank you." The desk clerk, dutifully, did as Anderson asked. Anderson then asked, "Can you show me the date Mr. Lusky's credit card was charged for the stay?"

Lusky, standing next to Anderson, grimaced, and tried to give the clerk a negative head gesture, indicating not to do that. The desk clerk never saw him and printed off the required screen shot. Anderson looked at it and said, "Wow. That's one expensive hotel room. Is it customary to charge the card immediately when the customer checks in?"

Lusky answered quickly, "I didn't have my card when I checked in. I left it in the car and brought it back the next day."

"Is that what happened?" Anderson asked the desk clerk.

The clerk said, "Yes. I remember now. We know Mr. Lusky very well. He stays here often. I trusted him, and he came back the next day with his card."

Anderson just shook his head in dismay. "How can you afford this place? Each night is almost my monthly salary."

This time Lusky didn't say anything. He didn't know why Anderson was suspicious of him. Anderson said, "Mr. Lusky, can you wait here or get something to eat or something? I want to ask your friend, Angel, some questions without you there."

Lusky didn't like that and said so. "I'd like to be there."

"Why? Don't trust your little Angel?"

"I'm just curious what she has to say."

"Well. I'd like you to stay away. I'm curious too, about what she has to say. Pretty little girl, isn't she?" Anderson started walking away, and Lusky followed him. Anderson turned around and looked menacingly at Lusky, "I want you to stop. I am serious. I am going to question her alone." Lusky stopped and turned around.

When Anderson returned to the pool area, Angel was again lying on her stomach, working on her back tan. He snapped a picture of her from the back. He wasn't sure why. Maybe just to show the other guys back at the station. Or maybe he had some intuition after his many years as a suspicious cop. He sat down on Lusky's chair and quietly whispered, "Angel. Angel. I need to talk to you."

Angel went through her bikini top pull-up procedure, turned over, and sat up on the edge of her chaise. She was no more than a foot from Anderson. He took out his notepad and tried his best intimidation voice, "You know I am conducting a police investigation. I will be taking notes. If you lie about anything, it's possible you will be charged with a crime.

I don't want to scare you, but you have to tell me nothing but the truth. The whole truth."

Angel did not look intimidated. She gave Anderson a coy smile. "I always tell the truth, officer. Always."

"State your name."

"Angel."

"Last name?"

"Just Angel. I go by Angel."

"Can I see your driver's license, please?"

She said, in a whisper, while looking down at her own body, "Officer, where would I keep my driver's license? I left it in the hotel room."

"Well, then go get it. I can wait. I have all day." Angel got up immediately, and Anderson watched intently as she walked away from him. She came back in under five minutes. Angel was prepared and had her "working" driver's license.

Anderson looked at the license, and the name said Angel Delight. He smiled. He could tell it was a legitimate-looking license, but had a few details that looked like it was a license one would pay about fifty dollars for online at various sites. "Your parents must have had a sense of humor to name you Angel Delight."

"Apparently they did."

"It's good you grew up to look like your name. Imagine if you were a fat hag and had that name. Life would be difficult." Angel didn't comment.

Anderson said, "Look, lady. I have been in this business a very long time. Tell me your real name and what's going on. NOW!" It was loud enough that those around the pool started staring.

Angel was scared and cracked immediately, "I don't want to get in any trouble. I am a student at Stanford, up the road. I make a little money on the side to pay for my education. Please don't get me in trouble. Please." She started to cry.

"What's your real name?"

"Emma Bradley. I'm from San Jose. If my parents knew what I was doing, they would disown me. I just needed more money for school. I'm not going to do this anymore after I graduate. I should be able to get a job in tech. What's crazy is that's not nearly as much as I'm making now."

Anderson reassured her. "I'm not here to make a prostitution arrest…"

"I am not a prostitute. Just a college girl looking to make a few bucks."

"No, lady. Emma Bradley. You can call yourself anything you want, but you are just a high-priced prostitute. A hooker, by any other name, is still a hooker. That's what you are. You get paid for sex. Nothing but a hooker." She started crying loud enough for other people at the pool to look over now in a concerned way. Anderson whispered, "Stop crying. Calm down. I'm not going to do anything bad to you, unless you keep lying. Just tell me the truth. Is Lusky your boyfriend?"

"He calls me his girlfriend. Yes."

"Does he pay for you?"

"Yes."

"How much?"

"I don't think you need to know that."

"Smart Stanford girl. You are right. I don't. I was just curious. When did your boyfriend check in to the hotel, and when were you with him?'

Angel/Emma didn't want to lie. "He says he checked in three days ago. I wasn't with him the first night."

"Were you with him the second night?"

"Yes."

"Did he tell you to say you were with him every night he was here?"

"Yes. He did."

"Do you know why he would ask you to do that?"

"I do not."

"That's all I have for you then, Emma. You have been a great help. Can I offer you some advice?"

"I don't want advice."

"Don't be a hooker. It's beneath you. And stay away from Lusky. He might be a problem for you. A real problem." Anderson paused, then said, "Don't tell him anything about what you said to me." Anderson walked away. Emma started crying again, walked slowly to the pool, and jumped in.

JENNY

Jenny didn't sleep well. She didn't think she slept at all. Angus was next to her snoring loudly. He didn't seem to be too worried about becoming a father. Jenny was thinking the worst about Chipper. She hadn't heard from him. She was planning on driving in and trying to get into the jail.

She was up early and wanted to do the morning shot. The only time she did it without Chipper was a few times when she came to visit Ben Morris, because Chipper couldn't come in the morning. She had fond memories of Ben and felt it would be a mood booster to get up and head to the backyard. It was very dark when she headed down the steps. Angus was ahead of her and bounded down the steps, headed immediately toward Stein and Debbie's place. Jenny had to yell for him to come back and chase her Slazenger golf ball.

Jenny grabbed the brassie out of the cabinet and took some practice swings. She couldn't see a thing, but it didn't matter. Routine was routine. She knew where the ball would go the second she hit it. She felt surprisingly strong this morning and debated using the long spoon, but after swinging the brassie a few times, she decided to hit it. Angus stood at the ready.

The ball exploded off the clubhead, and Jenny knew it would hit on the back of the green and roll over into the rough. Angus might have a hard time finding it. She started yelling to Angus, as Angus was moving at high speed toward the green. "It's over, Angus! It's over! Look for it in the rough!" Angus took a long time, an agonizingly long time, and ultimately came back empty. Jenny gave Angus his seven treats anyway, and they both started walking back to the house dejectedly. Then they heard Abigail bark and looked that way.

Abigail was heading toward them, and Jenny could see both Richard and Debbie walking toward her also. Richard yelled, "You're up early! Done already."

Debbie started yelling at Angus, "You horny dog! She's pregnant already! Stop it!" Jenny looked, and Angus was mounting Abigail. She was worried.

"Can he hurt her pregnancy? Crazy dogs. Stop it, Angus. Stop it."

Debbie said, "I don't think it will hurt Abigail. Not sure. I'll call the vet later." Angus and Abigail were done already and just lying next to each other on the lawn.

Richard said, "You have nothing to worry about, Jenny. I did a lot of research yesterday. Even if Chipper is put on trial, I can get him off, as it was a total accident. No problem. And if I don't, the most he can get is two years in prison, a $10,000 fine, and maybe time off for good behavior."

"Oh great, Richard. Is that supposed to make me feel better? It doesn't at all. Not at all. I'm going to drive in and see him. I hope they let me. Will you go in with me? Please. I'm going to get them to investigate Lusky for the internet posts, too."

Stein said, "I wish I could. Stevens is on the warpath. The Duke has sued us for hundreds of millions. If I leave the office for any reason, he'll fire me, too. Hundreds of millions."

Richard and Debbie both wanted to take the morning shot, but Jenny was already headed up the back stairs to the estate. Angus stayed on the lawn with Abigail, while Richard and Debbie were surprised that Jenny walked away from them. They reluctantly walked back toward their home.

JAILHOUSE SURPRISE

Jenny drove into town and toward the courthouse jail. When she arrived, she just parked in the red zone and walked in through the metal detector. The guard told her she couldn't park in the red, and she would get towed. She yelled, "I demand to see my husband!"

The guard stood in front of her and yelled back, "You are going to get in a lot of trouble, lady! You can't park in the red zone, and you can't just barge in here asking to see your husband. Who the hell is your husband?"

"Chipper Blair."

"That doesn't mean anything to me, ma'am. We have a lot of people in this building."

"He's in jail. He's being held for no reason."

"That's for the judge or the jury to say. I don't know him. You should just leave or phone the Sheriff's department to ask if you can see your husband. Just move your car, then call to find out if you can see him."

Jenny was frustrated, but headed back to her car and made the phone call. She was still parked in the red. No one answered. She didn't know what to do, so she called Richard Stein. "Richard, what can I do? I'm at the jail. They won't let me in. They say I have to call."

Stein simply said, "Go home, Jenny. Just go home or to work or to wherever you have to go. Try to stay busy. Don't think about it. I'll make some phone calls, then tell you what's up. Just go home and relax."

"How can I relax, Richard? You just tell me how I can relax. Fuck you, Richard. You should be doing something for Chipper. They can't just hold him forever. He didn't do anything. Help me, Richard. You are supposed to be a friend and you're supposed to be defending Chipper. You shouldn't be at work, Richard. You should be down here, not there." Then Jenny hung up.

At the same time, Chipper was being taken from his cell back to an interrogation room. This room was much bigger than before and had several strangers already seated in the room. He immediately recognized Officer Anderson and Officer Kennedy. He was surprised to see FBI Agent Tripp, from the San Francisco regional office. He was familiar with Tripp from his previous dealings with the Spanish Bay incident and Irene McVay's kidnapping. Tripp nodded at Chipper and did not seem antagonistic.

Chipper didn't really know what time it was. He was a bit upset that he was being dragged out of his cell, while he was only on hole four at Cypress Point in his mind. He was playing Cypress, swing by swing, putt by putt, in his mind and was three under after three. He was playing perfectly, and the way he was playing, he was sure to set a course record. Just as he had at The Hay and the other courses he played in his head.

Chipper was guided to a chair facing everyone, but he stood up for a bit and took a swing that, in his mind, was his tee shot on the short par-four fourth hole at Cypress. Not surprisingly, his shot landed over three hundred yards from the tee and in perfect position for his second shot. No one was laughing when Chipper took his swing, then smiled and did a fist pump, but one of the strangers said in a Scottish accent, "Aye, Laddie, good swing."

Chipper was excited to hear the accent and reached out to shake the man's hand. The man, dressed in a suit with tie, said, "Willie Sloane, Scotland Yard. Glad to meet ya, laddie, but nae under these conditions."

"Enough of the banter," said Officer Kennedy, "Let's get on with it now. Chipper Blair, this is highly unusual, but this is not a usual case. Not at all. Far from it. You met Mr. Sloane. The other two gentlemen you have not met are Jacques Beaufoy from Interpol, and George Addison from Lloyd's of London. This case has gotten very complicated. They just contacted me last night and filled me in. You might be in the clear, Blair."

Chipper didn't say anything at all. He was tempted to get up and hit his eighty-yard shot to the fourth green, but decided to just sit down and stay seated. He did say quietly, "Do I need my lawyer here? I didn't do anything."

Kennedy said, "No, you don't need your lawyer. No one needs

your lawyer. He's nothing but a gadfly. Strange man." He paused, then continued, "Mr. Blair, your fingerprints were not on the drone, but we did find some prints of the man you say was actually flying the drone, Mr. Nolan Lusky. But I remind everyone that no one saw Lusky at the scene, and only Mr. Blair's fingerprints were on the cell phone operating device. And…it was found in Mr. Blair's hands by the Pebble Beach security guard. Let's start with Officer Anderson, who interviewed Lusky a few days ago."

Anderson started, "Lusky seemed suspicious to me. Like he was trying to cover his tracks and create an alibi for himself. The Rosewood hotel clerk claims Lusky was there the night before and day of the incident, but for some reason they didn't follow their normal procedure of charging the room on Lusky's credit card the day he checked in. He also prompted a call girl to claim she was with him that night. She is a scared little thing and broke under my investigation and admitted she wasn't. Cute little girl. Also he created some, what I think are fake, emails that show Chipper Blair asking to use the drone. I know Blair from previous incidents. I don't think Blair is technical enough or interested enough to operate a drone. As I've heard him say, many, many times, he's just interested in golf."

Kennedy then said, "Your turn, Monsieur Beaufoy. Why are you here?"

Beaufoy began, "My organization, Interpol, was called in by my friends at Scotland Yard when they heard about the untimely death of the Duchess. Our agency is very misunderstood. We can't investigate, arrest, or prosecute in any case. We, however, have a very extensive eyes-and-ears network, and a huge database network. We can issue what we call Red Notices. We have been following this young man, Lusky, for a few years. He's rather criminal, dealing with foreign governments, getting payoffs, handling large payments of money from other nefarious sources. His new attempted drone business is a real threat to Western nations. Excuse my language, but he is an amoral son of a bitch. Has no conscience at all. Just cares about money. He made hundreds of millions from those Silicon Valley idiots who throw money around for bad ideas. Lusky knows how to work them. He is quite an operator."

Kennedy said, "Thank you, Monsieur." His pronunciation of Monsieur drew a grimace from Beaufoy. "Mr. Sloane, please."

Sloane started by taking a golf swing and looking Chipper right in the eye, "The Yard got called in initially because of the importance of the Duke and Duchess. And this was a horrible death. The poor Duchess. And in front of her children. We always get called in for these cases, even if they are not in the United Kingdom. Highly unusual case. We had been alerted a few years ago that the esteemed Duke of Irvingtonshire had some serious gambling and womanizing issues. Quite the rogue, that one. Bad bets on horses. Bad bets on football. That would be Soccer to you gentlemen. Trips to Monte Carlo. A constant loser. Tons of money on high-priced call girls. He is in serious money trouble..."

George Addison interrupted, "What is most interesting is The Duchess took out a rather large insurance policy on the Duke's life. Even for us, a rather large policy on the life of the Duke, just one month before the trip to Pebble Beach..."

Sloane interrupted back, "Quite a rogue with the ladies, the Duke. And the Duchess must have known about all his money problems."

Addison continued, "Lloyd's sent me out to investigate. My friends at the Yard very quickly informed me that the Duchess had two quick trips to the United States under an assumed name, Elizabeth Duker. Not much imagination there at all. Elizabeth Duker. These trips were a few months before the Pebble Beach golf visit. Guess where Ms. Duker visited both times?"

No one responded, and Addison said, "This one should be easy. Rosewood Sand Hill. I repeat, the Rosewood Sand Hill. Very suspicious. We think she met with the notorious Mr. Lusky and that this accident, or so-called accident, may not have been an accident at all. Not at all. Even worse, the Duchess seemed to have a proclivity for high-priced call girls, as well."

Kennedy said, "Oh, what a tangled web we weave. Cliché. I know, cliché, but..."

Chipper couldn't help but say, "So it seems that the Duke was the target, and Lusky missed, and that's why I heard him yelling profanities and running away?"

Kennedy continued, "But remember, this is all just speculation. Anderson, you have to head back up to Rosewood and find the girl to see if she spills on seeing the Duchess with Lusky. Blair, you are still the key to this. You are the only one who can say you are sure you heard Lusky's voice at the range. Nabbing him for this is really a stretch, but I have an idea. Live by AI. Die by AI."

Everyone looked at Kennedy for an explanation. He smiled and said, "We have your phone, Blair. We have a recording of Lusky's voice. We can make sure that on the day of the accident we have a record of Lusky's voice on your phone which you happened to turn on and start recording when you heard the yelling. And what was it, exactly, that he said?"

Chipper said, seriously, "Oh, shit. Oh, fuck. Oh, shit. Oh, Fuck. Or something similar."

Kennedy said, "That should be easy, then. Not very professional or kosher, but certainly in this case, the means justify the ends." Sloane, Beaufoy, and Addison all grumbled at the same time. Beaufoy started muttering in French. It was obvious they didn't like faking the voice using AI.

Kennedy took out his phone and said, "Take a look at this. Look what a sleazebag this guy is." He pulled up Cindy Springer's social media account and showed them what Lusky was suspected of doing. The men were quite engrossed in the video of a beautiful blonde girl and what looked like Rory McIlroy, having sex.

Sloane said, "That body doesn't look like Rory's. Too skinny."

Kennedy said, "And the girl's body doesn't look like Cindy Springer, either. Lusky created this. What a dick he is. Amoral."

Anderson quickly told Kennedy to put the video on hold, showing the blonde girl from the backside. He also took out his phone. "Now make the picture of her upper right leg, just below the butt cheek, larger. See that birthmark. Now take a look at this photo I took of the girl at the Rosewood. Same birthmark. That fucker Lusky used her body, for sure. No doubt about it. I'd like to wring that guy's neck."

Sloane immediately said, "You are a bugger, you are. Why did you take the girl from the backside? You didn't need to do that. You did that just so you could look at it. Who are we dealing with here?"

Anderson looked upset, "Just professionalism. Had a hunch that it might come in handy. And it did. For sure, it did. Pure hunch."

FBI Agent Tripp said, "Professional or not. Hunch or not. I'm going up to Rosewood with you. This is too important for you to go alone this time. Like the Yard guy said, 'what a bugger.' Whatever that means. Let's go. Time is passing by. We have to head up there now."

Anderson commented, while grumbling, "I can do this myself, Tripp. We don't need the FBI involved."

"Too late," said Tripp. "Let's go. I'll drive."

Chipper finally said, "Look, guys. You don't need me here. I'm no longer needed, right? It's all on Lusky now? Just let me go home."

Kennedy looked at him and said, "Well, Blair. You are now under protective custody. Still a suspect, as far as I'm concerned, but officially now you'll stay here a bit longer under protective custody. This guy Lusky probably knows you are the only one that can place him at the driving range on the day of the murder. I'm going to start calling this a murder, rather than an accident. Definitely suspicious. You're going to stay here longer for your own good."

"Can you get me some food, then? And a golf club? My cell phone?"

"Food, yes. Golf club, no. Cell phone, definitely no. We need it for a bit more."

Big Bill O'Shea was taking over Chipper's driving range duties while Chipper was in jail. He only knew to take over when Jenny contacted him. The Corporation said nothing to him. There were a few golfers hitting balls when Bill saw three MADRDI vans and one very long truck drive up onto the range, over the teeing area. The trucks parked near the right side of the range. Bill had no idea what was going on and walked over. The golfers didn't stop hitting balls and had to aim way left to avoid hitting the trucks and Big Bill. On the side of the trucks, Bill read:

MADRDI

In smaller letters underneath, the acronym was explained:

MODERN
AUTOMATED
DRIVING
RANGE
DEVELOPMENT
AND
INSTALLATION

Bill watched while twelve men in MADRDI-logo work clothes piled out of three of the vans, almost like a circus-clown performance. The fourth vehicle, a long flatbed truck, had a very large tarp over the back.

There was a big, long lump under the tarp that, to Bill, looked about fifteen feet high and fifty feet long. It hung a bit over the back end of the flatbed.

Bill approached the man who seemed to be giving instructions to the others and said, "Can I help you? I'm in charge of the driving range today."

The man, almost as big as Bill, said, "Didn't they tell you we would be here today? We're doing proof-of-concept for the Corporation and installing the temporary side mural as a demonstration." He then yelled to his men, "Take off the tarp and take the mural off! Be very careful."

Bill stepped aside and watched intently as the men lifted the tarp off and unveiled the rolled-up mural that was beneath it. The MADRDI supervisor then said, "Ok guys, now just roll it off the side of the flatbed. It's ok if it falls to the grass. It won't hurt it. Watch your feet." All the men climbed on the flatbed and quickly pushed off the entire roll to the ground. It made a large noise and created a little dust as it hit the ground. "Go over and touch it." The man said to Bill.

Bill walked over, and was surprised it was some sort of elastic material that was cold to the touch. It had some pine trees and greenery and blue sky in the mural. The part he could see looked like a photograph: very large and very vivid.

"Now comes the hard part," the supervisor said. The men went into one of the vans and brought out a large extension ladder and a hydraulic lift of some kind. They managed to get the mural roll on its end and get it on the lift. The supervisor walked over and inspected a few trees near the right side of the range, and when he found a mark he had left on one of them, he directed the men to put up the ladder and move the mural on the lift to the tree. Bill could tell this was a well-planned and well-rehearsed operation.

Six of the workers carefully climbed the ladder and were stationed at about ten-foot intervals in the air. Each had some sort of tool in their hands. The mural was raised on the lift, and each man did some sort of tacking or fastening operation of the end of the mural to the large pine tree. It didn't go all the way up but, as Bill estimated, about fifty feet up. Each man was asked in turn from bottom to top if his fastener was secure. Each responded in turn, "Secure." Each man then attached a rope to a hook in the mural near them. Then they descended the ladder.

The supervisor then walked down the right side of the range until he found another large pine tree with his previous mark. The hanging ropes from the six places on the mural were carried by each of the men to the new location. The rest of the workers moved the extension ladder to the new tree and put it up. Each of the six men climbed the ladder with their ropes.

The supervisor yelled, "This is the most important part! Be very careful! Don't pull too hard at first! Everyone pull at the same time and with the same speed! Be careful!"

Bill was fascinated as they pulled the elastic mural across the pines. As it spread out, he could see it was an exact photo of the right side of the driving range. Pine trees, brush behind them, sky, some clouds, and there were even a few deer, obviously Photoshopped in. It was easy to tell it was a photograph, but it was exactly like the regular scenery on the right side of the range. Bill was sure Chipper would hate it with a passion. With a passion. The MADRDI supervisor smiled and could tell Big Bill was impressed. "Great stuff, right?" Bill didn't respond. He didn't want to give the other guy any sense of satisfaction.

The man said, "Ok. Each of you now pull as hard as you can and fasten your part of the mural to the tree. Use extra fasteners, as many as you need. Pull the elastic as hard as you can. It's important it's very tight. No wrinkles. We want it to look natural. No seams. No wrinkles. Real life. Be careful. If you let go, the thing will snap back like a rocket. Pull it tight. Very tight. And don't let go."

Bill could see each man struggling to pull it as tight as he could and struggling more to hold it tight while fastening it with the machine in his other hand. Bill was surprised no one fell from the ladder. The supervisor yelled, "Keep holding on, even if you think you are perfectly fastened! Keep holding on!" He then went through the same drill as before and asked each man to verify before letting go of the rope. Each in turn yelled back, "Secure, boss!" Then they unfastened the rope and descended the ladder. The supervisor smiled at the company's work. It was magnificent.

He told Bill that the final mural would be one hundred feet tall and reach to the top of the highest pine. They then moved the ladder back to the beginning, and one man climbed and undid the six ropes. The mural was now hanging on its own. It was so tight that Bill could see the two trees at each end were bending toward the center.

The trucks moved away back to the parking area, and the supervisor returned and told Bill and the others at the range to try hitting some golf balls against the mural. The other golfers, still hitting balls, and Bill all started hitting drivers toward the mural. They bounced back on the range like a gymnast on a trampoline. Bill was able to hit some drivers over the mural fairly easily, but the MADRDI team wasn't worried. The real mural would be twice as high. It was only a demo. One of the guys on the range said, "I wish there were bounce-back screens on every golf hole I ever play. Wouldn't have to worry about missing the fairway or being in the rough."

The MRDRDI supervisor called CEO Stevens and told him the installation of the mural wall demo was completed. In ten minutes, Stevens and COO McDougall were on the range looking at the mural. O'Shea was standing beside them when they proclaimed that it was "wonderful," "couldn't be better." Stevens was ecstatic. He said to O'Shea, "This is truly incredible. It's the new era of driving ranges, and we are at the forefront. This couldn't be better. Look at that. It's just like real life. No hassle. A true driving range experience unlike any other." Stevens picked up a club from O'Shea and started swinging toward the mural. O'Shea laughed to himself at Stevens' attempts at hitting the ball. He had a good swing, but obviously hadn't played for a long time. He dribbled a few, but when he hit the ball and it banged against the elastic mural and bounced back in the range, Stevens exclaimed with joy.

O'Shea knew what Chipper's reaction would be if Chipper ever came back to the range.

THE ROSEWOOD SAND HILL

Tripp and Anderson took the Sand Hill Road exit off of Highway 280 and could see the Rosewood resort immediately off the freeway. Tripp was driving, and the ninety-minute drive from Monterey was strained. They barely exchanged any conversation at all. Tripp wasn't happy to be with Anderson, and Anderson wasn't happy to be with Tripp. They had no plan. Anderson, who had been there before, obviously had to take the lead.

When they arrived, Anderson headed to the front desk, and Tripp followed. He asked if Lusky was still there and received the response that he had left the day before. Anderson then headed out of the lobby and toward the pool area. Both men were dressed for something other than sitting by the pool. It was warm. They looked around, then sat in lounge chairs poolside in an area where they could see anyone approach the pool. They were under an umbrella. A few people were poolside and a few in the water. Tripp counted eight. The weather was Menlo-Park-perfect. About eighty degrees and windless. They relaxed in lounge chairs and waited. They were both sweating. The cocktail waitress came over and asked for an order. Tripp was reluctant, but Anderson ordered a gin and tonic, and then Tripp ordered the same thing.

Anderson asked the waitress, "Do you know Angel?"

The waitress smiled and said, "Everyone knows Angel. She's here a lot. She was here yesterday. I haven't seen her today. Do you gentlemen have an appointment with her?"

Anderson then smiled and commented, "No. We just want to talk to her. Was she here with Lusky?"

"I'm not sure I can tell you that. Who are you guys?"

Tripp showed her his FBI badge, and the waitress said, "Is she in trouble? She's a nice kid. Is No Load in trouble? I wouldn't doubt it."

"No trouble. We just have to ask her a few questions." Tripp took his phone out and showed the girl a photo of the Duchess. "Have you ever seen this woman around the pool or in the bar?"

"She looks a bit familiar. Hard to tell with that outfit she has on in the photo. Maybe if I saw her in a swimsuit or a more casual outfit."

Anderson googled the Duchess and didn't find anything other than formal photos online. The waitress walked away saying, "I'll bring you your drinks as soon as I can."

After about an hour, and two gin and tonics each, Anderson was dozing off when he felt Tripp tugging on his arm. Tripp said, "That has to be her, right? Beautiful girl." Angel was wearing a Rosewood-logo bathrobe and walking alongside a portly-looking man, also in a Rosewood bathrobe.

Anderson nodded and said, "Let's wait until they sit, then we'll go talk to her." Tripp was already on his feet heading toward Angel. Anderson was afraid Tripp would make a poolside scene, and he was right. He was ten steps behind Tripp when he saw Tripp pull out his badge and flash it at both Angel and her man of the day. The others at the pool were gawking when Tripp literally pulled Angel to the side and told the man to "beat it."

The date for the day said, "I'm not in trouble, am I? She's my daughter."

"You might be now because of your lying. Just go over to the other side of the pool and be quiet. You are not involved in this," Tripp said, threateningly. The portly man wandered timidly away, backwards. He was curious to see what was in store for Angel. He was still afraid of getting busted.

When Anderson walked up, Angel said, "I'm not in trouble, am I? You called in the FBI? I thought you said that I was ok."

Tripp motioned for her to sit on the side of a lounge chair, and he sat on the next one staring right in her face from about a foot away. He meant to be intimidating. Tripp said, "I know your background, young lady. Do you have a pimp, or are you on your own?"

Anderson grimaced and said, "That's not what we're here for, Tripp. It's just the Duchess and Lusky."

"Let me handle this," said Tripp, "we may be onto a prostitution ring here. I live for this type of investigation. Answer my question, young lady."

Angel was scared, "I'm on my own. I have no pimp. That word sucks. I don't even like to say it. I'm just making extra money for my school. I go to Stanford, you know."

"How do you get business, then?"

"Just word of mouth. I wouldn't lie to you. I wouldn't lie to anyone. Just trying to pay for school and make some extra money. Just word of mouth."

Tripp said, "You must be very good, then. Right, Angel? That's not your real name, right? You must be very good in bed."

Angel looked embarrassed and just said, "I do ok on the referrals. I think just because I'm young."

Anderson was getting upset, "Leave the poor girl alone, Tripp. Just get to the point."

"She's definitely not a poor girl." He took out a picture of the Duchess and showed it to Angel. "Do you know this woman?"

"Yes. It's Mrs. Duker."

"How do you know her?"

"She's been here a few times."

"Was she here with your friend, Lusky?"

"Yes. She was here with Mr. Lusky..."

Tripp interrupted, "How many times did you see them together?"

"Just twice."

"What were there conversations about?"

"There wasn't much conversation that I was involved in."

"Interesting," said Tripp. "Were you outside or inside with them?"

"Usually inside. I don't really want to talk about this. Do I have to?"

"Yes. You have to."

"What if I don't?"

"Then you will be in a lot of trouble, Angel." Tripp said, very politely.

"Mr. Lusky wanted me to have sex with Mrs. Duker. I don't like being with women at all. Not at all. Just thinking about it makes me feel bad. I need a drink of water or something." Tripp waived the cocktail waitress over and ordered water for Angel.

The cocktail server said to Angel, "Are you in trouble, Angel? I hope not. Can I do anything for you? She's a very nice girl, officer, or whatever you are. Just working her way through school. Never causes any trouble or anything."

Tripp said, "Yeah, the hooker with a heart of gold. Old story. Heard it many times. She's a hooker, a slut, any way you slice it." Angel started crying.

The waitress handed her a few napkins. Tripp continued, and Anderson just watched.

Tripp said, "What did you do with Mrs. Duker? She's now a dead Duchess, you know? Sorry for the alliteration." Angel started crying more.

It took a while for her to stop sobbing, and she finally said, "I didn't do anything, actually. I just lay there and let Mrs. Duker do whatever she wanted with me."

"And what did she do to you?"

"I don't want to talk about it. I really don't. It wasn't my best moment. Mr. Lusky paid me a lot of money. A lot of money."

"And where was Lusky?" asked Tripp.

"He watched the whole time. I don't want to talk about it anymore. Isn't that enough?"

Anderson said, "I think that's enough, Tripp. We have what we want. We have to go lock up this guy Lusky. We've got plenty on him now. Solicitation for prostitution, voyeurism."

Tripp answered angrily, "But we have to get this guy in jail for a long time. He's a menace. I want to hang the murder rap on him. Angel, thank you very much. Don't leave town. You can go back to your fat guy now."

ARTIFICIAL TURF

A few hours after Stevens left the driving range, O'Shea saw another MADRDI van pull up on the grass. The supervisor exited and told O'Shea, "I'm surprised Stevens gave us permission so quickly for this. We've got a bit more work to do. Won't take very long." He opened the back of the van. He only had three men this time.

Bill watched as they moved to the center of the range and measured out two areas with stakes that looked to be six feet by six feet. Two of the men had shovels and hoes and started taking out about three inches of turf in each location and cutting out the grass down to the dirt level. They then took two six-by-six-foot pieces of artificial turf out of the van and put them into the dirt. They spent some time making sure the artificial turf fit snug before they pounded stakes in each corner to keep them in place. They left room for wires that came out of the artificial turf and were lying on the ground to the right of each of them.

When they were satisfied the turf was secure, out of the van came two six-foot-tall pieces of equipment that looked like an upright stand-on bathroom scale that you would find in a doctor's office. The supervisor said to Bill, "These are our proprietary golf launch monitor standalones. They have the launch monitor at the bottom that measures eight key indicators, and the screen with the display is at eye level. Very easy to use."

The MADRDI workers took only a few minutes to install the equipment. "Try it," the supervisor said to Big Bill.

Bill took a five iron and some range balls and was fairly amazed that all he had to do was drop the ball on the turf, and after each hit he got a reading immediately on distance, swing speed, ball speed, launch angle, carry distance, maximum height, smash factor, and spin rate. Bill liked it, but he knew Chipper might smash the machines to bits when he saw them, as well as tear out the artificial turf. Bill knew he could never say anything good to Chipper about the new installations.

RELEASED

Officer Kennedy was talking to Chipper, "I'm going to let you go now. You have to promise me that you won't tell anyone about our conversations the last few days. Don't talk about Lusky. Don't talk about Interpol. Don't talk about Scotland Yard. No conversations about any of this. If I get so much as a sniff that you talked about any of this, I'll have your ass back in here so quickly your head will spin. In your words, you'll be back here faster than Bryson DeChambeau can swing a golf club. Faster than Tiger Woods can make a two-footer. Faster than John Daly can drink a can of beer. Faster than Craig Stadler can eat a hamburger..."

"Ok. I get it. Just let me go. I get it. I won't tell anyone. So what is your plan to get Lusky?"

"That's none of your business, Blair. You are free to go."

Kennedy handed Chipper back his cell phone and continued, "Make sure you don't erase the AI version of Lusky's voice on the phone. It's dated back to the Duchess's death date. Just remember, if anyone asks you about it, your story is that when you saw the drone head over the fence, you turned your phone on. That's all you have to remember. Can you remember that?"

"Don't patronize me, Kennedy. Just let me out. How do I get back home?"

"Officer Henderson is waiting for you. He will give you back your personal items and drive you where you want to go. He's in the corridor. I hope I don't see you again."

Kennedy opened the door to the corridor and put out his hand to shake, and Chipper walked right by him. Henderson was waiting and was talking to Sloane, Beaufoy, and Addison. When Chipper walked by, Sloane from Scotland Yard said, "Keep your eye on the ball, Laddie. Keep your left arm straight. Hit 'em long and straight."

Henderson, walking with Chipper, could hear Chipper whisper, "Fuck you." But no one else heard him.

Chipper called Jenny on his cell and asked, "Where are you now?" Jenny started sobbing again and didn't say anything. Chipper said, "I'm ok, Jenny. They are letting me out. Henderson is giving me a ride back. I'm ok."

She finally said, "I'm on the range at Spyglass. I'm giving a lesson to Mr. Takahashi…"

Chipper interrupted, "That's great. I'll have Henderson drive me there. I have to hit balls. I haven't hit a ball in three days."

She said, "I'm glad you have your priorities straight. Don't you want to see me first?"

"That's why I'm coming right over there. How is the weather there?"

"The usual. Foggy and cold."

"Damn. See you in a few, Jenny. I'm sure they'll let me use some clubs from the pro shop. I love you."

"Really nice to know you want to hit balls, Chipper. Really nice. I haven't seen you or heard from you in three days."

"I'm fine, Jenny. See you soon."

Sloane, Beaufoy, and Addison were back in the interrogation room with Kennedy. Kennedy was saying, "Now we have to draw Lusky out in the open. Anderson called and said that he left the Rosewood. He also reported that our contact there, Angel, verified that Lusky and the Duchess were there at the same time at least twice."

Sloane from Scotland Yard was concerned about Chipper. "Nice kid. He may be in danger if Lusky thinks that Blair might be able to identify him. Angel may be in danger, too."

Kennedy replied, "If he's not in danger now, he will be after I make a few phone calls. Remember, it's the real international meddling idiot, Lusky, who we're after. Who cares about a driving range attendant or a hooker, either? I'd sacrifice Blair and the girl for Lusky any day. Now, if you'll excuse me, I've got a few phone calls to make."

LOVE

Jenny was shouting at Takahashi when Henderson dropped off Chipper. Chipper walked to the driving range at Spyglass. He heard Jenny yell, "Same stuff, Tak! Move those hips! Get those hips out of the way! Turn them to the left! Don't sway! Turn! Turn! Try that again! That-a-boy, Tak!"

Chipper stood back and watched for a bit before he went over and hugged her. Watching her teach, just like when he first saw her on the range at Pebble, reminded him how much he loved her. Her passion for the game and her beauty captivated him. Chipper couldn't help but run over and hug her from behind. She turned and they kissed and hugged for a long time. Takahashi said, "Get a room. Get a room."

Jenny said, "I'd like to, but let me finish with Tak, first. He's a paying customer."

"And it very expensive. Each time more expensive. Not sure a few strokes worth all the money."

"You know it is, Tak. You know it is," Jenny said.

Chipper went inside the pro shop and went into the back. He didn't even acknowledge the pro behind the counter. He quickly went in and grabbed a few clubs, a bucket with some range balls, and a windbreaker. He put on the logo windbreaker and carried out a nine iron, five iron, three metal, and a driver. He walked to a range spot a few over from Jenny and Takahashi, so he could hit balls and still watch them.

He stretched with his nine iron behind his back, swung it a few times, and lamented how stiff he felt after three days off. He vowed never to miss three days again. Never. Jenny kept smiling at him from behind Tak. Before hitting his first shot, he stretched and took practice swings for about fifteen minutes. Chipper was relishing hitting his first shot. He scraped over a range ball with his club and was happy to hit a solid first shot with his nine iron. Dead straight. Solid. He couldn't help but saying, "I love this game." Takahashi and Jenny both turned around. Chipper exclaimed again, "Love it."

He always felt an immediate sense of calm when he started to hit golf balls. It was a feeling like no other when the club hit the ball solidly, and he just stood and watched the ball's flight against the cloudy and foggy sky. It was magic. No cares. No worries. No jail. No Lusky. Complete freedom. Chipper was in control. He went into a trance and hit about a dozen balls with the nine iron before he heard Takahashi yelling in front of him. "Damn! I hit that one! Hey, Jenny girl! Senior tour for me!"

Jenny said, "Not quite yet, Tak. Not unless you can hit three hundred in a row just like that one. Turn around and watch how Chipper gets his hips out of the way."

"But he younger than me. A lot younger. My hips don't move so good." Tak said.

Jenny commented, "But just watch and try that."

He tried and didn't hit a good one. "I too much concentrate on hips and not ball. No good. I not Chipper."

Jenny said, "Let's end on a few good ones. Just swing hard and smash it, Tak."

He hit ten more balls before he hit two in a row just right. He was happy. Jenny was happy. She walked over to Chipper and watched him hit a few, then walked around behind him and clung to him from behind. Takahashi said again, "Get a room."

Jenny said, "Let's get a room, Chipper. Let's do that. I missed you."

"Just let me finish hitting the bucket, then we'll play a few holes, then head home. I want to stop at the range at Pebble to see what's going on, also, before we head home. Also want to go to the pro shop to see what's up with Roger. Did Richard get him his job back?"

"Let's just go home now, Chipper. No golf. No range. Yes, Richard got Roger his job back. Let's go make a baby. Let's go make Annika."

"Ok. You talked me into it. I just want to drive by my range, though, on the way home."

Jenny had heard from Bill about the range and definitely didn't want to show it to Chipper. Chipper took the borrowed clubs back to the pro shop, took off the windbreaker, and they headed home. He protested when Jenny didn't drive by the Pebble Beach driving range, but could do nothing about it. He wasn't even suspicious or curious. He rubbed her thigh when they drove home.

She asked about what happened in jail, and Chipper just said, "I don't want to talk about it. I'm not supposed to talk about it. Maybe in a few days." Jenny knew that bugging him for more would be fruitless, so she didn't ask again.

Angus was waiting in the entry hall when they came in the front door. Angus barked and rolled over, but both Jenny and Chipper ignored the poor dog. They almost didn't even make it to the bedroom as they shed their clothes going up the stairs. Angus was barking loudly behind them as he stepped over two shirts and a pair of pants. He continued to bark and jump on the bed as Chipper and Jenny enjoyed their first attempt of the late afternoon to make baby Annika.

Between the first and second attempt, the poor dog jumped on the bed and enjoyed belly rubs from both of them. The belly rubbing didn't last long, as it wasn't long before Annika-making started again. Angus knew it was time to leave the room.

LUSKY AND THE NEWS

Nolan Lusky was home and slept very well. He felt confident that his tracks were covered and that there wasn't anything anyone could do. He thought about Angel when he went to sleep. He woke up groggily when he heard what sounded like the front gate intercom squawking several times. He glanced at the clock and saw it was ten A.M. He had slept for almost ten hours. He pressed the button near the bed and heard a voice say, "Premier Auto Restoration here. Your car is back."

Lusky was amazed that his beloved Pagani was back already. He had paid a fortune for quick service, but this was incredible. He said, "I'll buzz you in. Hold on a few minutes, and I'll be right down." He jumped out of bed, put on some shorts, sandals, and a tee shirt and came scrambling down the staircase, rushing to the front door. When he opened the door, there was a large flatbed truck with his Pagani Huayra on the back. He started weeping.

He ran up to the man, who had just exited the truck, still weeping and said, "Thank you. Thank you. This is amazing. I can't believe it's been shipped back and fixed so soon. Let me examine it."

The driver, in some sort of dark blue uniform that was starched and pressed, said, "We aim to please. You paid the company enough money to get great service, and that's what we gave you. Let me back it off the truck, so you can examine it, then sign the paperwork."

"Be careful," said Lusky.

The uniformed driver just laughed. When the car was sitting in the driveway, Lusky started slowly walking around the car. Very slowly, he examined the area where the key marks were. He got down on his knees and examined every inch of the door panel. The driver waited patiently as

Lusky started humming and continued his examination. It took a good twenty minutes. The driver didn't say a word.

Lusky said, "Wait just a minute, and I'll be back to sign the paperwork. It looks better than new. Better than new." Then he went inside and brought back cash to pay the driver a tip. He signed off on the paperwork, took the keys, shook hands with the driver, and handed him a wad of bills.

The driver said, "We don't take tips. We are just happy you are happy. What a great car this is."

Lusky said, "I insist you take the tip." The driver finally looked at the stack of bills and saw they were hundreds. At least the one on top was.

"Well, if you insist," said the driver, expecting the hundred to be the only one, and the others to be ones or fives. When he looked, after he drove off, he found Lusky had given him ten thousand in cash. All hundreds. He was astonished.

Lusky was eager to drive his car and wanted to show it off. He went inside and put on his driving hat, a wide-brimmed straw one that barely fit inside the car. He headed out the 17-Mile Drive to the Carmel gate and drove up and down Ocean Avenue several times. He had his driver's side window open and was waving to people and driving very slowly. He would yell at several walkers, "It's a gull-wing." Or "It's a Pagani." Or "This car cost me over three million dollars." He did get a lot of stares and some applause. He then drove out to the south of Carmel to Rio Road and headed to the Carmel Valley Coffee Roasting shop in the Crossroads Shopping Center.

He knew that he could park his car in front and have coffee outside while looking at his car, so it would be safe, and he could impress the gawkers who might stop and look at the car. The barista was attractive, and he talked her into coming outside to take a look at the Pagani. She refused a ride, "I have to work. I am working." Lusky sat next to a group of five older men who were holding court around their usual table.

"See that car," he beckoned, pointing at it, but still seated. "It's mine. It's a Pagani Huayra. Cost me over three million. Has gull-wing doors. Only a few made."

One of the older men said, "What kind of gas mileage does it get?" and Lusky ignored him, and went back to sipping his coffee. There was a Monterey County Herald at the table next to him. He grabbed the Herald from the table and gasped when he saw the headline. His gasp was loud enough for all of the old men to turn around and look at him.

The headline said, "Horror at The Hay." Then Lusky read the article.

HORROR AT THE HAY

MONTEREY HERALD

BYLINE DEVINE

Murder at the Hay

Although the Pebble Beach Corporation tried to keep this out of the local news, this reporter has uncovered more insider information on an international incident that occurred at The Hay golf course last week. We received an anonymous tip from a reliable source indicating that a drone struck and killed the Duchess of Irvingtonshire while she stood on the putting green watching her two children take a lesson. The impact of the drone was so devastating that she died instantly.

This was originally thought to be a dreadful tragic accident, but it has become a murder-for-hire investigation being handled by several local police agencies as well as the FBI, Scotland Yard, Interpol, and the prestigious Lloyd's of London. Insurance fraud may be the motive of the murder-for-hire.

Our local driving range attendant, Mr. Chipper Blair, who seems to be in the middle of every incident in the Forest, was arrested and interrogated as a material witness. He has not been charged with anything, but may be able to identify the drone operator. His corroboration and testimony will be key in any follow-up investigation or court case. This reporter's phone calls to the Pebble Beach Corporation, the FBI, and Chipper Blair were not returned.

Lusky put down the paper and gasped again, then said to the old men. "Did you see this headline? Can you imagine?" He held up the paper and one of the men handed him a Monterey County Weekly and said, "Read the Squid column. It's back on page twelve. Same thing. What a nightmare."

Lusky turned to page twelve and started reading.

MONTEREY COUNTY WEEKLY

THE SQUIDFRY

This Squid was just swimming calmly, when I was approached by a shark with a whale of information. The water became turbulent when the Squid heard the news. The shocking death of the Duchess of Irvingtonshire (I kid you not — there is, or was, a Duchess of Irvingtonshire) at, of all places, the putting green of The Hay golf course in Pebble Beach. A drone, no less. Yes, a drone to the head. Wham Bam, Thank you, Ma'am. You're dead as a mackerel swimming with sharks. The drone came from over the fence at the driving range where you-know-who, Chipper Blair, was working. Blair was arrested but, of course, claimed he knew nothing about it, although he was holding the drone cell phone commanding device in his hand at the time of his arrest. But wait, there is more seaweed in this story. Blair claims he knows who did it. Of course he does. Murky waters now. Interpol, Scotland Yard, and some big insurance company from over the big sea are all involved. Can Blair swim out of this one? Will he identify the real crab that killed the Duchess? Murky and deep waters await.

Lusky quickly rose from the table and left half of his cup of coffee sitting there. He ran to the Pagani and yelled at the men at the table, "Watch these gull-wings!" before he made them operate on both sides, although he only needed one to rise for him to get in. He then gunned the engine and backed out.

One of the men said to his cronies, "Strange man. Wealth is wasted on the young."

ONE MORE TIME

Jenny awoke first and tapped Chipper on the forehead, "One more time, Chipper. I think it's gonna work this time." Then she climbed on top of him.

"I have to get up, Jenny. I don't even know if I have a job. I've got to get to my driving range."

"It's early, and your driving range will be there all day. Bill's got it under control. And it's still early. Just concentrate on me for a bit. One more time, Chipper."

Angus was now sniffing and licking Chipper's face as Jenny positioned herself for another baby attempt. Chipper started laughing, then stared into her face and said, "You truly are beautiful, Jenny. I'm a lucky man. I hope Annika looks just like you." He tried to bring her head closer to his to give her a kiss, but Angus got in the way.

"I feel good about this, Chipper," she said, after they were done. "I think we may have done it. I feel hopeful. I feel really good. Quite a night."

All Chipper said was, "I'm very hungry."

Jenny replied, "Maybe we'll see Richard in the backyard this morning. I hope so."

When they got out of bed and headed for the shower, Angus bounded joyfully out of the room. He was waiting by the back door when, in the shower with Chipper, Jenny said, "One more time, hon."

Angus waited patiently by the back door while Chipper finally was able to grab something to eat in the kitchen. When they opened the back door, Angus flew down the stairs looking for Abigail. Abigail was walking with Richard and Debbie toward the estate backyard, and Richard yelled, "Good to see you are home, Chipper! Very happy to see you."

Debbie yelled, "Angus! Let poor Abby alone. Leave the poor girl alone." But it was too late.

Jenny whispered to Chipper, "Maybe we should try it like they do." Chipper headed for the club storage bin and pulled out the brassie and the long spoon. It was a rare clear day. He had four Slazengers in one pocket and several dog treats in the other. He was as eager to hit the morning shot as Angus was to mount Abigail.

Richard said, "What happened after I left? You were there an awfully long time. You should have called me."

"They had my phone. Wouldn't let me use it."

"Highly irregular. Do you want me to file suit against the Sheriff's office?"

"I just want to forget about the whole incident. Everything. I just want to hit golf balls," Chipper said, as he swung the long spoon. After a few practice swings he hit what he thought was a perfect shot. "That's got to be very close. Got to be." Angus and Abby took off running and playfully bumped into each other as they disappeared from sight on their way to the fourteenth green. Chipper ran up the stairs quickly and peered through the telescope. He yelled down. "Two feet right! Exactly pin high." Jenny was disappointed that the ball wasn't in the hole, as it would have been a good omen for her pregnancy.

Surprisingly, Abigail came back with the Slazenger, with Angus, looking proud, right next to her. They both sat next to Chipper and waited for treats. He took several out of his pocket and dropped them on the green. Angus waited while Abigail had a few, then Abigail stepped aside and let Angus gobble up the rest. "Quite the pair," Stein said. "Quite the pair."

Stein continued as Jenny took her practice swings, "I got Roger put back on, Chipper. Really no problem. Have you been to the range yet?" Jenny stopped swinging and looked at both Chipper and Richard. She put her index finger to her mouth and looked at Richard with the "hush sign."

Chipper said, "No. What's up with my range?"

Richard took the hint and clammed up. "Just curious, Chipper." At this point, Chipper knew to expect the worse when he arrived this morning. He didn't know if he had a job and didn't really care, or he would have asked Richard, but he did care if something happened at the driving range. Clearly, because of Jenny and Richard's actions, he knew something really bad was going on there.

Chipper kissed Jenny and took off in his cart. He didn't even wait for the other three to hit their golf balls. When he hit his shot to fourteen from the middle of the fairway, he saw one golf ball, which was Jenny's, on the green. Abigail and Angus then picked it up and headed back. Chipper played fourteen, fifteen, and sixteen with three pars, then headed into what he was sure was awful.

DISTURBED AT THE DRIVING RANGE

Big Bill O'Shea arrived early at the Pebble Beach driving range in anticipation of Chipper arriving. Bill wanted to be there earlier than Chipper, because he expected the worst. He had to try to control Chipper's worst instincts, which he was sure would involve destroying the two constructed fake-turf stations and the photo mural along the right side of the range. Bill was waiting with feet apart and arms crossed, standing steady like the rock of Gibraltar in the middle of the driving range near the new turf installations. He could see Chipper approaching in his cart from a short distance.

When Chipper drove up, he stopped short of Bill and said, "I'm tired, Bill. Jenny had me up all afternoon and all night trying to make a baby."

"Too much information, Chipper, but I hope it works."

Chipper looked around and didn't immediately react to the driving range changes. All he very calmly said was, "I expected worse. I can get rid of this stuff very easily. No problem."

"You can't do that, Chipper. You know that. I respect you too much and won't stop you if you do anything, but when the boss asks, I have to tell the truth. Just have some patience, Chipper."

"Patience isn't my best quality. You know that, Bill. What the hell does Stevens think he's doing here? That screen on the right is a monstrosity. And anyone can hit balls over it. It's a fucking photo mural. It's awful."

Bill said, "It's only a mock-up. The real one will be one hundred feet tall. This one is just to prove the concept. Stevens was over here and loved it."

All Chipper said was, "He would. I'm sure he would. For you, Bill, I won't do anything. Do I still have a job?"

"I don't know, Chipper. I was told to work here until I heard something."

Chipper phoned Richard, and as he did, he said, "I should have asked him this morning. I saw him early. I was just anxious to get here. It's worse than I thought, Bill. Much worse."

Stein answered, and Chipper said, "Am I still employed? Am I still working at the driving range?"

"Not sure, Chipper. You are still on the group email, I just checked this second. Let me check with personnel. You haven't been charged with anything, just a material witness. I don't think there are any grounds for firing you. I'll fix it if I find anything else, Chipper. I'll text you or call you or maybe come over later. I need to try out the new hitting mats."

"Fuck you, Richard," was all Chipper said. Chipper then turned to Bill and said, "Who has to pick up balls that are over that disaster screen on the right?"

"They've hired a kid to pick up range balls. He comes over after school at RLS. High schooler. Nice kid."

"How many balls are in the shack, Bill?"

"No way of knowing. There are probably fifty buckets full, maybe fifty to a bucket. Twenty-five hundred, maybe."

"I've been literally caged up, Bill. I'll take a few buckets and hit them. Really need to hit some balls."

Big Bill watched as Chipper took two buckets and went to the grass just to the left of the first artificial-turf hitting station. Chipper warmed up by swinging what looked like a sand wedge and swinging as close as he could to the outside of the artificial turf. His divots were deep in the surrounding real grass. Then Chipper started hitting a short iron toward the offending mural. Every shot went over it. About every ten shots, Chipper would grab his sand wedge and take more divots around the artificial turf. Bill didn't do anything.

In less than a half hour, Chipper walked over to the shack and brought back his two empty buckets and grabbed two more. In the next half hour, he repeated the same drill as with the first two. Now there were two hundred balls in the trees and rough over the screen.

Bill walked over, finally, and said, "You are being childish, Chipper. The poor kid is going to have to hunt around in the deep grass over there and find all those on foot. He'll be here until dark." Chipper didn't reply, but took his two buckets back to the shack and grabbed two more.

"This will be it, Bill. I'm too tired. And take a look at this turf mat installation. They didn't secure it very well. It seems to be moving around when someone walks on it. It's very loose. If someone hits balls off of it, it looks to me like it will move."

"You are lucky I consider you a friend, Chipper. Not only are you trying to have a baby, but you are a baby."

When Chipper was hitting balls and Big Bill was jawing at him, neither saw the Pagani Huayra drive by the range. Lusky was doing a surveillance run, and was very happy he saw Chipper back on the range. It made things a lot easier for him. Lusky drove back to his estate smiling.

LUSKY AT HOME

Nolan Lusky opened a bottle of Rye, even though it was just a bit after noon. He sat on a sofa on his private deck and put the film he had surreptitiously taken of Serena Antonelli and her boyfriend on a loop playback on mute on his eighty-inch TV on the outside deck wall. He poured some of the rye into an orange juice glass and took a small sip. He rolled it around in his mouth and felt very content. He was too smart to be baited into going after Chipper right away. He suspected that the Squidfry and Devine columns' information was leaked by someone who was out to get him.

He was enjoying Serena's antics on the screen while he made his first phone call to his drone supplier. He talked to "his man" at the office, Gopal, and explained his specifications for small explosive devices with big impact to be suspended in the under carriage of each drone. It was time for a test that would surely increase his chances of selling the drones to the North Koreans and the Chinese. Gopal said he needed Lusky to email some more details about the amount of explosives and Lusky's specifications.

Lusky was impatient while he sent what he needed via text. He received some smiley emojis back almost immediately. His second call was to Angel. "Hi, Angel. Talk dirty to me."

"I can't, Nolan. I'm on my way to class. I only have a few minutes."

"Then text me dirty stuff during class, my Angel. I'm sitting here drinking rye and watching that Serena girl do her stuff. She is truly amazing."

"I have to go, Nolan. I have to concentrate in class. No can do what you want. Goodbye." She hung up abruptly.

Lusky poured more rye and laughed when he received a text from

Angel that was a gif of some pigs rolling in the mud, and her comment was "something dirty." He was startled when he heard the front gate entrance intercom make a buzz, then a voice came on saying, "Mr. Lusky. Please open the gate."

Lusky stood and went over to the intercom box on the deck. "Who is this?"

"It's Officer Anderson. We met at the Rosewood resort. I'd like to ask you some more questions, please."

Lusky said, "This isn't really a good time." He was hoping to avoid another round of questioning.

Anderson said, impatiently, "Lusky. I'm afraid this has to be the time. I have some others with me, and the timing is important. Please let me in. Now!"

Lusky said, "Give me a few minutes, then I'll let you in. No problem." He then rushed around trying to think about what might be a problem. He stopped the film and turned off the big screen TV. He didn't feel he had anything else to hide. This was going to be a breeze. He thought about changing his clothes, but decided not to. Then he pressed the button on the intercom to open the front gate. Lusky walked to the front door and opened it.

Anderson was driving a Monterey County Sheriff's van, and Lusky was surprised when several men exited the vehicle. Anderson exited the van and came around, but didn't shake Lusky's hand. He pointed toward each of the men in turn. "Officer Kennedy from my office. Mr. Sloane, Scotland Yard. Mr. Beaufoy, Interpol. Mr. Addison, Lloyd's of London." There was no additional handshaking.

Lusky didn't know what to say and was getting nervous. He had a bit of a buzz from the rye. He thought he'd try a bit of attempted humor. "Well, the gang's all here. Why do you all want to talk to me? Should I have a lawyer here?"

Kennedy said, "Do you think you need a lawyer?"

Lusky pointed at the Pagani, about ten feet away, and said, "You gentlemen ever see a silver and gold Pagani Huayra? Over three million. I paid cash."

Kennedy took that as an opportunity to start immediate questioning,

"Didn't you sue Chipper Blair for keying your car? Isn't the suit still ongoing?"

"I have to answer yes and yes on those."

"Why did you let him use your drones, then, if you had a lawsuit against him? Didn't you also have a restraining order on contact with him?"

"Good questions, Officer. I think I would like to put my lawyer on speakerphone, just as a precaution. I don't want to get anyone in trouble, including myself." He called his attorney and explained who he was with, then turned on the speakerphone. The attorney said, "I would advise my client not to say anything to you gentlemen. It's highly unusual for so many different jurisdictions to be together. Do you have a reason for talking to my client about anything?"

Kennedy said, "Just routine questions. Lot of things going on around Mr. Lusky. We need some explanations." He continued, "Please answer the question about Chipper Blair."

Lusky said, "The drones are my pet project. I love this high-tech stuff. I also want to be friendly to people, even if they do bad things to me. Blair insisted on using the drone. I thought maybe he had a new use for the technology that would help me sell them. He said he wanted to use it to pick up golf balls. Crazy. Even though I was suing him, I wanted him to try it."

"Are you aware the Duke is suing the Pebble Beach Corporation for negligence in the death of his wife because of the drone accident?"

The lawyer on the phone said, "My client has no knowledge of any of this."

Kennedy said, "Isn't it strange you aren't being sued for providing the drone? You have deep pockets, as does the Corporation. I'm surprised the Duke didn't include you in his lawsuit."

Lusky was quiet, waiting for his attorney to say something. There was an awkward minute of silence until Kennedy said, "Did you ever meet the Duke or the Duchess?"

Lusky quickly said, "No. I never did. Too bad about what happened. That Blair is a loose cannon and a maniac. He should be locked up."

Addison said, "Did you know that the Duchess had taken out a life insurance policy for a fortune on her husband? Very strange that she should die in the accident. Maybe it wasn't an accident? Maybe the Duke was the one who was supposed to be in the accident?"

An angry voice came on the phone from the attorney, "My client knows nothing about any of this. Nothing. I advise him to say nothing else. Nolan, don't answer any questions at all. You men should leave unless you have a specific reason you can give me for badgering my client. He hasn't done anything. Do you have a search warrant or anything?"

Kennedy reached out and grabbed Lusky's phone and turned it off. He yelled, "Don't leave town, Lusky! We think you are a scumbag. We'll be back. We're on to you, man."

Lusky was nervous and instinctively walked over between the men and his Pagani, afraid Kennedy might run over and key or violate his car. He watched as the men climbed into the van and drove away.

As he drove out of the driveway, Anderson was angry, "Why don't we just arrest the asshole? We've got plenty on him. I'm tired of Lusky. Damn idiot spent more on his car than I will make in my lifetime. What a waste. What an asshole. Let's go back in and rough him up a bit. I bet he'd start crying, break down, and confess to everything."

Sloane said, "Aye, man. Be patient. Justice works in strange ways. I'm sure he'll get what he deserves. We Scots have a saying 'Whit's fur ye'll no go by ye.' It means what's meant to happen will happen; there's no escaping fate."

THE WAITING

The next few weeks were great for Chipper. He was officially back to work. He was back to his routine. He wasn't worried about anything. Not so for Jenny. She was worried about everything. Was she going to have her period? When were the legal cases against Chipper going to hit? She couldn't stand the waiting. Chipper didn't want to talk about either, but she made him have conversations about both. He was eager to be a dad now and did have fears about what was going on with his legal issues. As long as he was working and able to hit balls, his world was wonderful. He spent many hours hitting balls over the screen mural. He spent an equal amount of time taking big divots around the artificial turf.

When golfers bought range balls and wanted to try the mats, Chipper tried to dissuade them. If someone was on the turf, he would walk by and say, "Real golfers don't hit off artificial turf. Real golfers hit off grass." Or "Be careful about falling. The mats don't seem to stay put when you swing. Don't fall." Chipper made sure the mats were not solidly in the ground. He was surprised no one from the Corporation or the MADRDI Company came by to check on everything. He spent some time every afternoon posting anonymous comments on social media, or in made-up names, about how bad the mats were and what an abomination the fake landscape mural was.

He noticed that the ball supply was going down. Where there were once fifty full buckets each morning, there was now only thirty-five. He rarely saw the ball collector boy but the few times he saw him very late in the afternoon, he told him he didn't have to pick up the balls in the rough. The boy was happy. Chipper was happy. At least for another day or so.

LUSKY PREPARES

Nolan "No Load" Lusky was nervous since being visited by the authorities. He wasn't sleeping. He was drinking more rye. Angel wasn't answering his phone calls. He continued to watch porn. His lawyer had nothing good to say and stopped returning his calls, also. Three prototypes of his drone with the bomb holder on the bottom arrived by Federal Express, and this changed his mood.

Shortly after receiving the drones, there was another ring on his estate gate intercom. He was expecting this one. Gopal didn't want to mail the explosives. He had to deliver them himself. He was carrying a sack about the size of a brown lunch bag full of what looked like Tide detergent pods, each about the size of a golf ball. They would each fit into the carriage below the drone. "Be very careful with these, No Load. They are very powerful. Let's go into the back of the house for a demo. How close are you neighbors?"

Lusky was intrigued. "No problem." They headed to the back of the house where there was a few acres of space. The next-door estates could not be seen in any direction. Gopal left the regular pod-size balls inside and had a small backpack hanging on his back. He pulled out a packet with very small teardrop-size packets and handed one to Lusky. "What the hell is this?" Lusky said.

Gopal said, "Throw it out in an area where there are no trees. Throw it as far as you can, then cover your ears."

"But it's so small."

"Wait until you see what it does. Make sure you don't get it near any trees, please. Make sure you cover your ears. Throw it as far as you can."

Lusky fired the little pellet toward a large dirt area, aiming for a target about sixty yards away. He was short of the dirt area, and the pellet landed on a cement walkway just short of the dirt area. Lusky failed to cover his ears while Gopal was ducking and covering his head with both arms. The explosion was enough to make Lusky feel the impact and be pushed backwards. The cement cracked and rose into the air, and the dirt below it blew up into the air. When the dirt and cement lifted, there was a three-foot-by-three-foot crater, about a foot deep into the ground. Lusky couldn't hear anything but could tell Gopal was talking.

"Fuck me!" Lusky yelled, "Why didn't you tell me that would happen?"

Gopal was talking again, but Lusky still couldn't hear him. "Let me try one more, Gopal. One more. That had to be heard all over Pebble Beach. I hope the fire department or security doesn't come out."

Gopal handed him one more and said, "Try to reach the dirt this time, No Load. And cover your ears this time."

Lusky didn't hear him, but this time Lusky ran about ten yards ahead when he flung the pellet, then he ducked and covered his ears. He was careful to watch the result this time. The explosion of dirt seemed even worse than before. It was like a mushroom cloud of dirt that rose about thirty feet into the air. Lusky walked over and found a six-by-six depression in the dirt that was over a foot deep. "Very impressive," he said.

Gopal walked over and stood in the depression. He waited until Lusky signaled him that his hearing was back. It was several minutes. "Pretty impressive, huh, No Load?"

"Yes, sir. What happens if the regular-size pods explode?"

Gopal said, "Six times worse. Six times more noise. Six times more destruction."

"How big a pod can you make? And how big can the carrier be on the drone? This will really sell to the Koreans and Chinese. You've really done it, Gopal. Really done it this time."

Gopal said, "It's kind of unlimited. Tremendous amount of damage could be done."

"I'm going to send you a big bonus, Gopal. Really big bonus. I thought this would be like my former stuff, where some VC pays me huge money for just the concept, and I make hundreds of millions, and it really never works right. This time we've really got something."

"Just be careful with those pods. They really shouldn't be all together. As soon as you can, make sure you separate them."

"Why don't you come in for a drink, Gopal?"

"I don't drink alcohol."

"Let me show you some videos you might like, then. I'll have a drink, and I can show you some stuff you won't believe."

Lusky poured himself some rye and showed Gopal the bottle. It was a Rittenhouse Single Barrel 25-Year-Old Rye. "I paid fifty thousand for a case of twelve of these. You should have a sip."

Gopal just said, "I don't drink alcohol."

Lusky made Gopal sit down and turned on the Serena video. As soon as Gopal saw the naked woman, he turned around and said, "Holy God, No Load. I can't watch this. This is an abomination. An insult to God. I have to go. I have to go immediately." And he walked out.

Lusky said to himself, "To each his own. To each his own."

LUCID LUSKY

Lusky woke late the next day and was panicked when he read a text message from his attorney. *Nolan. I had a visit from an FBI agent named Tripp early this morning. A complete surprise. I didn't answer any questions. Attorney-Client privilege. I think they are close to arresting you for a variety of things. Erase this message after you read it. I highly suggest you flee the country immediately.* Lusky immediately called back, and no one answered. He started yelling into the phone, "Pick up! Pick up! God Dammit! Shit!"

He wasn't thinking straight. Needed coffee. Needed to take action. Needed to do something. Lusky didn't know how to make coffee. He dressed quickly and drove the Pagani a short distance to the Lodge. He parked right near the front steps to the protests of the front door guys, ran inside, went to the complimentary coffee canister near the front desk, and poured two cups each three-quarters full, so they wouldn't spill in his car. Made sure to cover them and headed back outside. The front door guys were walking around his car, and Lusky said, "Nice car, huh? It's a Pagani Huayra. I paid over three million cash for it."

One of the guys said, "Where'd you make your money?"

"Glad you asked, sport. I'm very smart. Tech businesses. Very smart."

He didn't head straight home. He had to get his thoughts together. He just roamed around the 17-Mile Drive and tried to figure out what he had to do. He didn't want to take his lawyer's advice. He would never flee the country or flee his wealth. When he drove by Cypress Point, he couldn't stop thinking that Chipper Blair was the cause of all his problems. If Blair was out of the way, everything would be fine. When he drove past Spyglass Hill, he turned up the hill to home and felt better about his prospects.

When he drove back into his driveway, he started implementing his plan. Before he exited his car, he made two phone calls. The first was to the Rosewood front desk. "Hi, Tony. It's Nolan. I'm just up the road and going to be there in a little while. Can you check me in, please? My usual suite." Then he read his credit card number to Tony. "Angel will be by to pick up the key. If anyone ever asks, just tell them I checked in and picked up the key, and you saw me and Angel around the pool and the bar today. Thanks, Tony. There's some money in it for you. I'll see you later today. Two nights, Tony."

Then Lusky called Angel. She didn't pick up. He went into the house and called her at five-minute intervals for thirty minutes. She answered and said, "Nolan, you should write down my class schedule. I was in class."

"Angel. Very important. I need you to head over to the Rosewood and get the key to the suite from Tony as soon as you can. I'll be there this evening. If anyone asks, I was in the room with you all day."

"This is getting too much for me, Nolan. I don't want to lie to the police or anyone anymore. I think they are going to get me in trouble anyway."

"Just do this, Angel. Very important. I'll pay you extra. Just relax, lay by the pool. Remember, I was with you from now until later. See you later. Enjoy. Charge anything you want to the room."

Then Nolan Lusky grabbed three drones, and carefully, very carefully, put the larger explosive pods into the carriers. He didn't know what to expect from the larger pods. He considered trying one in the backyard, but didn't want to draw any attention. If they were what he expected, any explosion in the backyard using the big ones would certainly draw more attention than he wanted.

He said, "This is going to be fun. Very fun. Goodbye, Chipper Blair."

BOMBS AWAY

Unsuspecting Chipper Blair and Jenny Nelson took their morning shots as usual. When Angus approached Abigail, Debbie Rogers, was worried. "I think we should keep Angus away from Abigail for a bit. He trots over during the day and pesters her when she's resting. Look at her belly. I think she needs rest now. Can one of you take him to work today, or lock him in the house?"

Chipper said, "Why don't you just lock Abigail up in the house? It's not fair to Angus to lock him up. He's used to running around. You are being too careful with Abigail. She'll be fine."

Jenny shrugged and said, "Heartless, Chipper. I'll take Angus and tie him up. He can watch me give lessons at Spyglass. He might enjoy it. I'll bring him over at noon and see you for my lesson with Cindy."

"Thank you, Jenny," Debbie said. She gave Chipper a harmless punch on the arm and said, "Heartless."

Chipper played his way into work and was happy with the way he hit the ball. He striped one down the middle on fifteen and made birdie with a great nine iron to two feet. He birdied sixteen, also, and decided to play seventeen to see if he could birdie all three of his morning complete holes. He hit six iron to the right hand pin to ten feet, lined it up carefully, but missed the putt on the high side. He thought to himself, "This is going to be a great day." The fog was lifting, and the sun was creating long shadows of trees. It was magnificent when he arrived at the range.

In between golfers hitting balls on an abnormally crowded day at the range, he spent the morning lobbing wedges over the mural and taking divots around the turf mats. Several players tried hitting off the mats and getting readings on the tall screens. A few came over to Chipper and asked what the numbers on the readout meant. "What is smash rate? What kind of spin rate am I supposed to have? Are the distance readings correct?"

Chipper's response usually drew some laughs, "It's all bullshit. Nothing but bullshit. Doesn't matter. Just play golf."

When Jenny arrived at the range a few minutes before noon, she let Angus out of the car and let him run over to Chipper. Angus was happy and rolled over on his back. Chipper knelt down and petted Angus for a long time while Jenny walked over. The usual crowd of onlookers for the noon lesson had gotten smaller, but still was about forty every day. They weren't as noisy or raucous each day, but still gave catcalls to Jenny when she walked. Jenny was able to ignore it. Not so when Cindy and Duncan exited their car.

Duncan could never live down the video that was still on the internet. Many yelled, "Premature Duncan! Hey, Cindy!" They tried to ignore the yelling.

Angus kneeled near Chipper while Jenny started giving Cindy her lesson. Cindy was hitting it very well lately. She could fade or draw the ball on command. She could hit it low or high. On the CSUMB golf team, she was battling Serena and Maya for the number-one spot. Cindy had become very serious about her game and knew exactly what questions to ask Jenny about her swing. Jenny just had to stand by and make occasional comments during each lesson.

They were set up, as they always were, about twenty feet left of the installed turf stations. Chipper was standing about ten feet back with Angus by his side, and Duncan was beside Chipper. There were a few others hitting balls on the far right side of the range, and one golfer hitting balls on the left piece of artificial turf.

No one saw Lusky drive up the 17-Mile Drive and pull his car onto the dirt on the other side of the mural. He parked behind some trees and carried his three drones over behind the very far side of the screen mural. He had them each set up in a row. He peeked around the mural, careful not to be seen, and realized the screen was going to make this very difficult. He was happy to see Chipper, Jenny, Cindy, and Duncan standing so close to each other. He still remembered that Cindy had defied him and put her foot up on his car, despite his protestations. They all deserved their fate for crossing him. He set the dial on the drone to slow speed, as it would be easier to control. He would be better able to stand behind the screen and see the path with his cell phone.

The driving range was calm as the drone went over the mural and slowly went toward the group of four. One of the Cindy crowd was the first to see the drone approaching and yelled as it sped up. The yell was loud enough that Chipper and Duncan looked toward the drone. Jenny and Cindy were concentrating on Cindy's shots and didn't pay attention. When the drone sped up, Chipper had just enough time to run over between Jenny and the drone and took her to the ground. This was just before the drone, fortunately, flew directly into the upright tower and screen of the right turf position. The explosion was deafening. Cindy and Duncan were knocked to the ground by the sound concussion. Chipper lay on top of Jenny when they were covered with dirt that was descending from above them. Chipper looked up just in time to see the dismembered arm of the poor man who was hitting on the other mat. It landed near them. The golfer on the mat had no chance. He was instantly killed.

The two artificial-turf hitting areas and tower screens were no longer there. Just a large hole in the ground and some debris. Chipper yelled, "Run! Everyone run toward The Hay!" Jenny and Chipper were able to get up. Duncan had to pick up Cindy. Her leg was bleeding from a cut where some metal hit her. They ran, hobbled, and shuffled toward the trees on the left, toward The Hay, for some cover and protection. The crowd behind the range, watching Cindy and Jenny, all took off running toward their cars.

It didn't take long for Lusky to peek around the mural again. He grabbed the next drone. He was laughing at the damage that he had seen. These would certainly sell to anyone. He felt he should be filming to show the capabilities. Chipper and Jenny had just reached the trees when Jenny looked back and yelled, "Angus! Angus!" Angus was covered with dirt, but she saw the brave dog creeping slowly in the other direction toward the mural on the side that was closest to the hitting areas. He wasn't following the others. She saw him run behind the screen. Jenny was terrified, more for Angus, than for herself. Cindy, being helped by Duncan, finally made it to behind the trees.

Lusky peeked around the screen again to get his bearings and see where the group was crouching behind the trees, then crept behind it before setting the drone on the fastest speed. He sent it hurtling rapidly toward the group hiding behind the trees. The drone, fortunately, hit a pine tree about twenty feet away and exploded with another deafening roar. They all ducked and covered their heads and ears. A small fire broke out in the brush at the bottom of the tree. The tree itself was burning, as well.

Lusky was now panicked and frustrated. He realized that in order to control the final drone properly he was going to have to try to do it visually and not with the small cell phone screen. He knelt down and crawled around the last tree holding the end of the mural and backed up against the mural, near the tree.

Cindy was bleeding badly from a piece of the tower that had scraped her leg. She still had her five iron in her hand, holding it protectively. Chipper grabbed her five iron while Duncan consoled her. Jenny was still yelling and completely panicked. "Angus! Angus!" They were now sitting ducks, with Lusky coming out from around the screen on the other side of the range. He had the third drone, and when they saw him coming out, Angus was right at his feet, trying to bite his leg. Lusky was kicking Angus to try to make him stop.

Chipper realized that at this point he had no choice. He started running across the driving range with the five iron in his hand. He tried to keep himself on a direct line between Lusky and Jenny. Jenny was yelling and crying, "No! Chipper, No!" Where the last drone had exploded into the trees, there was now a larger fire burning in the brush. Lusky had the drone on slow speed again and was controlling it with his sight as he had it going toward Chipper. This was going to be easy.

When the drone was three feet away from Chipper and hovering his way, he took a wild swing with the five iron. He wasn't sure if it would immediately set off the explosives. He didn't care. He had to save the others. By sheer luck, his five iron swing hit the drone and not the explosive carrier. Chipper cringed, closed his eyes, and expected an immediate explosion, but all he heard was the whirring sound of the drone. He opened his eyes and watched the drone, now completely out of control, circling around and heading back toward Lusky and Angus. Chipper yelled for Angus to run.

Lusky was equally surprised and stunned. He was standing in front of the mural and couldn't believe what was happening. He leaned back against the mural screen, about ten feet from the end. Angus started running out on the range toward Chipper. Chipper watched as the drone headed toward the left side of the screen, but thirty feet into the air. Chipper wasn't sure if Lusky had any more drones or not. He couldn't see one in Lusky's hand or near him.

Chipper and Lusky made eye contact as the drone hit the side of the screen that was attached to the last pine tree with the five tethers. When it exploded, three of the tethers came loose immediately, and big flames were creeping toward the other two. Lusky covered his ears and watched as the fire approached the other two tethers. When the tethers broke, the straining, tightly-pulled screen immediately started collapsing and rolling up. Lusky didn't have time to move and was rolled up in the screen as it rapidly headed back to its original tree. The screen was on fire, both top and bottom, and the flames quickly engulfed it. Lusky could be heard screaming inside it as it sprung back to its original rolled-up shape and completely burned down. Nothing but ashes. It happened so quickly that all Chipper and Angus could do was watch in amazement. When he thought about it later, Chipper was surprised that the mural material used was not fire-retardant. He turned around and saw his wife and friends retreating back from the trees on the left side of the range. There were fires burning on both sides of his driving range, and sirens could already be heard getting closer. One of the usual crowd had called 9-1-1.

Pebble Beach Fire was the first to arrive and drove right on the range and had no problem putting out the fire quickly near Jenny, Cindy, and Duncan. The paramedics worked on Cindy's injury, as well. The fire on the right side of the range was more problematic. The brush was denser, and the flames quickly spread before the fire brigade could get over to the other side of the range. The brush was burning ominously toward the Pagani Huayra, soon engulfing it in flames. When it blew up like a fireball, the fire spread in all directions. Monterey Fire and Seaside Fire were on their way.

Cindy's wound was cleaned and treated, wrapped in several layers of gauze, and she was able to walk to The Hay with Chipper, Jenny, and Duncan. They sat outside, decompressed, and sat in complete silence as they tried to watch the attempts to put out the fire. The fire suppression chemicals were being used to try to confine the fire to the trees and brush on the driving range and not let it cross the 17-Mile Drive and threaten nearby estates on the other side of the road. Chipper was still holding Cindy's five iron. Jenny was holding Angus in her arms.

A Pebble Beach-logo van drove up and parked on the road near The Hay. The uniformed driver exited and opened the van doors. CEO Donald Stevens, along with General Counsel Richard Stein, exited and started walking up the path to The Hay patio. When Stevens saw Chipper, he started walking faster, then jogging toward Chipper, yelling, "I heard you caused all this! It's your fault, right? It's always your fault!"

Angus jumped out of Jenny's arms and started growling at Stevens. Stevens backed off, but Angus charged at him, still snarling. Stein stepped in front of his boss, and Angus stopped, rolled over on his back, and expected a belly rub from his friend, Richard. Stevens kept up his grumbling and ranting at Chipper.

REDEMPTION

Everyone on the outside deck at The Hay turned around and paid close attention when several cars with sirens came driving up and parked on the road behind the Pebble Beach van. Only two of the cars were police cars. There were three others with no markings, but with loud sirens blaring. Stevens stopped ranting and turned around with the rest of The Hay patio crowd.

Stevens only recognized Officers Anderson and Henderson, in their Deputy Sheriff's uniforms. They walked right by Stevens without a glance and approached Chipper with big smiles and hands out in greeting. It was high fives all around, and Anderson said, "Nice job, Chipper. Well done." Stevens was mystified.

Then Officer Kennedy, also in uniform, came up next and actually hugged Chipper before apologizing, "I'm sorry for the way I treated you in jail, Blair. You are a hero now. We heard about what happened on the range. You are a true hero. Very lucky, too. As I understand it, Lusky is, literally, toast." Stevens tried to step around Stein, but Angus immediately stood up and growled.

Still behind Stein, Stevens said, "What's up, here? What are you guys talking about?"

Kennedy said, "I'll let these other guys tell you." And he pointed at the very casually dressed men walking up to The Hay from the plain cars that had sirens. Kennedy introduced each one, in turn, to Stevens. "This is Mr. Sloane from Scotland Yard. This is Monsieur Beaufoy from Interpol. This is Mr. Addison from Lloyd's of London. And I think you know FBI special agent Tripp."

Stevens was overwhelmed as each shook his hand. Tripp spoke first,

"Mr. Stevens. Your boy Blair just ended what could have been a very serious international incident by taking down Lusky. Lusky has been dealing with known terrorists from North Korea, Iran, China, and other bad characters trying to sell his speedy drones. They obviously now have explosive capabilities." He then pointed at the fire on the other side of the driving range. "We've all been watching Lusky. Also the incident at The Hay, right here, where the poor Duchess got killed, was not an accident. Lusky had conspired with the Duchess to kill her husband, the Duke, for a big life insurance payment…"

Stevens interrupted, "But it was the Duchess that got killed."

Tripp continued, "Exactly. Lusky missed." Then Tripp started laughing, almost maniacally. When he stopped, he said, "Fucking Lusky missed. He killed the poor Duchess. Missed the Duke. Can you imagine that? The drones he developed had problems. Hard to control. Very hard to control. Too fast. Might have been really good if he had sent a bunch to the international terrorists. They might have killed themselves trying to use them."

Anderson broke in, "And every one of you knows what an amoral asshole he is, or, I should say, was. Paying young prostitutes, filming strangers and using AI to post on the internet. Didn't care about anything but making money, then telling folks about it. Chipper, you are a true hero for taking a chance and taking him down. Mr. Stevens, your driving range guy deserves a raise."

Stevens didn't know what to say. He didn't comment at all. He just turned around and headed back to his van. "Stein, are you coming with me?"

Stein said, "I think I'll stay here a bit." Then, when Stevens had his back to the group, Richard Stein gave a thumbs up to Chipper and commented, "I guess the MADRDI screen is out. I can't imagine why it wasn't fire-retardant?"

Chipper finally said, "I'm hopeful this is over. It seems like the fire and smoke are dying down. I think we should head back to the range and hit some golf balls. I just want to hit some golf balls." Jenny gave him a hug.

HOPEFUL AT THE HAY

Six weeks had passed. Cindy only missed a few days of golf. Her wound was superficial. Ian Osterholm had confessed to keying the late Lusky's car. Osterholm was unhappy with the way Lusky was treating Merlene at the party. Lusky was ashes, and the car was burnt-out scrap. The lawsuit against Chipper was dropped.

Jenny and their friends were meeting at The Hay for what they hoped was the first of monthly get-togethers with their new puppies. Abigail had five puppies. Stein and Debbie kept one female and named her Annabelle. Chipper and Jenny took a male and named him Shlomo. Irene and Bill took a male and named him Dom, after the champagne bottle that Irene used to save her own life and escape from her kidnappers. Emily and Takahashi took a male and named him Ohtani. Emily Hastings had no idea why, but Tak insisted on it. Cindy and Duncan took a female and named her Andie. It was an ode to St. Andrews, where they met. Angus and Abigail were standing by the table looking over the puppies, who were in a small fenced area that Stein had created to keep the dogs in one place.

Everyone was drinking, except Jenny. She had missed her period and the previous morning had some morning sickness right after the morning golf shot. She hadn't taken a pregnancy test yet, because she didn't want to be disappointed. But she was pretty sure she was pregnant. She already had several heated discussions with her mother about baby names. Her mother still wanted Shlomo for a boy and Sadie for a girl. Jenny told her mother she would not ever name a son Shlomo, but they would give that name to the new puppy. A boy would be Ben Nelson Blair: Benny Blair. A girl would be Annika Nelson Blair. And she would be called Annika and never Annie. That was the end of the discussion, until her mother brought it up on the next phone call.

Chipper was happily back at work daily. The automated driving range project was scrapped. Even the automatic ball machine was taken away. Chipper's course record at The Hay had been accepted, and there was a small sign near the starter's desk recognizing his course record. He had received an apology from Donald Stevens when the Duke's lawsuit was dropped. The Duke was now suing Lusky's estate. Stevens even named Chipper the Pebble Beach Corporation's employee of the month. Chipper skipped the presentation ceremony. As employee of the month he had a free parking spot with his name on it near the Lodge for that month. He never used it.

The FBI also awarded Chipper a very-rarely-given Shield of Bravery. It was only the second time in history that a non-FBI agent was presented one. They wanted Chipper to fly to Washington, D.C. for a special presentation, but he refused. They mailed it to him. Jenny placed it on the bar in the Dreel Tavern replica room in their estate.

After Lusky's untimely death, Stein immediately called Lusky's lawyer to see if there was a will. It could have been a great opportunity to pick up another Pebble Beach estate at a bargain price. No such luck. The attorney confided to Richard that Lusky was estranged from his parents, had no siblings, no real friends, and had left everything to Angel. There was likely to be a prolonged legal case with the parents questioning their son's judgment in leaving his substantial wealth and estate to the young girl. Lusky's attorney also told Stein that he was preparing a several-hundred-million-dollar lawsuit against the Pebble Beach Corporation as well as the MADRDI Company for his client's untimely death.

Stein was going to be busy, as the family of the unfortunate golfer that was on the MADRDI piece of artificial turf hitting balls when the first drone tore him apart was also filing a large lawsuit against the Corporation and MADRDI, as well. Several of the young men who were regular Cindy and Jenny watchers at the driving range were also filing a class action suit for trauma and duress from having viewed horrible scenes on the range.

None of this mattered to anyone on the deck of The Hay. After several drinks, the group took the puppies over to the putting green and let them roam loose. The dogs ran around randomly with the adults trying to corral them and keep them from running away, or out onto the street. It was chaotic. Angus and Abigail sat quietly and proudly watched their pups. Great energy from the puppies and the adults. New life. New beginnings.

While the others ran around, Chipper grabbed a putter similar to his own and some golf balls from the rack next to the green and started practicing five-footers. He made four in a row and missed the fifth. Shlomo, who was running loose nearby, saw the golf ball near the hole, sniffed it a few times, then attempted to pick up the ball in his mouth. When he finally had a good grip, he carried the ball back to Chipper and put it down at his feet. Then Shlomo rolled over and expected a belly rub.

Printed in the United States
by Baker & Taylor Publisher Services